IN THE SHADE OF THE GOOD TREES

EWA PRUCHNIK

First paperback edition April 2021

Editor: Jerry Dean
Translator: Aleksandra Kocerba
Cover design by: Damonza.com

ISBN 978-83-956113-2-2 (paperback)
ISBN 978-83-956113-1-5 (ebook)

CONTENTS

PROLOGUE

THIS STORY WAS supposed to have a very different ending. It carried me for months, as I was taken by familiar currents through familiar waters. Just when I thought I would slowly reach the shore, imagining a friendly pat on my back – "Man, didn't I tell you that could do it, congratulations!" – a storm came raging. Mad at fate, the world, myself, him and her, I threw a silver fountain pen at a glass wall and howled like a wounded animal.

It is so hard to believe that any of these unpredictable events did not prevent my story from finally reaching the destination, even if in the beginning it was gravitating towards a whole different place. Why, having put aside all the grievances, resentment and remorse, did I decide to say it all – for which I was partially responsible?

I realized that among all the stories that I carry, I have to share this one with you.

Standing with his hands in his pockets, he was waiting for everyone to take their places. They were settling down: young faces, rebellious conquerors of the future. In a reflective mood, he started to suspect that everyone looked at him as if he were a burnt tree with that one last, dry leaf about to effortlessly and elegantly fall off. Smiling at his thoughts, he reminisced: nobody would even suspect that having been deeply immersed in this world of prestige and scientific achievement, it was music that filled his heart.

Granted, he might have been a little up in the years, but does age really matter? Not at all! With such a heart, such a soul, mind and body, he was a unique genetic blend of two humans that were connected, high on wine and a balmy, summery Parisian night, by the mischievous fate that mocked all the prejudices, stereotypes and social divisions.

"Ladies and gentlemen," he finally broke the silence, "this is my last lecture." A gasp of disbelief swept through the audience. "Your reaction is certainly flattering, although I do have a feeling that after you listen to the lecture, all of you – and I know you well – will chip in for a ticket and send me to the airport, begging me, for heaven's sake, not to come back. Or, at most, to return as a tourist."

Upon concluding the lecture, as always full of digressions and wandering away from the main topic, when he arrived at the grand finale to underline all the highlights that he methodically headed to, silence ensued, leaving the audience motionless. He intensively gazed at these faces, as if looking for consent, acceptance, understanding. In this very place, where for years he would bare his soul, juggling the abundance of gray matter in pursuit of truth, tackling moral issues along the way, he could not want anything more at that moment. These young people were like his daughters and sons. People that we build relationships with, shape and release to the world.

He closed his eyes for a moment and upon opening them, gazed at the students; slowly, meaningfully, questioningly, fondly, finally finding what he's been looking for.

Hoping that it was not his mind bringing up distorted memories, emotions and elations that once struck a chord, he wanted to retrieve all the moments that were carelessly overlooked. So he went out into the world. Treacherous fate, however, like a mischievous goblin, managed to stir things up for the professor. Despite his incisiveness, intuition and that whole Philo-Sophia thing that he used to encourage and invigorate young, rebellious minds to think, he had no idea his journey would unfold in such a critical moment for humanity. A moment when separation, isolation and covering one's face with a mask would be the greatest manifestations of love.

Roaming around lifeless interiors, she touched nearly every single thing, as if she were looking at old, discolored photos in a family album; page after page, accompanied by the quiet rustle of parchment. She was wondering what should she do with all of this. This building. This whole inherited estate. At her fingertips, every memory came into focus; here she grew up, dreamed and was then forced to abandon the place. Deep silence made it seem like everything around her was slowly and unavoidably collapsing into a profound stillness, as if disappearing. It could be almost perceived in a physical, tangible, painful way...

She thought this had to be the way that abandoned houses

die, burying all the secrets of the former inhabitants, carefully passed from generation to generation.

But this white house with a copper roof was a tough one. Before taking its last breath, it fought its fate.

The history of Joanna's family home is inextricably linked with the consequences of a horrifying war catastrophe, which like an apocalyptic hurricane violated, destroyed, and moved the territories of many countries, finally finding the acceptance of their recent allies. The Polish borders were moved westwards, while the Soviet Union took over most of the country's eastern area. The local population, which had lived there for years, was relocated to the Reclaimed Territories.

All these historical maneuvers gave Joanna's grandparents a significant role in the reconstruction of Wrocław; a city that ceased to exist, a city that World War II turned into rubble. For a long time, they couldn't get used to the new home, naively hoping that sooner or later they would return to the sacred city of Lviv and all the family graves they left behind. To this phenomenal place, where so many cultures and religions could coexist. Where even rain respected tolerance, fairly dividing the streams pouring down the churches' roofs into two parts: one supplying the warm waters of the Black Sea and another feeding the cold currents of the Baltic.

As time passed by and hope for a better future started to fade away, Joanna's grandparents – with piercing melancholy in their hearts – started to slowly blend into their new life, becoming acquainted with unfamiliar buildings, rubble and gothic inscriptions. Józef Lubczyński, Joanna's grandfather, who before the outbreak of the war had held the position of a professor at the University of Lviv, was part of the intellectual elite. The very same elite that later on lived in suburban homes that resisted the Siege of Breslau. Village and town people inhabited burnt townhouses in the heart of the city center.

Józef, his wife Kazimiera and their teenage daughter Hanna moved into a small, post-German villa. The building, untouched by artillery fire, was located in Pawłowice near Wrocław. Tormented for a long time by unimaginable remorse that they are sitting at someone else's table and sleeping in their bed, they found solace in the birth of Hanna's daughter, who was given the name Joanna, and finally felt at home. In a truly beautiful home. Boasting a bright façade, copper roof and an old buckeye tree whose leaves, pushed by the wind, filled the windows with waves of green.

"Mom?" She flinched as Adam touched her shoulder. "Everything okay?" he asked immediately.

"Oh, yes. Yes," Joanna patted his hand. "I got lost in my thoughts... not that it was necessary."

"How so? It's your family home after all, part of your life story," he started looking around the living room, "the furniture, paintings, great-grandfather's books... are you sure you want to sell it all?"

"I will do it."

Trying to come up with a thoughtful way to make her reflect on the subject, he nodded his head in reaction to the decisive 'I will.'

"Just like that?" was the best he managed to conjure.

"Just like that. Obviously, we're talking about the building here, not the belongings. These..." Joanna shrugged, "I don't know. I will definitely keep the books."

"Don't be in a rush. You don't have to make decisions ad

hoc. It's a beautiful house. A unique one. They don't make them like they used to do."

"Beautiful, but…" she searched her mind for some 'but', "but I feel it's so neglected and needs lots of help. Oh, it's not that important to keep thinking about it. Hopefully, we will manage to find a buyer real soon."

She knew she could afford such harsh words in the presence of her son, even when talking about the place where she had spent her childhood and early adulthood. Its dark history was no longer mysterious to him, even if he had been spared some details.

"Oh, sure," he nodded, "a whole bunch of buyers. For the time being, there's only one, the unbreakable village administrator Banaszczyk, who eyed the property even when grandpa was still alive. Listen, mom…" moving one step closer, he raised a hand towards her neck to fix a twisted string of pearls: a gesture from childhood which never failed to move them both, "what about you wait for a while? We could renovate the house and sell it at a better price. Or, who knows, maybe you will like it so much you will keep it."

"Oh, come on! Keep it?! For what purpose?! I don't plan to move from Warsaw to Pawłowice, there's no way I could leave my students and their competitions… it would be desertion! Adam…" she caressed his cheek with the back of her hand, "honestly, I don't even need the money from selling this house. You and Konrad, though, could certainly use them."

"Mom, come on!" Adam sighed, looking at this petite, dainty woman whose personality made quite a lot of heads spin. A truly extraordinary creature where the sensitivity of an artist collided with a cold breath of harsh reality. "Speaking of the piano… follow me!" He took her hand and, using a narrow, 'stone staircase with a well-worn metal railway, led her upstairs and through a tiny corridor. "The mystery room" he stated. "Whenever grandpa chased me away from here, I would wonder why. Why wouldn't he allow me to go inside?" Adam gently pushed the ajar white door, which opened wide with a creak. "My childhood imagination was a source of abundant possible scenarios. This included a skeleton in the closet. I guess grandpa just wanted to hide this piano from me, but am not sure why. Do you have any idea why would he do that?" He gently placed a hand on her elbow, a gesture encouraging her to move further. She did not do it, though.

The interior emanated the atmosphere of unfinished human history, suspended in the air with the smell of dust, mothballs and a sweet scent of rotten fruit; the scent of oblivion. The room was bathed in dimmed light coming through the grated window. It was Joanna's father who mounted these iron rods that scared intruders away like the teeth of an enraged beast. He did it shortly after driving her, distraught and shattered, to Warsaw, fearing a man he had never met, yet was ready to kill. A black grand piano with peeling paint and copper pedals dominated the modest constellation of furniture: an ascetic bed with an iron headboard, a two-door wardrobe with a somewhat austere look and the only stool in the room, a wooded Thonet chair with a bent backrest. All of this gave the room a tad quirky, slightly eccentric vibe. A truly grand instrument, worthy of concert halls, standing in the middle of a rather humble setting. How was it even placed here?! The door is too narrow, the window too small.

A minute, maybe two passed when Joanna, relaxing her breathing, dared to make the first step. Then a second. And a third. Pushed by the memories she walked towards the piano. Reaching it, she stopped and gently caressed the keyboard, as if trying to understand or capture something. She sat on the bench, with hands raised and wrists straightened when suddenly she was overpowered with the impression of that oneiric, mysterious presence that came out of nowhere. Her hands dropped to her knees.

"Mom... sorry, I did not know that..."

"Hello? Anybody here?" Someone's voice from downstairs burst into their intimate moment.

"Ah, that must be Banaszczyk," Adam concluded, "I'm going to welcome the honorable administrator. We barely placed an ad and he's already here. This guy must be very determined. We'll see how much."

"I don't want to talk to him." Joanna said, turning on the bench to underline her decisiveness.

"Sure, that's understandable. Stay here, I will take care of everything. I beg you to do just one thing: think carefully about whether you would really like to sell all of this. Remember that you can withdraw the offer at any time, alright?" Adam crossed the room, buttoned up his jacket and closed the door behind him.

Again, she was all alone in the room. Sitting on the bench she felt like she experienced that moment of awakening when time plays with the feeling of here and now, leaving us all unsure whether we are still asleep or already awake. She raised her head towards the window, where the tangled branches of the buckeye tree curiously peeked inside. How many years have passed? How many? She went back down memory lane, as far as she could. As a little girl, she would lie in her wrought iron bed and gaze at the swaying leaves, with twinkling, clear stars and a curious moon shining through them, waiting for a good sleep. Good things happen in the shade of the good trees, her mom said once. But when she looked into more recent memories, she reached a point where the old buckeye tree and its tangled branches complicated her life again, bringing so many consequences. And there was this question that roamed in her mind again... If she could turn back time and close the window, or maybe not open it at all, what would she do? And there was her answer again... She would go back to this rainy summer when the days dragged on and the nights were too short, and do exactly what she did: open the window wide and wait. She waited with the very same feeling of undefined anxiety, fear and happiness, among the sounds of the piano and raindrops falling on the window sill, waiting for the good tree – the mystery of life, death and fertility – to bring her not good sleep, but that mysterious presence permeating the room that breathed a new life into her so many years ago. Metaphysically and physically...

PART I

JOANNA

HE DREW THE curtain and silently jumped from the stone windowsill into the dark room. Turning on the flashlight a dim light traveled across the walls, ceiling and then on the floor. 'What the heck is this?' he thought to himself upon seeing an object the size of a bear cage, 'A grand piano?!'. A hopeless sigh broke the silence when he noticed that the walls were entirely bare, like a shameless prostitute. Not a painting in sight, not even a tiny one. He got so mad! Where is all of this freaking furniture with its drawers and secret compartments? Just this musical monstrosity in the very middle. To the left, against the wall, he noticed a wrought iron bed with unmade bedding. 'I better be careful!', he thought. Some sleeping prince could appear out of nowhere and make some noise that's bound to get him in trouble. In such a situation he would be forced to smack him upside the head. Slowly, he approached the bed. Well… no, it looks like it's a classic sleeping beauty. The bedding was not only clean; it even smelled like an ocean breeze. For a second he wrangled the thought whether he, a nomadic wizard and a wild pauper could sleep in a place like this. A shiver of comfort traveled up his spine and he could not resist the temptation anymore, finally sitting down on the soft mattress. Trying to avoid the undesirable reaction of any of the springs, he did not move an inch and slightly closed his eyes. It was so pleasant that he smiled under his breath and let out a content murmur. Suddenly he noticed something by the headboard; something that resembled a book. He put the flashlight in his mouth to free the hands and was about to open the rigid, thick cover, when he heard a barely audible sigh and saw the door open. He... she... or maybe it... this whoever or whatever entered the room. He was not sure anymore whether it was a sleeping beauty prince or princess. This someone was not too big but wore pajamas that were too loose and resembled a jail uniform. Skinny as a toothpick, with an unnaturally long neck and short hair that accentuated the flawless shape of the head. He broke out in a cold sweat, as this someone walked past him unfazed, as he sat still on the bed, like a new piece of furniture in the room. Moving just his eyes in the dull silence, with a lit flashlight still in his mouth, he followed this someone's smooth movement. The book remained in his hands. The scrawny one, not even noticing him, approached the piano and sat on the bench. The moonlight coming through the window cast a silvery halo over an unnaturally impeccable profile with an extended neck. The thief's attention was averted from this hypnotizing view by three gentle sounds that tingled in the air like tiny bells. And then, upon the touch of these skinny fingers, exploded music so loud that it made the thief uncomfortable, fluttering inside his chest like the echo of an alarm. Suddenly the creature stopped playing (as the thief held his breath for a moment, with the flashlight still in his mouth), lifted itself up and marched past him towards the door, gently closing it behind.

Meanwhile, after having shaken off the feeling and before escaping through the window, he made sure he left no trace of his thievish presence. It wasn't until he jumped from the tree and landed on wet grass that he noticed he was still clutching a black leather-bound book.

About ten minutes later, a young, short-haired girl wearing boy's pajamas returned to her room and despite the deep darkness in the room, moved around with the grace of a swan. When she approached the piano so grand, that she looked like a 10-year old next to it, something visibly upset her. Seemingly nothing has changed. Everything was as usual. Empty silence within bare walls. Yet something bothered her. Had someone been there?

It was a Saturday morning in August when Joanna woke up to the sound of a tree branch hitting the window. The rain was ceasing but it was still windy when she came downstairs to the kitchen, where Kazimiera has kept herself busy since early morning. As usual, she wore her red and white polka dot apron.

When Joanna pulled out the chair to sit at the table, a black cat trotted over to her and after weaving a double figure eight between her feet, jumped on her knees.

"Hi there, kitty," she scratched him behind the ear, just like he liked it, "thanks for the gift".

"Did he bring a dead sparrow again?", Kazimiera inquired, setting a plate with a bun before her, "Dear Lord," she suddenly seemed concerned, "you're red as a beet, you aren't coming down with something, are you? Feeling feverish?"

"Not at all! I'm great," Joanna assured, taking a hearty bite of a warm roll. Last night's events clearly worked up her appetite, "Today Sphinx brought me not a bird but a tiny mouse. The poor little thing was dead," she added emphatically with her mouth full.

"Such a dumb creature, this cat!"

"Sphinx is everything but dumb!" Joanna growled. "That's how he shows me what I mean to him. It might be quite a cruel way to express it but it's in line with his feline nature."

"Oh," Kazimiera froze while raising a glass of water to her mouth, as the familiar sound of a turning key could be heard from the door, "your father is so kind to grace us with his presence".

"I really don't like it when you talk about him like this, grandma."

"Talk like what?"

"You know. Mean."

"I met Kramer," Zygmunt declared, entering the kitchen. He took off a thin shell jacket, hung it over a chair and sat at the table opposite his daughter, "he said that you gave quite a concert in the dead of night. Didn't you?"

"Was he complaining?"

"Well..." he downed half a liter of soured milk, taking big, careless gulps, "was it complaining? I think he likes it when you play," Zygmunt wiped his mouth and leaned back.

"And I'm telling you, for God's sake, stop with these concerts!" Kazimiera turned off the heat under the frying pan and approached the cupboard to take out a plate. "You won't let people have a good night's sleep. Why don't you play during the day?"

"It's not the same. Daytime distracts me."

"Mama should be the last person to complain about it. Mama's dear hubby also liked to busk underneath the moon and stars, bringing the great works of culture to simple people just like me in our neighborhood," he raised his brow as if waiting for a retort.

"I beg your pardon!" Kazimiera grasped a wooden spoon and put scrambled eggs on a plate, which she not so nicely set before Zygmunt.

"What? I'm telling the truth."

"Listen…" she began and stopped, taking a quick gulp of water to chase a handful of colorful tablets, "I don't want you to call me mama!"

"And why is that?"

"Because you say it in a particularly sarcastic manner."

"Sarca… what?"

"Here we go, that's my son-in-law! With all the learning gaps and shortcomings in upbringing."

"Thanks for the breakfast," Joanna pushed her plate away and got up from the chair, "I'm going to my room!"

"Joanna! What about the scrambled eggs?"

"Thank you, I ate a roll and that's enough for me."

"Jesus Christ!" Zygmunt scowled at Kazimiera. "Can't you let it go for once?"

"You shall not misuse the name of the Lord your God in vain, you pagan!"

"Please… please… please!" Joanna ostentatiously covered her ears. "I don't want to listen to this anymore. You know what?" her arms fell to her sides, "it's a shame I'm not deaf.

Instead of being blind. I'm going to mom!" she picked up the white cane which was leaned against the table and left the room. Hungry Sphinx followed her.

The cane wasn't even necessary. She knew every bump and every hole on the narrow gravel path, a shortcut leading to the gates of a local cemetery that she would tread almost every day in pursuit of freedom – for among the countless paths in the world, this was the only one she could walk on her own.

Her mother passed away due to a "female disease". Such was the cause of death that spread by word of mouth among her family and neighbors. The core of a catastrophe that had shaken her world remained a mystery, but she perceived it as something inconceivably terrible. This "female disease". She was seven when her mother was buried in this grave. She remembered that it was raining that day and actually it made her happy because it made it easier to hide the tears or, rather, lack thereof. Not a single tear was shed during the funeral. She just couldn't, even though she wanted to. Not for herself, not even for her mom. But for grandma and dad, so that they would have no doubts how much she loved mom. Death was just something so unreal that it did not convince her that mom has ceased to exist. Just like that. Ceased. She thought it would be just for a moment. A second. That mom will be back. She had so many things to do; fix a hole in her white tights, cut her bangs "because it keeps falling into your eyes and you're squinting all the time", cook noodles on Saturday. What would Saturday be without milk soup with noodles? But most important of all, it was mom who was supposed to walk her to school on the first day. And what now? How would it be without mom around?!

It was bad without mom. And finally, the tears came. A whole ocean of them, because even if she could feel her mom's aura, she could neither hear nor touch her. Soon people would start talking that poor little Jo missed her mommy so much that she bawled her big, blue eyes out.

Optic neuritis turned the rooms, furniture and objects scattered around the house into the number of steps counted to measure distance. Outside she was forced to follow handrails, curbs and fences. No matter how hard she tried to find herself in the new reality, she would keep on stumbling over her own shadow, collecting even more painful bruises. But she didn't complain. Instead of going to school, she would tickle the ivories of the grand piano. At first with a dash of nervousness and anxiety. Then gently, subtly and gracefully. People passing by their home would often stop and listen. Who is playing so beautifully? Little Jo? Isn't she blind, though?

Her dad drove her to specialists who said the disorder was only temporary and it would pass. But it did not. And then they stopped saying it was "temporary". While it might have been ten years that she spent moving around this world in darkness, she was able to sense it deeper than anyone else. An heiress to her grandfather's genes that she could neither willingly accept nor refuse with disdain, from whom she inherited remarkable sensitivity – a source of extraordinary human capabilities. Józef Lubczyński was a physics professor, but he also happened to be a romantic. One that reveled in stargazing. It's been so many times that his wife Kazimiera saw him coughing, with an unbuttoned sweater, as he chased his beloved Orion nebula across the fall sky with the vintage telescope. She never missed an opportunity to reprimand him to stop risking his health with these useless nighttime investigations of silent stars. The professor, however, admired music the most. When he would sit at the piano, the sounds that flowed not only conveyed a particular melody composed years ago by some musical genius but were also a means to translate his own emotions, mood, a type of commentary to everything that was happening in his heart and mind. He would always return to the same pieces by Chopin, Beethoven and Dvorak, always finding something new in them. These pieces deeply moved his soul and triggered nostalgia.

The dignified and wise life of Joanna's grandfather echoed widely in the hearts and minds of his students and colleagues. The University of Wrocław dedicated a commemorative plaque to professor Józef Lubczyński; a prominent physicist, who organized the Polish university on the ruins left by the Siege of Breslau, along with a few dozen other scientists from Lviv. Even though Joanna did not really manage to befriend her grandpa, as he passed away when she was two, she vividly remembered the unveiling of the plaque, which made her so proud. Some important person said that history destines people like professor Józef Lubczyński for challenging, yet extraordinary endeavors.

Following her mother's death, Joanna's upbringing was entrusted to two eccentric individuals that stood in stark contrast, namely her grandmother (Kazimiera) and her father (Zygmunt). Kazimiera believed in God and all the Saints, reverently kissing any paintings, pictures, sculptures and kitschy figurines that portrayed them. She never hesitated to get on her knees and kiss the floor where holy water had spilled, participated in the life of the parish community, sang in the church choir and prayed the rosary every day. Even though she attempted to live out the ten commandments, she never missed an opportunity to show great disappointment and spite to her son-in-law (that her nobly born, educated daughter once fell head over heels in love with) usually doing so in an extremely suggestive way, resembling a painful and unexpected stick of a pin in one's side.

Zygmunt, on the other hand, believed in Marks, Engels, Lenin and social equality, and on top of that was a gambling addict. After the death of his wife, Hanna, he drowned his sorrow in vodka and never really got closure to his mourning. When dealing with his mother-in-law, he employed mocking and a corny sense of humor, but Kazimiera was not afraid to hit back. As he would sometimes (oftentimes, rather) walk unsteadily home, she would direct a torrent of abuse at him, comparing him to their neighbor, Kramer. Zygmunt would rack his brain, trying to figure out why Kramer, as the neighbor was abstinent.

"Hammered again like Marian the lush!"

One day, awaiting the return of her son-in-law with a bowl of cold soup, a truly devilish idea emerged in Kazimiera's mind – to redecorate the space shared by all family members, a small lounge where the three of them would sit on Sunday after-noon, giving the impression of a normal, functioning family. The rearrangement, albeit small, almost knocked Zygmunt off his feet. The walls that he recently painted were now adorned with scenes from the Bible and portraits of saints he didn't even know existed.

"What is it!" he exclaimed.

"Saints!" Kazimiera snapped back. "Who you should pray to every single day and thank for having a daughter like you do! And on your knees, I should add."

Zygmunt nodded his head, which might have seemed like humility and repentance, but the portraits of the saints and Biblical scenes vanished on the next day and were replaced with other artwork.

"What is this!?" – the woman was shocked, as all the famous faces representing the communist ideology gazed upon her: Bolesław Bierut and his mustache, bald Józef Cyrankiewicz and Władysław Gomułka with horn-rimmed glasses. All three were surrounded by solid, black frames made of high-quality wood.

"See, mama, these are my saints! But there's no need for me to pray to them or mama's saints, because when it comes to thanking for my daughter..." his voice started breaking, "I thank Jo's mother for her every day. Not on my knees, but here..." Zygmunt beat his chest and a hollow thud was heard, "here, inside, in a place not worthy of neither her nor our daughter. In my rotten heart."

"Oh...," the woman rolled her eyes.

Something, however, united them over all these worldview differences, divisions and spite. Joanna was that connection. Together, they created for her a home where she was supposed to safely wait out her whole life as if she were in an air raid shelter. By doing so, they limited her space in nearly every dimension one could imagine.

Joanna, however, was so eager to discover the world that they shut tightly before her that she started asking, and then begging them to at least let her learn to read. Soon, twice a week Mrs. Wodecka – a particularly strict teacher from the school for the blind – would arrive in front of their house, announced by a high-pitched screech of her bicycle brakes. For Joanna, this piercing squeak was the most anticipated sound.

Excellent orientation within the top-bottom and right-left planes helped her learn to read and master all the combinations of raised dots. Fluency in Braille not only liberated her from illiteracy; it also turned out to be her magical potion for independence. To keep her skills up to date, Joanna would pore over thick pages of the Gospel of Matthew, a birthday gift from Kazimiera. It was a unique, huge volume bound in black leather, filled to the brim with dots. Joanna adored the book as she would hold it and wander around the house and garden, read it, open, close and tenderly caress, making Sphinx jealous.

The weather on that day was awful, with clouds hanging low and a morning storm rolling in. Joanna was not afraid of storms, as afterward the scent of tranquility filled the air, unlike the deep sadness that saturated every tiny corner following an argument. As she strode with Sphinx along the narrow, gravel path leading to the parish cemetery where her mother had been laid to rest, her thoughts anxiously revolved around the last night; she felt someone strange roamed the house, but the anxiety neared excitement rather than fear. Finally, something was happening.

Suddenly the tip of the white cane hovered over the ground, making her feel horrible as if someone had deprived her of navigation. Sphinx did not like it either, demonstrating it with a throaty growl escaping his open mouth. That's how he would behave upon noticing Roman Banaszczyk, who has been following Joanna ever since she learned to walk. Even her blindness did not discourage him. Sure, she even liked him in the past. Particularly when they hanged around the neighborhood from one tree to another, collecting chestnuts to donate them to the zoo. He would pour the chestnuts into her basket and she would repay him with a charming smile. One time she added to the smile a kiss on his radiant cheek and then held his hand. Roman became the happiest nine-year-old on the planet, as he believed that this pretty six-year-old lady loved him and before the blush even left his face he decided he loved her. Joanna, on the other hand, was not even aware of this budding, yet mighty love. She wasn't even aware that Roman was her sweetheart.

"Good Morning, Jo!" He greeted her with mock politeness, chewing on a blade of grass.

"Certainly it will be good as soon as you let go of my cane," Joanna grunted.

"Why are you so moody today? You could hold my hand instead of this stick. I'll lead you everywhere, I would even go to the ends of the earth for you."

"No, thanks. Too far away." She sullenly replied, attempting a joke.

"Oh, Jo! Come on. Sooner or later we will be doing it anyway."

"Excuse me? Doing what?"

"Well, holding hands. But first... phew!" he spat the blade of grass out, "you have to recover your sight. I don't mind your blindness at all, I mean, you're so pretty anyway. But my father... well, you know how he is. He wants everything to be the best, his daughter-in-law too. It's the eighth today, isn't it?"

"I don't know, I didn't look at the calendar."

"I didn't look at the calendar," he repeated, "good one! You sure like to crack a joke, just like your father, right?"

She didn't answer.

"Alright, it's the eighth. The eighth! Do you know why it's so important?"

"What about you tell me about it some other time," Joanna said, wanting to be left alone.

"You don't know? Your father and grandma didn't tell you? Okay, listen! I'm going to tell you. In twenty days, something important will happen in your life. Mine too. Damn, I'm so hyped about it..."

"I will ask them about this important event as soon as I return home. Now leave me alone."

"Why, do I bother you?"

"I want to pray at my mom's grave."

"I will stand by you. Very quiet. You won't even notice... that is... you won't sense my presence."

"Go away! Come on, now!" Joanna said, losing her temper.

"Alright, alright, don't get so mad. And remember to ask them!"

When he finally left, Joanna sat on a small green bench near a gray tombstone, overcame with a conviction that the twenty-eighth day of August does not hold any good for her.

"Come here, kitty!" Moving with feline grace, Sphinx obediently jumped on her lap, kneading her body for a while before settling down.

Petting him behind the ears, she started wondering what was it that her grandmother and father did not tell her. Does it have something to do with Roman some time ago talking non-sense about their life together? It seems like the youngster has been teasing her forever, with her father always nonchalantly brushing it off and making it clear to stop his pathetic advances. Last summer, however, something changed. He started being kind to Roman and once he even invited him home and offered some vodka or rather got him blackout drunk. Father was fine, after all, he was a seasoned heavyweight drinker. When the old Banaszczyk came to pick up his son, vodka flowed in amounts sufficient to kill a horse but not certainly not enough to knock them out, as the two managed to drag unconscious Roman back home. Two days later Roman followed Joanna all the way up to the cemetery jabbering something about their life together and a famous ophthalmologist. Joanna was fairly sure he was still intoxicated from the previous night. The friendly relation between their fathers was even more surprising, as the two had been rather distant and cold towards each other; it was after that drunken night that their relation bloomed like a snowdrop kissed by a wayward ray of the winter sun.

August twenty-eighth, the sound of it resonated annoyingly in her mind. Instinctively, she felt there was something unsettling about it, but did not ask her grandma or father about it. She'd rather stay out of their sight in fear that they might discover the missing Gospel. Someone took it, and it meant so much for her! She liked having it with her, roaming around the house and garden clutching it to her chest. For her, this unique book bound in black leather was like a jewel box, opened sporadically only to feast your eyes on a diamond hidden inside and gently caress it. Using a red ribbon, she marked the page where the following words could be found: "FOR TRULY I TELL YOU, IF YOU HAVE FAITH THE SIZE OF A MUSTARD SEED, YOU WILL SAY TO THIS MOUNTAINS, 'MOVE FROM HERE TO THERE' AND IT WILL MOVE; AND NOTHING WILL BE IMPOSSIBLE FOR YOU'." She would open the Gospel in that very place, and tracing the embossed quote, strengthened her faith. Not her faith in God, but in science and medicine. The doctors who handled Joanna's case for years could not understand why she couldn't regain her vision, so they stated it was time to humbly accept something, which was there to stay for good. Unless a miracle happens and these sure happen in medicine, they would say, awakening hope.

Joanna was a carbon copy of her grandfather; a man of extraordinary musical sensitivity and a deep belief in the phenomenon of human reason. Deep inside she also carried that grain of faith, believing not in miracles, but in the driving force of science, medicine, advances and human thought that will one day move her evangelical mountain from here to there, and colors will flood her world again, she will see Sphinx and the faces of her loved ones.

Irritation fueled by the encounter at the cemetery and general anxiety surrounding the twenty-eighth of August kept Joanna wide awake. On top of that, the room was filled with heavy air before a storm. She grabbed a book and ran her fingertips over the raised dots. Suddenly, she felt thirsty; after completing the sentence, she got up and went to the kitchen. Having returned to the bedroom, she grew weary and slowly closed her eyes. She was floating somewhere between the realms of dream and reality, glancing over the projections of dark shadows in her head when a mighty thunder rolled and resonated in her body. Joanna jumped from her bed and headed towards the window, but instead of closing it, she reached out of the window, trying to collect the cold raindrops in her hands. After standing there for a good five minutes, Joanna, wrapped in freshness, wetness and with her mood elevated, approached the piano and started playing Chopin's *Raindrop Prelude*, pouring all her sensitivity and soul into it, uniting with the world outside the window: the calmness, serenity, and subsequent dark, unsettling sounds. All of it was a mere introduction, for it was followed by a gloomy, yet moving memento for the unfulfilled musical feeling of a musical genius; the first tones of *Moonlight Sonata* filled the space. Not even taking a break after Beethoven, she smoothly moved to a monumental piece that stunned with its raw emotion – *Hammerklavier* – putting into it all the depth of her emotions.

When she was done, the last chord still hung in the heavy air. Joanna seemed to be exhausted as if music had drained all her energy and strength. Suddenly she raised her head, adjusted her posture and played Dvorak's *Humoresque*, her petite fingers creating an artistic vision blending into a rhythm of joyful jumps of a little girl, who occasionally stops in her tracks to gaze at something in amazement. The grimaces, tension and spasms faded away from her face, giving way to brightness.

Indifferent to the view and sounds, Sphinx was sitting on a chair, slowly licking his paw. But there was someone else in the room. Standing in a dark corner, listening and forgetting to breathe.

In the afternoon, Zygmunt was roaming the garden. Pruning shears in hand, he was cutting faded flowers and overgrown branches.

"What in tarnation... who broke that?" he stopped underneath the horse chestnut tree, staring at its crown.

"Broke what?" Joanna asked, petting Sphinx who was comfortably seated at her shoulder.

"The chestnut branches."

"Must have been a squirrel."

"A squirrel?" Zygmunt looked at her, as if she were dumb. "What on earth are you talking about, Jo?! Have you seen... have you heard about a squirrel as heavy as hell?"

"No, dad," she giggled in a charming, girlish way, "I have not heard about a squirrel this heavy, nor have I seen one, as far as I remember."

"All joking aside, this is a serious problem and suspicious. Damn..." he cursed, stroking his hair, "what if it was a man?! Huh?!"

"A man? What for? Why would someone climb our tree?"

"Who knows!" Zygmunt shrugged. "Maybe it was a thief?"

"If it were a thief... Sphinx!" Joanna shouted, turning her head towards the cat when his predatory instincts took over and he jumped down, running somewhere, probably chasing a mouse again. "If it were a thief," she addressed her father again, "he would probably steal something. Is anything missing?" she inquired, immediately thinking about her Gospel.

"Don't know yet..." Zygmunt responded, lighting a cigarette, "I'll look around. But," he exhaled the smoke," "if not a thief, then who was it? A peeping Tom? Phew!" He spat under the tree, "Freaking perv!"

"Dad, you're so suspicious. It doesn't make any sense, who would he watch?"

"Who? Certainly not grandma! That would be one great perv!" Zygmunt grimaced and with his finger removed a tobacco particle from his tongue.

"Oh..." Joanna's deep sigh resounded, "looks like it's going to rain. I'll get the laundry." The girl walked past the porch, where the clothesline was hung.

"Jo, wait!" Zygmunt held her arm as she was returning with a bundle of white shirts and blouses. "Sometimes I act like a jerk, right?"

Silence ensued.

"Listen..." he rubbed his nose, "don't tell grandma about the tree, you know how she is. Panic will start, a heart attack or something even worse will happen." Zygmunt puffed on a cigarette.

"Worse?" Joanna repeated worryingly.

"Yeah..." the man disappeared in a cloud of smoke, "maybe she will buy herself some lace lingerie! Perhaps red...?"

"Dad, come on!"

"Where are you going? You were supposed to help me in the garden!"

"I was wrong, it's not going to rain today. I'll put the laundry in the basket to be ironed and go to the cemetery."

"Go! Sure, go, complain about me to your mother. To hell with these women!", said Zygmunt, crushing the cigarette butt with his shoe.

Joanna walked on the winding path in the old, post-German part of the cemetery, with tall and sharp lettering on the graves. Mom once explained to her that it was Gothic script. While lighting candles for grandpa, they would always stroll here. Mom and grandma would discuss some important, adult stuff as she held their hands tight. It wasn't her favorite moment; she was afraid of tripping and falling on one of these scary, stone graves, and then whoever was buried there would surely drag her in and either eat her or force her to become his wife.

"Jo, don't be afraid…," mom would try to calm her down, "the deceased won't hurt you."

"And you, mom, did you like these people who are buried here?"

"I didn't know them. But if I did, then who knows…? I guess I would." And that was enough; the great fear of a little girl had disappeared.

Loss of sight made it impossible for Joanna to observe how time turned this place into ruins, with all these forgotten and abandoned graves among strangers.

Deep in her thoughts, she suddenly felt a pebble thrown at her back and reflexively clutched her cane.

"Who is it?" she strained her ears, trying to calm her breath.

"Damn, Jo! I have never seen you so petrified!"

"Roman! Why did you do that?"

"For fun."

"If you think this was funny, then..."

"...it wasn't supposed to be funny."

"You know what, you have changed."

"Changed? How?"

"You used to be different. So nice. And now...? Now you're rude and unpredictable. I never know what's going to pop up in your mind. Remember when we were kids? Do you remember?" Joanna enquired, moving one step closer. She looked like she was trying to figure out what impression did her words make. "We used to be friends. Why are you constantly scaring me?! Why? And now..." not waiting for an answer, she lowered her head, "will you be so kind and leave me alone? I want to be on my own."

"Sure, princess, here we go with the bossy tone again. I will not be taken lightly!", Roman was bordering on rage, "Because I'm a grown, adult man, do you understand?! And a man cannot be a soft loser. You better play it nice, because you're at the mercy of everyone else. You're blind. And I'm not saying that because it makes me happy, quite the opposite. I hate your blindness because it made you forget me. And for your question, obviously, I remember when we were kids. Do you remember, though? Do you remember how I taught you how to swim? Or when we were walking around collecting chestnuts and you held my hand and... God, I was a nine-year-old brat but I suddenly felt the blood drain from my face. And now..." he hesitated, not sure how to express it, "now I'm following you like a stray dog and you keep pushing me away. Instead of me you just pick up this cane and walk around with it as if you were treasure hunting... Wait!" he yelled, grabbing Joanna's hand when she turned around to leave. "Where are you going?", his fingers clenched around her wrist, "I'm not done yet!"

"Let go!", demanded the woman, trying to escape. "You're crazy. Don't you dare follow me."

"Sure, princess!"

With the white cane nervously hovering just above the ground, Joanna was returning home in the shade of trees shivering in the wind. The familiar voice of the radio presenter welcomed her home, announcing Vivaldi's *Summer*. She leaned against the wall, absorbing its soothing, cold calmness, while the sounds of the radio – joy, sweltering heat, the melody of a cuckoo's singing and a summer storm – enveloped her and lifted her high above all that had happened at the cemetery, above all her sorrows.

"Jo! C'mere!"

And here it was. The moment was gone, she sighed and entered the kitchen.

"Dad, you're drinking again."

"I drink... 'cause I want to!', Zygmunt slurred. "Toasting myself! Not the ladies! And ya... why...?' he stared at her absently, "why the pout? Ahh! Alright...' the man nodded his head like a bobblehead toy, "you visited her. Your mother."

"Dad...," Joanna pulled the chair out and sat next to him, "do you hate me?"

"What? Whatcha talking 'bout?"

"Do you hate me because I'm blind?"

"Don't say: blind!" Zygmunt uttered the words with excess clarity. "Watch your words! You are not allowed to talk like that, do you understand?! I'm asking, do you understand?! I'll do anything, look, I'll rip these veins out of my arms. You see them"? as he pointed his wrists toward her. "What the hell am

I saying, you can't see. Listen, Jo. Listen," he propped his arm on the back of her chair, "We won't go back to these... freaking quacks who took away our hope! Do you understand?! Hope, Jo! Hope!... If there's no hope, then... then what, the hell?!" Zygmunt almost broke into tears. "I talked to old Banaszczyk, he has... you know... connections. He made an appointment for you... with a real eye specialist. A guy known world-wide, an American professor, but I will tell you more...hic... once I get better," he said and slammed headfirst into the table.

"Sure..." Joanna sighed, getting up from the chair. Before heading off to her room, she felt around and found two bottles on the table. The empty one landed in the container, where glass waste was stored for recycling. The second one she tilted over the sink underneath the window and poured the remaining vodka down the drain.

Joanna was sitting on the edge of the bed and started mechanically petting Sphinx who was lounging in the sheets. *Someone was here again*, she reminisced about last night. He broke the branches, but more importantly, returned the Gospel. What kind of thief steals and returns things? A remorseful one? Did he take pity on a blind girl? How generous of him! And then he just sat in the corner and enjoyed her concert. Did he also watch her in her sleep? Probably. His scent was noticeable, but it seemed to be different than the one accompanying the first visit when he had fled with the Gospel. And what if there were two people? One who stole and another who returned it? The idea seemed reassuring, like a warm, kind embrace. When night fell, Joanna opened the window wide, indulging in hope, mystery and uncertainty. That night, however, nobody came to visit.

Father's indisposition continued until the next day.

"You're hammered again! Like that Marian! The town drunk!" Kazimiera kept on whining as she hustled in the kitchen. "Christ, mama!" Zygmunt winced, placing a wet towel on his forehead. "My head is gonna explode. Show some empathy, please, alcohol poisoning is a sickness after all, why make a scene? Does mama have to yell like that? I had a valid reason. I had something to celebrate."

"Celebrate, celebrate… you will be sacked in no time, and what will you do then? Huh?!" she enquired with hands on her hips. "How will you support your daughter? Your blind daughter at that? Will you send her to work?"

"I will not send her anywhere. She will choose her profession on her own, but first… oh, damn!" Zygmunt adjusted the towel, "first she has to regain her sight and finish her education. No big deal, she will make up for everything. She's bright. Just like her mother and mama's honorable husband."

"Well, definitely not like you."

"That's for sure. And with all due respect…," a sly smile appeared on his face, "not like you also, mama. We graduated from the same elementary schools. I mean, mama completed the elementary school, I finished vocational training as well."

"Vocational training! While Hanna had a double major, dear Lord!" Kazimiera rolled her eyes. "That's the blockhead that my only daughter married. God only knows what she saw in you. And I'm telling you…," she wagged a disapproving finger, "stop giving Jo hope. She's never going to… again…, " the woman fell down on a chair and buried her face in her hands.

"Let go, mama," Zygmunt spoke softly, "I talked to Banaszczyk yesterday. This twenty-eighth of August is certain. We'll all go. You, me and Jo."

"And then what?" She clasped her hands on the table. "Huh?

Will you give her hand away to Banaszczyk's son? Roman? She will hate you!"

"I'd rather she hated me than not give her a chance. Roman is a decent guy. With a temper, but really decent and he won't hurt her. You have to understand, mom, that we have to give her that chance. And even if nothing comes out of it, she doesn't regain her vision and will be at everyone's mercy until her last days, at least there will be someone accompanying her. A husband who will care for her, provide aid and support in sickness. Otherwise, what fate awaits her? Hm? Can you imagine? They will find her dead, clutching the tales of Saint Matthew, surrounded by wild cats. That's what awaits her. I won't let it happen!"

"Blasphemies again! Just stay silent, for heaven's sake!"

Roman's father, Stefan Banaszczyk, was a well-connected man who eagerly used his contacts, boasting of his personal relations with influential people. People such as a surgeon from an oph-thalmology clinic in Silesia, a fellow avid fisherman. The Silesian clinic, cooperating with famed specialists from both East and West, provided world-class care. Thanks to Stefan's efforts, an appointment was scheduled for Joanna on the twenty-eighth of August; on that day, she was supposed to see an American professor who supposedly treated the eyes of victims of the Hiroshima and Nagasaki atomic bombings. The consultation alone would not restore Joanna's sight, but Zygmunt hoped so much it would help that he was ready to give his daughter away to a man who was not a good match for her. Not at all. A certain belief based on his own marriage occupied his mind; a marriage that so many people considered to be so incompatible, against everything and everyone. He, a smugly nonchalant roll-ing stone, and Hanna, a reasonable and orderly girl. Thanks to these differences they enriched and complemented each other. This love was grand.

Hanna did not have lofty ambitions that would push her into a sense of her own helplessness. In her case, being born into a family of a recognized professor was not enough of a reason to feel better than others. She did what she had to do and kept a low profile. Graduating with a double major was a sort of gratification for her mother, Kazimiera, who married a much older man at the humble age of seventeen, becoming a housewife deprived of anything more than elementary education.

The decision to marry a sly-smiled carpenter, who had just completed vocational training, was Hanna's independent and conscious choice. Her parents did not interfere, not even when their future son-in-law expressed excessive interest in gambling. This family order of letting the relatives live their own lives existed until the death of Józef. However, once Hanna passed away, it all collapsed like a house of cards, exposing hidden human shortcomings. Kazimiera and Zygmunt engaged in a war of mutually denouncing each other's sins, mistakes, faults and vices, all of which happened in the presence of helpless Joanna.

It was the warmest night of that rainy August. Every single rustle of a leaf in the wind drew Joanna's attention. She was thinking about Sphinx; previously curled up on her neck, he was now gone, so lying still underneath the duvet, she was wondering where could he have disappeared. As anxiety overpowered her, she finally gave in and went to check in the garden.

"Here, kitty, kitty, where are you?"

Joanna found him under the horse chestnut tree.

"Come here, you little adventurer." The girl picked him up and kissed him on the cool, wet nose.

She didn't feel like sleeping or returning to her room. The air was filled with the sweet and spicy scent of the garden; the place, where the paths of her nighttime walks among the chestnut tree, azalea and rhododendron bushes could be unmistakably found. Joanna looked up to the sky and tried to imagine what is up there, in heaven. It was one of these August nights that people say the sky is crying with the tears of Saint Lawrence. Her imagination brought up images of sparks falling from the dark sky, every single one accompanied by a dream. A dream one thinks of very quickly before the star crashes to the ground. At least that's what she thought once, that it would crash… She also remembered that some of them shone brighter than the full moon and left a gleaming streak while falling. And so it was on this very night. This exact picture of a sky stretching above her appeared just before she closed her eyes. Something was moving on its every single piece. Shiny, deep blackness. Sphinx is blackness. Stars are sparklers. Long, shimmering wires held by revelers next to a Christmas tree, always with a dash of uncertainty in fear of getting burned.

"Can you see all of this, cat? Up there? Look to the stars! Tell me, tell me what you see," Sphinx purred impatiently in a response, "Oh, you…," Joanna cradled the cat against her chest, "you ignorant thing you. No respect for beauty. No scratching! Or I will play *Hammerklavier* for you!"

After entering the room, Joanna felt the presence that concerned her over the past few nights and pleasantly distracted her loneliness. Without even thinking, she could point her finger at the corner by the wardrobe and say: "Here you are!". Hiding inexplicable joy, she pretended to be unaware of someone watching her, passed by and sat down on a stool next to the piano. The moon, flickering through the waves of green, surrounded her emotionless face with an unearthly halo.

Graceful like a swan, she raised her hands and suddenly, like a new dawn, the air was pierced by the sweet thrill of the thrush's song, quarrels of the robins, interrupted whistles of blackbirds, branches moved by a gentle wind, a rustle of leaves, melodious shouts of male crickets and grasshoppers, even the woeful buzz of a fly caught in a spiderweb, as well as a fast-flowing creek and a tiny, forest brook.

The music exploding at Joanna's petite fingertips, moving with extraordinary speed, was an expression of joy, the state of her heart pumping vital blood into every single piece of her young body with immense pressure. At the same time, a desire was awakening in someone hidden in a dark corner, watching her with admiration. What desire? He could not really tell why. Love? Love that changes everything and makes one do good? He was too young to understand what was he looking for in a strange, dark room in a foreign country, well after midnight. He was mature enough, however, to notice the outline of shapely breasts underneath the funny striped pajamas worn by the genius creature conjuring up a mystic atmosphere with Grieg's *Morning Mood*.

"You didn't let people sleep again!" Kazimiera scolded Joanna, setting a tin mug with morning coffee before her. "Oh dear, dear, they will send militia after us for not respecting the peace during the night. You will see! Playing a bit too long and too loud."

"A bit?!" Zygmunt laughed, mouth full of food. "She fucking banged on them keys like crazy!"

"Don't be vulgar."

"Who...," he wiped a droplet of oil off his beard, "who's being vulgar? Me? Look, I hardly opened my eyes after a sleepless night and a nighttime concert that my own daughter served me under my roof, and mama's at it again."

"What is it? Herrings?" Joanna caught a familiar smell.

"That's right, darling, your hungover father is eating herrings for breakfast."

"And what am I supposed to eat, as mama didn't make breakfast for me?!"

"Just as we agreed. I told you – if you go to bed drunk, there's no breakfast and dinner for you the next day."

"Yet somehow mama managed to wake me up for work. And you swore you would never do it again!"

"And it was the last time, I'm telling you! Wake up on your own after a drunken night!"

"No problem, mama, will do!"

"Sure! Will do. You won't wake up on your own!"

Joanna jumped up from her chair with an expression on her face as if she wanted to say something, but words were stuck in her throat. Instead, she approached the staircase, her movements almost noble and dignified. Sphinx followed her, a manifesto of silent solidarity.

She was moving around the room, roaming the squeaky floor and scolding herself – how could she ever have hoped everything will be alright! That wise doctors would find a great cure for her eyes and normal life would return to this house. How could she dream in such a naïve, infantile way?! Hostility is the only thing that feels at home here! A hostility that holds her back every single time she feels powerful enough to try again.

Sphinx, crouching like a black panther, followed her movements with his keen eyes.

Standing by the bed, she heard the shuffling slippers followed by knocking. She chose to stay silent. For ten seconds.

"Come in."

"Honey, you did not eat anything." Kazimiera was standing in the doorway with a kitchen towel in hand. "Will you come downstairs or should I bring it here? Father's gone, he's left for work," the woman added upon Joanna's silence.

"I'm not hungry, thank you," the girl replied a few seconds later.

"Jo, what's going on?"

"Nothing."

"What, you don't want to tell me?" Kazimiera waited for a while. "Oh, I don't blame you. At all. To have a father like this!..."

"You think he's that bad?"

"Ahh!" she waved the towel. "Bad or dumb, what's the difference. He's just hard to live with. But you shouldn't lose your sleep over it. What's between me and him is none of your concern."

"None of my concern?" Joanna took a brave step forward. "Grandma, what are you talking about? How can you even think like this? When I was younger, I would take all the blame. I thought it was all because of me! Your constant fights, the bickering. Lord, I wanted to be able to see again so very badly! I thought that maybe if I recover my vision, there will be peace at home again. The way it used to be. When mom was alive. But you know what? After years of blaming myself for your hatred, I finally realized the problem lies with someone else. You two are the problem! You! The joke is on you because fate made you a family despite your opposing characters. This should have never, ever happened. And I'm so, so sorry for you. God...," Joanna held her face in her hands, "it must be so depressing. Such a dreadful feeling to be stuck in such an unhappy predicament.

So I guess that's why you're constantly trying to escape! Escape each other. And me." Sorrow traveled through her like a violent wave and left her speechless as she fell back on the bed.

Kazimiera broke the silence after a minute, not sure what to say.

"I'm not trying to escape."

"You are running away, grandma. Your daily visits to church are nothing else but an escape. And dad? Dad is trying to do the same with gambling and vodka."

"Not at all, sweetie! You're wrong! I go to church to pray. Because I have a lot to pray for! Your father, for example."

"God himself wouldn't be able to talk some sense into him."

"Don't say that, Joanna!"

"Anyway… nothing and nobody will ever be able to talk some sense into him," Joanna admitted miserably, hanging her head, "One day he's going to drink himself to death…"

"Every single day, when I pray, I'm not asking God for your father's abstinence. That's something he can cope with on his own."

"On his own? He can do it by himself? How do you know that?"

"Well, I know him."

"Then what is it that you are praying for? What is it?"

"I've got to go, I'm running late. The mass starts in a second. Please, come downstairs and grab something to eat. You can't worry so much."

"Gran?" Joanna called.

"Yes?"

"You didn't answer me. You know that I'm going to think about it all the time. Don't leave me hanging. Tell me, what is it that you think about when you pray for dad?"

"Inquisitive like your grandpa," Kazimiera said, grasping the door handle, "always on a quest to find an answer."

"So?"

"Every single day I pray to God that your father would not suffer." The woman quietly closed the door and set off, shuffling her slippers.

The cemetery was wrapped in silence, which was broken only by the gasps of trees swaying in the wind. Sitting like that by her mother's grave, Joanna would often think of heaven. Is mom there? What is it like? It's so tough to imagine something you cannot touch. For her, heaven was driving rain on her face, the touch of sun on her skin, sometimes the cold fluffy snow. She saw what she felt. But what does heaven look like? The place her mom is in? Joanna had no idea what could she compare it to. How could you wrap your mind around or comprehend something that you do not see when you're alive, but you touch it? Blue, gray, black. Colors in general. These were fading away too. Everything she remembered from childhood was disappearing into the void – methodically, piece by piece, slowly and inescapably. She used to dream in colors, pictures, friends' faces. And now... now her dreams were barely visions and touch. Sometimes so painful, as if she was experiencing it physically. Images, images... these fade away too. But one impression was engraved in her memory like a thorn, bothering her, frame by frame, till the end of her days. Her mother's death. A priest came with Zbyszek Maruszczak, an altar boy ringing a tiny bell. The priest was saying something, mom was just looking, grandma was crying while dad left the house and did not return until the next day. Drunk, he immediately started yelling at grandma because he did not like the fact that she had covered the large mirror in the hallway with a black shawl and stopped the large pendulum clock. Grandma just took his hand and said: "Let's go, we have to wash her." Then they placed mom in a brown coffin and people who gathered around sang sadly. Only dad didn't sing. He was wearing a dark suit and a tie and kept looking at mom's face lit by two big candles standing next to the coffin. She still remembers the fear that mom's hair would catch on fire. That was the only thing she could focus on – her own fear. And then it got even worse. The funeral was grim. It was raining and mom's coffin was lowered into a very deep hole using long straps. Suddenly, as soon as mom disappeared under the surface of the earth, she became the center of attention of all the attendees. Affectionate cheek pinches and forehead kisses ensued. "Poor baby! Poor, little Jo!"

"So, did you ask them?" Roman's voice broke into her memories that weren't even pleasant, but somehow always managed to sneak into her mind like an unwanted guest that you are still expected to be nice to.

"I don't understand, what are you talking about?" she responded carefully.

"The date. August twenty-eighth. You were supposed to ask, remember?"

"I didn't do it."

"Too bad," said he, sprawling on the bench with his hands in his pockets. Meanwhile, Joanna sat still, clutching her white cane as if it were a lifeline, "really too bad. The clock is ticking and you don't even know what joy awaits you."

At this point, Joanna remembered the conversation with her father that they were supposed to finish when he feels better. But it's been a long time since he's been supposed to get better.

He swore to do everything so that she could see again. He'd rip his veins out! And then he mentioned an American professor.

"Tell me about this joy," she requested, pretending to be polite.

"Girl, you're about to meet doctors," as he nudged her and leaned back, he added: "doctors that will cure you."

"How do you know that?" Joanna, still as a statue, seemed to stare into the distance.

"How do I know? And who do you think managed to schedule that appointment for you? Your alcoholic father? Or crazy grandma?"

"Don't talk about them like that!" She stood abruptly, letting go of her white cane.

There was something raw and adamant about her emotional stance. Like a mother wolf or bear ready for a fatal battle to protect her young. In fact though, without a cane, she was more of a helpless puppy rather than its dangerous mother.

Joanna fell on her knees, desperately trying to feel for the familiar surface of the cane. Embarrassment and humiliation overpowered her. She always tried so hard to hide before other people, and especially before him, her weaknesses, her awkwardness imposed by her disability, attempting to show her strong side, beaming with pride and independent of anyone, particularly him.

"Hey!" A painful nudge on her back. "How is it without your metal detector? Much harder, isn't it? But if you ask nicely, I'll give it back."

"Please."

"I said, nicely."

Joanna stood up and held out her hand.

"Nicely."

"You're so funny, just like your old man. But…," Roman looked her up and down and smiled, "at least you're much prettier. But really, you don't dress very nice. Always in those dungarees! Dear Lord, you look like a handyman's assistant. And your hair…," the man ruffled her bangs, "did it stop growing or does your grandma trim it with a chainsaw?"

"Touch me one more time and I'll gouge your eyes out!"

"Well, well…," he said, taking away his hand and pushing it in his pocket, "what a lioness! And about these doctors for you, my old man arranged everything. He's a good sport and has a heart for people. Everyone from our town owes him something."

To be honest, he was right. Using his extensive connections, Stefan Banaszczyk helped many people and then made them all dependent on him. Those who refused to accept the aid had it even worse, as Banaszczyk was the vindictive type. Kazimiera would call the man a "primitive communist", while Zygmunt was quite fond of him. And out of this sympathy, he let him win when they played cards together. Twice.

Information about the appointment with the American professor gave Joanna hope. For her, hope was never "the mother of fools"; she disregarded this disrespectful phrase that deprived people of the will to live. For her, hope was the air she breathed.

Every single day, early in the morning, before grandma and father would wake up and everyone would meet at the breakfast table, Joanna would sit at the foot of her bed and attempt to imagine how life will be when she recovers her vision. Won't her senses go mad in the mixture of colors and chaos of shapes? What about the music? And the piano? And if her sight takes her hearing away? So her Chopin and beloved Dvorak? Now seeing meant touching. How would it feel to look and actually see, with all the emotional baggage evoked by the image?

Faces... she would never touch people's faces. This aspect of their physicality was never that important for her. The voice meant way more. Nervous character, shyness, empathy, vanity – a conversation was enough for her to read it all in someone's voice.

But there was someone who aroused her interest without speaking a word. And this interest grew in her, irritating or even sharpening the senses. It had a certain aura of surreality. As if someone, lured by the sound of her piano playing, fell into a trap and she – hiding somewhere in the darkness – would look at them, observe their behavior and attempt to create the profile of their character.

In the dead of night, the person would enter a stranger's house through the window, ignoring the rain, storm and thunders outside. His strong, distinct and warm scent deconcentrated and invigorated her. Apparently, he liked piano music and, most of all, he returned the Gospel that must have been stolen by someone else.

Judging by all these behaviors, Joanna imagined the person to be a reckless young man, eager to take risks, brave, agile, honest; someone with a sensitive, artistic soul.

She always sensed the moment he slipped in, quietly, without a sound, somehow making his way around the squeaky floor. Sometimes he would hide behind a curtain, sometimes in a corner behind the wardrobe. He would sit on the floor and listen to her playing the piano as if it were a slowly unfolding tale. At that very moment, Joanna was overcome with an infantile desire to make him stay there for as long as possible. When she was finally going to bed, dead tired, he was still in her room. And that realization, that a stranger is watching her sleep, brought certain unsettling thoughts to her mind: what if I snore? Like dad whenever he drinks?

"Do I snore?" Joanna asked her grandma as the elderly woman was preparing to leave for the evening mass.

"Do you what?" the woman responded as she crouched and leaned against the wall to put her shoes on.

"Do I snore?"

"What is up with you? What would you need that information for?"

"It's just that dad snores and you don't. I'm curious how is it with me."

"With you? No. You don't snore."

"Are you sure? I mean, you do wear earplugs. So you could be wrong."

"Well, right," grandma sighed slowly, "had it not been for these earplugs, I couldn't sleep because of your father. Can you see it? He's bugging me all day and night. Back to you, however... I'm not wrong, my dear, you don't snore. You're always quiet and fast asleep."

"Mama is never wrong!" Zygmunt's ribald and slightly mischievous voice came from the kitchen. "Remember, Jo. Your grandmother is infallible. And saint at the same time! The Pope himself could take a leaf out of her book."

"I made a mistake once, indeed."

"No way! What was it? Did I miss something?"

"When I let my daughter marry a lush like that Marian!"

"Oh, why does mama insist on comparing me to Marian...? That's offensive! He doesn't drink! And such a loser."

Kazimiera shook her head, waited a while, and went into the kitchen.

"Tell me, what do you think it takes to be a loser?" As she waited for the answer, Kazimiera tapped her fingers on the table-top. Zygmunt's booze breath nearly knocked her off her feet, but she braced herself, closing the eyelids for a while.

"Dear mama, a loser…," the man swirled the glass in his hand, "is someone born with a kick me sign the size of Jo's piano on their back."

Kazimiera waved her hand impatiently as if wanting to say, *Oh dear, you're never going to change!*. Then, she proceeded to tie the black headscarf under the chin and clutching her prayer book, she left for the evening prayers at the church.

It was raining cats and dogs. Despite the humid and chilly weather outside, the window remained open. Joanna sat on the edge of the stool, resembling a stately waterbird. Soon, Edvard Grieg's *Morning Mood* lit the space wrapped in a heavy, dripping night, from gentle piano to joyful, luscious sounds.

Upon finishing, she remained motionless in the same stately pose, amid the flurry of chords in the air. Then, resembling the sails on the stormy sea, the curtains flapped, bringing a breath of humid wind throughout the room. The sound of a closing window and a firmly turned handle sent shivers down her spine. He stood right behind her, close as never before, smelling of the chestnut tree and cold, fresh rain. An undefined energy pierced her as if someone had suddenly turned the lights on and inten-sively, precisely investigated all the defects of her body and soul. Dear Lord! Dear Lord, give me the wisdom to know what should I do now. The chords still fluttered in the darkness of the room.

❦

Even when he would leave and escape in an unknown direction – another street, another city, another country, maybe even a star or planet – her room remained lovingly lively. She could feel the smell of rain, wind, the horse chestnut tree, as well as a wide smile on her face as happiness crushed her ribcage, invariably ensuring her that he's bound to return the following night.

What impression does she make on him? Who does he see when he's looking at her? A pianist? A girl? A blind girl? Or maybe a tomboy?

A tomboy. She heard someone calling her that for the first time one summer. Her grandma and father had some errands to run and left her at home with aunt Albina. Albina was one of these women who simply are the epitome of class, always looking great and being able to hold an intellectual conversation. Succinct, straightforward, with defined cheekbones so red they made her seem permanently embarrassed.

While it was just the beginning of summer, it was scorching hot. Standing near a stunning pink azalea bush and holding the suspenders of her gray dungarees, Joanna was heartily laughing at something that sat at her nose – and what might have been a butterfly.

"Joaaaanna… have you ever considered growing your hair out?" she heard aunt Albina call out from the porch, where the woman was resting on a striped orange lounger, wearing a straw hat and sipping yellow lemonade.

"No, auntie! It flew away! Was it a butterfly? Oh, what a pity… No, I have never thought about that."

"Jo, haven't you thought about buying a skirt? Or a dress? I'm sure you would look charming!"

"No, aunt, I haven't thought about that either," Joanna admitted politely, plucked an azalea flower and secured it behind her ear.

"Oh!" Albina raised her sunglasses to the forehead, "you look so pretty with this flower, finally like a girl."

"And without the flower?"

"Without the flower? Well… without it you look slightly different. Like a child. Or not… not like a child. Like a tomboy."

"Does it mean I look like a boy?" Joanna's mouth dropped open.

Albina, holding with her hand the straw hat on her head, approached Joanna.

"A very gentle boy, though." The aunt led her to the porch, where they both fell into deep loungers. "No offense, dear, but these pants do no good to any young girl. Neither does this boyish hairstyle. You look like a child. A woman your age…," she hesitated for a second and inquired further: "How old are you?"

"Fifteen."

"See, almost sixteen," she chirped, "so you are a young lady and you should take care of your appearance. Do something with your eyes, lips…"

"Do something with my eyes?! And lips? Is something…," Joanna appeared to be devastated, "wrong with my natural ones?"

"Nooo," Albina giggled, "I mean make-up. You know, black mascara, red lipstick… that's our feminine weapon!" She added teasingly. "*Sex appeal is our best weapon…*" she quietly hummed like in the old cinema.

"Well, that would be problematic," Joanna responded, "I don't have any weapons, so I'm unarmed."

"Oh," the woman covered her mouth, "I'm so sorry. Dear Lord, I keep on forgetting that..."

"...that I can't see. No worries."

"Jo, you certainly don't take yourself too seriously," Albina stood up from the lounger and crouched next to her, "and that's good. I want you to know that no matter what you're wearing, a skirt or these damn dungarees..." she pulled one of the suspenders, "you are a beautiful girl. Don't ever forget about it. Ever. Your face, but most importantly this," the woman poked Jo's forehead with a finger, "right here, is your weapon."

"Thank you, auntie."

"Anytime, sweetie."

"You know..." Joanna broke the silence after a long moment of relaxing stillness: scorching heat, lazily sipped lemonade, chestnut leaves rustling in the wind, all the scents, "oh, it's nothing. Never mind!"

"Go on!" Albina said, raising slightly from the lounger.

"I don't want to come across as vain..."

"Come on! What's going on?"

"Sometimes I wonder how do I actually look. You know: my face... body... I think I missed all these changes," Joanna attempted to joke, but there was a tone of sadness in her voice, "I know for sure that I have a long neck. Dad says that my neck would certainly be the envy of giraffes, and..."

"No more of this nonsense!" Albina protested, waving her hand as if she were chasing away an annoying fly, "and your big eyes would be the envy of frogs. Sounds like your father and his subtleties! There are no words for this man!"

That night, when the stranger decided to come out of darkness, Joanna felt the intensity of his gaze on her neck and the conversation with aunt Albina came to her mind: the boyish haircut, a neck that giraffes would envy and those big frog eyes. And she deserted, suddenly storming out of the room and leaving the stranger in a trance. When she returned, he was gone. Struck by her own cowardice, Joanna fell onto the bed and buried her face in the pillows, as if taking a plunge into the darkness.

The home was quiet, except for the ticking of the old clock. Hunched over the piano, as if she were delving into a complicated passage, Joanna played some measures with her finger, doing her best to think clearly as her mind run wild, but they stubbornly went in the wrong direction. Deep inside she was certain that the stranger wouldn't appear again, which would be a devastating loss. His mysterious visits fueled her dreams of sold-out concert halls; she was supposed to emerge from hiding and unleash her talent before other people. These night visits made her feel like she had spent her whole solitary childhood preparing for this very moment.

Twelve strokes of the clock, sudden as a cup of cold water thrown into one's face, were followed by heavy thunder. Awakened by the sounds of a storm, she tucked herself in bed. She wasn't afraid. For her, the sound of thunder always reverberated with warm sounds that lighted up the memories of her mother. "Don't be afraid Jo, there's a grand, good tree in front of our house. Only good things happen in the shade of good trees. Even when the storm is raging."

She quickly fell asleep and dreamed of her mother's voice. Its strangely realistic sound was abruptly stopped, replaced in the ethereal sequence by the distressing noise of an axe chopping down a tree, the sound of a breaking trunk and a tree crashing to the ground.

Joanna woke up suddenly, crushed in her dream by the fallen chestnut tree. What is all of this supposed to mean? Anxious and drenched in sweat, the woman was engrossed in her thoughts when she felt Sphinx's warm body around her neck and breathed a sigh of relief.

"Sorry to interrupt your sleep, kitty. What a nightmare it was! I need to drink something."

Before venturing to the kitchen, she approached the window and opened it, wanting to check on the tree. Quietly and majestically, it enveloped her face with the scent of rain and the rustle of leaves. Barefoot Joanna went downstairs to the kitchen and returned five minutes later with a glass of water. Sphinx, previously curled up in a ball on the bed, was now weaving between her feet and nervously meowing, as if excited by something. And then, as she bent over to pick him up with her free hand, she felt it. The stranger was standing in front of her, so close she could touch him. She held her breath, and so did Sphinx. Joanna panicked, suddenly turned around and, as if she had just remembered something, slipped out of the room again. It wasn't until she reached the bathroom and closed the door that she started breathing again, thoughts frantically running through her head. What now, Sphinx? Huh? Tell me! These horrible pajamas! And her hair was certainly a mess. For a second she even thought about taking a bath... but no! He will know that she knows. What a predicament! She chugged a glass of water, choking and coughing. Sphinx hissed. Alright. No bath then, and she won't even fix her hair; he would notice that she tried to make herself pretty. A sudden realization came to her mind: she was wasting valuable time. He could have disappeared already like he did the previous night. Joanna left the bathroom in a hurry, slamming the door with the confused cat inside. Her heart fluttering and hair a mess, she dashed into the bedroom and stood by the piano. It all felt so uncomfortable. She knew he was there, but couldn't really tell where. In which corner? Where are you? Where?! She couldn't focus. Heavy rain raged behind the curtains blowing in the wind, hitting the leaves of the chestnut tree and making it impossible to focus. Joanna moved towards the window, pushed it and turned the handle. And then, leaving behind the shame, insecurity and all the feelings that inhibited her, faced someone who leaned against the wall and – holding his breath for a while – suspended his existence. Joanna lifted her head high and blew. The stranger closed his eyes and smiled.

The days dragged on like Sunday afternoons. At night, Joanna and the mysterious stranger became entangled in something she struggled to define. It delighted and disturbed her. Slowly, she gained certainty that it was neither Chopin, nor Dvorak, nor any other great musician that set the tone of their meetings. A sense of mutual closeness and fascination grew in the intimate silence between them. She was trying to force herself into thinking that it was enough. But it wasn't, she wanted more; Joanna wanted to touch him and explore his face. Ever since he had appeared, some undefined and understated happiness filled every corner of the room. Gently crossing the invisible borders of their relationship, the stranger unveiled before her such reactions of her body she was entirely unaware of. A few times he blew on her hair, ruffling her bangs; one time, when she hunched over the keyboard, absorbing the sounds of Beethoven's bagatelle, she regularly felt his warm breath against her neck. Cold shivers, running up her spine, tangled up her fingers as she hit wrong notes. How could she have known all of this was barely an overture...

∾

"Can I have another one?"

"There you go," Albina said, pouring more tea into a mug and setting a plate with one more slice of warm bread before Joanna.

"Mmm... so delicious! Did my mom bake bread too?"

"Honestly... I don't think so. But I'm not sure about it, maybe I didn't have the chance to see it myself. She passed away so young. But you know what, your dad can. Or at least he could at some point in the past."

"Dad?!"

"Yes," Albina took a big sip of coffee. "Can you imagine? This boor would make a sourdough starter, knead the dough after five days, pop it into the oven and bake it. Our grandma taught us how to do it, we called her Nusia," she added with a nostalgic smile.

"Dad kneading bread dough..." Joanna got lost in her thoughts.

"See?! Sometimes we know so little about those closest to our heart. Even our parents. Ah," she waved dismissively. "It's all water under the bridge now. He always preferred to mess with wood anyway."

"That's why he's a carpenter," Joanna added. "People even say he's the best... we still have a cradle he had made for me when I was born. It's somewhere in the attic."

"I remember it. Hanna wanted a crib, as it would be more practical, but Zygmunt insisted on making a cradle."

"Now my old dolls and Leopold the bear sleep in it. Do you remember Leopold?"

"Gosh, I sure do! Leo! I thought he vanished somewhere."

"How would he dare? You know, you raised him really well."

"Oh, I can't really take credit for that. Before he landed in my lap, and then in yours, he belonged to my older cousin, Irena."

"Oh dear, how old is he?"

"God only knows… he's old, it's simple as that. All that I know is that his name used to be Konstancjusz."

"*Konstancjusz?*"

"What a silly name, right?"

"Not really? *Konstancjusz.* It has a nice ring to it. And sounds so regal."

"Oh please! It sounds horrible as a name for a teddy bear. Can you imagine it? A toddler talking to their stuffed animal: *My teddy, Kon-stan-cjuuusz!*?"

"Well…," Joanna wondered, rubbing her arms, "…not really!"

They both burst into a hearty, gleeful laugh, like old friends.

"You know, auntie, I don't think I ever had a chance to see any other things dad made apart from that cradle. It's a pity."

"It is, indeed!" Albina wiped smudged mascara off her face. "You should definitely see them. He's really good at it."

"I really regret that I can't."

"Oh, Jo…," the aunt shook her head. "I'm such a… sorry, honey."

"No worries!"

"Christ, it's so easy to forget it when you're around. To forget that you have trouble seeing."

"Trouble seeing, you put it in such a nice way. I'm blind as a mole! Though I don't even know...," Joanna made herself comfortable in the chair, "what does a mole look like."

"Nothing to regret here. It's a kind of a bigger mouse, except instead of paws it has shovels and a long nose. But wait...," uncertainty sparked in her eyes. "Do you remember what a mouse looks like?"

"Sphinx reminds me of that all the time."

"Good! And regarding your father... he could do other things as well. Quite a talent, this one. He used to be a great painter."

"Painter? As in, painting pictures?"

"Mhm," Albina murmured, propping her chin in the palm. "He used to draw as well. Your father is a classic example of wasted talent," she rubbed her finger along the rim of a glass as she spoke. "Unfortunately, it's quite common. Wrong paths, bad choices, lack of care, support, money... on the other hand, had he made different choices, we wouldn't be sitting here right now... together."

"Sure. Probably I wouldn't be here at all."

"That would be a huge loss for mankind, my dear," Albina chuckled.

"What do you think, what would he be doing right now? Who could he be?"

"I don't know. But you can speak about certain possibilities. Maybe a painter? Or a baker? But would he be happy then? When it comes to life choices, I think it's fate that decides for us. It throws particular events, phenomena, and people in our way… and we don't really have much choice but to instinctively surrender."

"Instinctively? What about reason? Shouldn't we follow our reason?"

"Well… perhaps? It would be best to follow our reason, intuition, and – of course – heart, my dear, our heart! Do you even know how did your parents meet each other?"

Joanna knew:

Every Thursday, Józef Lubczyński would host cultural bridge sessions for his university colleagues – like him, they were all professors and truly astute minds. During one of these meetings, a young carpenter recommended to the Lubczyński family by one of their acquaintances, was making minor repairs of their worn-out furniture. As he made his way through the living room, driving a nail here, putting some varnish there, the youngster was preoccupied with the players. Hammer in his hand, nails in his mouth, he was carefully observing the men. Suddenly one of the scholarly players, visibly moved, had to quit the unfinished game, leaving behind an empty chair standing by the game table. When the disappointed professors got up to say goodbye to the host…

"I can stand in for the gentleman who had to leave," a young carpenter proposed.

"Dear sir," started one of the scholars, dropping cigarette ash into a crystal ashtray. "No offense, but it's a really demanding game!"

"Demanding, elite, only for those from a good home with pre-war traditions," Kazimiera added, placing empty cups and dessert plates on a fine Chinese tray. She definitely had no idea that this blithe remark paved the way for the future tumultuous relationship with her son-in-law.

"Let's not exaggerate!" Józef interrupted the two. "Bridge does not require coming from a good family, just a bit of passion and gray matter. And you, young man," he carefully inspected him, "look like a person who has what it takes."

"I have all that." Zygmunt boldly rubbed his nose.

He had a great passion and an abundance of gray matter. Apart from that, there was an endearing sharpness and wild look in his eyes. And that was precisely what Hanna had seen in him, as she observed Zygmunt bid, take all the tricks and ruthlessly write something down on a worn-out sheet of paper with his yellow pencil. All with a mischievous grin of a hungry wolf.

She was twenty-five when he saw her there for the very first time. Beautiful, aloof and unavailable. As it soon turned out, not for him.

"And so in every spare moment, whenever he wasn't constructing furniture or outplaying people from their salary, he would grab a pencil and draw a portrait of Hanna. That's how I realized that my big brother lost his heart to someone, he was madly in love," Albina concluded. "Here you go," she handed Joanna a cotton handkerchief.

"Were these drawings nice?", she enquired, blowing her nose.

"They were, but he refused to show them to anyone. And when Hanna died, he destroyed all of them. All that's left is that pencil."

"Which pencil?"

"You know, the yellow one. The one he constantly puts behind his ear," she blurted out blatantly.

"He's carrying a pencil behind his ear? A yellow one?"

"I'm sorry," Albina closed her eyes and slowly opened them again. "Damn it, I can't get used to it. Listen, what about we stick some kind of note on your forehead for my sclerosis, huh?"

"No way," Joanna shook her head. "I like your forgetfulness. It's contagious. When I'm with you, I forget that I'm blind. It's a pity that grandma and dad are immune to it. Ouch! Auntie, you're going to squeeze the last breath out of me!" Joanna made a friendly attempt to resist, feeling Albina's strong embrace on her neck and the way she buried her face in her arm.

"You're so sweet," Albina admitted, returning to her chair. "Your father got a little bit lost on the way. He is doing his best to take care of you. And grandma... oh, this grandma of yours! It's better if I just stay silent."

"Grandma is doing her best to take care of me too."

Albina's eyes narrowed; her gaze uncertain.

Back then Joanna had no idea it was her last conversation with her beloved aunt. Albina's fate was no different from that of thousands of single women, who left the country hoping for a new life, and maybe even love. At first, she arrived in Italy, where she cleaned offices and pharmacies. She remained in good health, retained her dignity and class. An American lawyer of Sicilian origin fell in love with her; a widower of twenty years, he was visiting his brother, the owner of a pharmacy in a tiny town of Castelmola. And he took her back to the States, where they married.

She barely managed to close the door behind her, when someone aggressively dragged her into the kitchen.

"Where the hell have you been!"

Father's booze breath wafted on her face.

"Dad, don't scream, please. I was at aunt Albina's."

"Christ, why did I not know anything about it?"

"You weren't here yesterday when she came to pick me up. Grandma knows where I've been, she let me stay overnight. Didn't she tell you?"

"Not yet."

"What do you mean: *not yet*?"

"I mean *not yet*! I have just returned. Grandma must be at church."

"You were not home last night?"

There was no answer. Instead, she heard her father pull out a chair and flop on it.

"I don't like it when you're visiting Albina," he stated finally.

"Dad, she's your sister, after all... you don't like her?"

Silence ensued as he was trying to come up with an answer. The sound of an opening door and the shuffle of elderly feet on the concrete floor penetrated the stillness of the house.

"God bless you, mommy! What a cute sweater you have here!", he mocked his mother-in-law.

"Dear Lord!", the woman groaned and immediately hit back. "You look like you've been just released from the drunk tank!"

"Come on, mama, you're overestimating my possibilities, I'm no Lord. But yes, mama is infallible as usual. I did return from the drunk tank indeed. Not alone, though! With my best friend, Stefan Banaszczyk. At first, we had a cultural discussion over a beer, then we continued our discussion al fresco, by the Oder River, and then... whatever, never mind what happened after that. What really matters is what we had agreed on. So, should I satisfy mama's innate curiosity and tell her what did we arrange with my dear friend Banaszczyk?

"I don't care!"

"And you should! Mom," he started, his voice taking on a serious tone. "It concerns our Jo. And Roman. Take a seat," Zygmunt pulled out a chair next to him, "we have to talk. Jo, you take a seat as well."

"Me and Roman?" Joanna's mouth opened slightly.

"Zygmunt...," Kazimiera looked around in panic, as if she were afraid that by sitting next to her son-in-law, someone could get hurt, "not now. I'm going to tell her, but later."

"But what?! What do you want to tell me?" Joanna enquired.

"Later! Later!" Zygmunt nervously took a cigarette out of the pack. "It's for her good, don't you understand, mama?"

"Dad, but..."

"Go to your room, upstairs, now!"

The way to her bedroom seemed particularly long. She fell on her bed, burying her face in the pillow, Sphinx emphatically scratching the back of her neck.

She slept a restless sleep that infiltrated from reality; she could feel the scents, hear the steps and voices... "It concerns her and Roman. It's for her good, don't you understand, mama?!". In this dream, she was falling head-first and wanted to come back to reality so very badly. When she finally woke up, a painful echo of the nightmare lingered in her head and she could sense a gentle touch on her cheek. Panicked, Joanna sat up and froze on the edge of the bed and gasped for air, trying to come to herself and understand what was happening.

"Dad?" she asked with uncertainty in her voice, as he hasn't been to her room in years.

Joanna placed her fingers where she felt the touch in her dream. Now it seemed even more realistic. In some intuitive way, her hand found a way to someone else's warm and soothing palm. An enormous wave of emotion overcame her; she was very well aware that this hand represented all the best moments of this rainy summer. The sensation was accompanied by a profound belief that this touch is good. It won't bring harm. And that she was safe. A few moments later a thumb started moving across her knuckles. For the very first time she wanted to talk to him and tell the stranger in short, simple words, how happy his visits make her. But she was unable to put her thoughts into words. Their fingers intertwined and he held her hand ever so tightly. A sudden thought prevailed; a belief that a new chapter in her life has just begun, and she has to bid farewell to the old one, all by responding with an embrace to the stranger holding her hand in this firm and soothing way, anticipating her response. She was not ready for it yet – she could not and did not want to do it – so she clumsily took her hand away. Panicking, Joanna pulled her knees up to her chin and embraced them with her elbows, covering her ears with her hands. What now, she thought. It's all because of this shield. A shield built of distance towards people, events, the world. The world that could not infiltrate the impenetrable dark curtain that covered her eyes, to reach deeper into her soul and body. She paid for it with loneliness and the general opinion of being slightly crazy in her work pants, the Gospel clutched against her chest and a black cat weaving between her feet; found either at the piano during the night or at the cemetery during the day, like a gravedigger's daughter. Except for Albina, no one took her seriously. And then he found a way and crept into her life, turning it upside down. He noticed her and then, even if only for his own pleasure, dragged her out of the shadows. No matter how hard she tried, she couldn't logically describe it and find a deeper meaning in this situation. Joanna just felt as if someone perceived her distinctness as if it were a blossoming exquisiteness. Sitting by his side she had no idea what should she do and how should she act; on the one hand, she wouldn't like to hurt him, on the other, she wanted to play it safe. She swung her legs off the bed.

"Do you want me to play?", she asked, immediately regretting that the question sounded so stiff. Joanna interlaced her fingers on her knees.

A gentle blow of air in her face was an answer. She approached the piano, sat on the bench, but upon playing the first notes, another waft of air followed.

"Oh, not this piece?!", she responded, slightly disappointed. "So what?" Joanna put her hands between her knees and waited. The room slowly filled with tense silence. His stillness unsettled her, as she finally understood not a word would come from him.

"Will you say something? Even just yes or no. I'm not insisting, but it would make the communication between us much easier. Though I have to admit that...," she felt a warm breath on her neck. "Mhm. That was nice! Out of all the signs you're giving me, this is the most pleasant. It feels like thousands of tiny pinpricks that pleasantly tease me every single time I think about you." Joanna admitted, displaying a disarming honesty. "So I tend to think about you a lot. I've got so many questions for you. Why do you come here? And why through the window? You could try another way, a more traditional one, by using the door... do you like taking risks? Aren't you afraid? All that fuss with tree climbing, it must be dangerous, what if you fall? Or someone notices you and treats you like an ordinary thief?" His silence bugged her and slowly grew to be too much to handle.

"Do I know you? Do you live somewhere in the neighborhood? And it wasn't you who stole the Gospel, right? You know who did it, but it wasn't you. I'm sure of that. You just brought it back. Thank you, it means the world to me. Or maybe you are a runaway? Hiding from someone? Alright, here's me chattering all the time, and you're silent. They say silence is golden, but now I beg to differ. I'm not going to play the piano today; I don't feel like it. So...," the woman shifted on the stool. "Are we going to sit here in silence like this? You know... I have this idea. Probably crazy, but since you dig the risk so much...?"

There was a chair underneath the window; Sphinx was taking a nap on a pile of folded clothes. Suddenly Joanna removed the pajamas, first the top, then the bottom, as lightly, naturally and confidently, as a child would do in the presence of its mother. And so she was standing there in the moonlight, completely naked – as Joanna was entirely unaware of her appeal, the impairment depriving her of that guardian protecting the nude body against mockery, rejection and violation of dignity that sighted people call shame. As the flooding moonlight mercilessly highlighted the beauty that up to now was hidden underneath funny striped pajamas, someone gazing at that extraordinary scene was standing nearby glued to the floor, refusing to breathe, slowly falling apart into tiny pieces. Joanna apologized to Sphinx, who obediently jumped down from the chair, and then put on a flannel shirt and gray dungarees, evoking a groan of disappointment, or maybe rather a sigh of relief in someone; anyway, she did not hear that. She put her finger to her lips and gestured him to follow her as they took the stairs and went outside.

The night smelled of ripe summer.

"Hold on to me and don't be afraid of anything," Joanna

said over her shoulder, "my sight is equally good in the dark and in the day." As he persistently kept quiet, she had no idea how did he like this joke. From time to time, she would only hear him trip over something.

Suddenly he stopped in his tracks, realizing that the sight of crosses against the night sky was slowly looming on the horizon. He remembered about the flashlight in his pocket – naked Joanna still occupying his mind – and followed its light as graves emerged between the trees; those made of stone and those mounds of earth resembling people sleeping underneath thick blankets. Further on, neat rows of graves overgrown with weeds could be seen; ruthless evidence for the presence of the worst enemy of human remembrance. The passing time.

"Here lies my mother," Joanna remarked once they reached a modest terrazzo grave. "And my grandfather is buried closer to the old part of the cemetery. People say his grave is the most beautiful in the area, made of real marble. It was funded by his friends, professors and students. He was also a professor himself. A physician, mathematician, he also played the piano... so beautifully. Unfortunately, my recollection of him is very weak, he passed away when I was two, but you know... I feel like he's still present in my life. Maybe it's because of the piano? I'm not sure, he used to own it. I also have his vinyl collection. Chopin, Beethoven, Mozart, Rachmaninov... apparently he particularly appreciated Dvorak, I enjoy his pieces as well. So joyful and moving at the same time. You know, in a few days I'm off to a clinic in Katowice, some famous doctor is supposed to check my eyes. If he cures me... God, I don't know...," Joanna shook her head. "I just don't know what's going to happen then. I keep on asking this question to myself. Maybe it would be better not to change anything? Will I gain or lose more? Truly a Shakespearean thought, isn't it? *To be or not to be?* I know one thing for sure. I know what I'm going to do once I regain my vision. I'm going to go to a concert. A true concerto with the whole orchestra... a viola... cello... double bass... trumpets... kettledrums... glockenspiel... the harp... and obviously a grand piano. A grand piano and a violin. I adore the violin; don't you think they can wail in the most beautiful way? I know how the violin sounds, but I have no idea how does it look like. My aunt says it has the shape of a little woman, that's why it keeps on moaning. Apart from the grand piano, I don't know the shapes of any other instruments."

Joanna stopped talking and sat on the edge of a bench made of wooden planks. Engrossed in her thoughts, perhaps partially absent. The stranger sat next to her and looked into the sky, not a cloud in sight on that night, and got mad at it for displaying all of its stars with no empathy for those unable to see. He turned off the flashlight.

"I come here often when loneliness kicks in. So basically I'm here every single day... When I lost sight after my mom's death, I stopped playing with other children. Or maybe they did not want to play with me anymore? Well, apart from Roman, he keeps on following me. I've got a feeling my dad wants me to marry him. Grandma doesn't want me to know about it. But I already know, I don't need to be told. I can understand a lot of things, I can guess... dear God," Joanna, startled, suddenly realized something. "I don't want Roman! I'll never get married, it's so horrible. When one spouse dies, the other person hits the bottle or becomes a religious bigot. And you have to have children. I don't want to have kids at all. What if they lose sight? Like I did? Anyway, I don't think I would be able to take care of them. And you," Joanna turned her head towards him, "do you have a wife?"

Silence.

"Alright, you don't. Why? Are you ugly? I've heard it's tough for ugly people to find someone who would love them. Sometimes I wonder what does it mean to be unattractive. I just know that being ugly and blind is one misery. Both destine you for a life of loneliness. People don't know us. So? Are you ugly and lonely?"

Silence.

"So, you are unattractive, lonely, and music fills your heart like it does mine... You know, I think that beauty and ugliness could not exist without each other, as one is the evidence of another, isn't it?"

His concern overwhelmed her; nobody has ever listened to her half as closely as he did. On the other hand, she had never spoken this much to anyone.

"I have a request...," Joanna straightened up. "It's just that...," she ran her hand across her forehead as if trying to set free the thought that bothered her, "...that I don't know what your reaction will be. I don't want to offend you, hurt you or violate your intimacy... Usually, I don't do this for faces aren't interesting to me. The human voice is far more intriguing, but since you refuse to speak... I would like to touch your face. May I?" Joanna stretched out her hands with her fingers extended. "May I?", as he remained still, she closed her hands and felt horrible, awkward, pushy and greedy.

"You know...," the girl continued, trying to sound carefree. "That night you appeared at my place for the very first time, I came here and told her about you. She told me: *he won't hurt you if he appreciates music*. Obviously, I did not hear it, that's how I imagined it. She was right…," Joanna turned her face towards the stranger. "You are a good person. Like my grandpa. I think I'm a good person too, right? What do you think about all of this? Do you think so too? Alright," she sighed, "you just won't say a thing. So I won't say a thing too. Although I'm not sure if I can do it with you."

"You know…," she continued after five seconds. "I enjoyed being quiet with you. I came to the conclusion that it's not necessary to fill the void with just about anything. Just like silence should not be filled with mere words that convey little meaning, that won't teach us anything, but can only irritate us. What do you think?" Silence. "Oh my God…," Joanna suddenly realized something, "I know! How could I have not thought about it before? Are you mute?! Because if you are, we are quite a couple. A blind one and a mute one." Her pearly laugh resounded in silence. "I'm not wrong, you are mute! But your hearing is really good. And your sight. Oh no," the tone of her voice suddenly changed as Joanna extended her hand, "there you go! Did you feel it too? I felt a raindrop, I think we should go back, it's going to start raining soon. Thank you for coming here with me, it was very nice of you. If you let me," she took his hand, "I'll guide you. Oh! Your hand is so strong and coarse, like my dad's. You have to work hard. Don't you think it's funny? A blind girl guiding a mute one. Or maybe you are guiding me? You know…," she stopped and gazed upwards, seemingly looking him in the eye. "I want to tell you one more thing. I really like having you by my side. So come to me, please, as often as you can. And if you won't be able to… well, I will be waiting anyway."

And then the rain poured down. There was something joyful in the escape from the downpour as if they were not trying to run away from it, but chasing happiness instead.

The next day, Joanna was wandering around the garden, humming under her breath, smiling to herself and playing rough with confused Sphinx. She just couldn't help it.

The evening came. In the stuffy lounge, the only sound was the slow tick-tock of a wall clock, making it seem as though time was passing slower. Kazimiera's mouth moved in the devout silence, following the mute and repeated prayer to the rhythm of rosary beads moving between her fingers. Entrusting her granddaughter's sight to Hail Mary, deep down she was cursing her son-in-low, who had certainly already hit the bottle! In the morning he promised he would come home straight after work so that they could carefully prepare Joanna's medical records for tomorrow's visit at the clinic. Meanwhile, the glowing sun was vanishing behind the horizon and he was nowhere to be seen. Joanna sat in the armchair opposite her grandma, her Gospel in hand, so absorbed in her thoughts. She was obsessively thinking over and over again about the same thing.

"You will wear a dress." Kazimiera broke the silence, having quickly but devoutly kissed the rosary and placed it in a small brown box.

"Excuse me?" Joanna's mouth dropped open.

"You will wear a dress to the appointment."

"Grandma, a dress? Where am I supposed to find one? I don't have any! Not even one!"

"Oh really? Right, you don't." The woman admitted after a while. "Wait, wait!" She quickly got up and went to the hall, approaching a mahogany wardrobe inherited from previous owners. The creek of the old door followed. "Your mom was quite an elegant dresser," Kazimiera spoke loudly as she moved the hangers: floaty dresses, woolen skirts, two house dresses, everything in mint condition, "…and took good care of herself. You know…," she continued, "the war was barely over, dear Lord, everyone was dirt poor, but somehow the most recent fashion trends seeped through the Iron Curtain in no time. Women started sewing, their sewing machines were constantly rattling… and they still do, up until now," Kazimiera's petite hand, covered in a net of veins, stopped over a short, A-line dusty pink dress. She took it off the hanger and passed it to Joanna. "Here, try this one on. It's nice, so girly. Your mom liked it very much, and she designed it herself."

Joanna removed her denim dungarees, put the dress on and then slowly turned around.

"So…," the girl spread her arms, "…how do I look?"

"Dear God…," Kazimiera covered her mouth with her hand, shaking the head. "You look like her!"

"Like mom?"

"Mom too, but more like… you know…?," she was trying to recall something. "Oh dear, it's on the tip of my tongue… I saw this actress on the cover of a fashion magazine, Albina showed me. She had hair like yours and generally resembled you. And the dress! Almost identical! What fate! Ah, see, I can't remember. Or actually… wait, wait… Twegg, Twagg… something like this!?"

"Was she pretty?"

"Thin as a toothpick, with huge eyes. Like you! Alright, let me see! Turn around once more. Oh, see?! Much better than in those pants your father forces you to wear."

"He doesn't force me," Joanna protested. "I like these pants. And in this…," she took a few steps forward, "I feel weird, as if my legs were bare. Am I not going to be cold?"

"Child, it's summer. It's warm."

"But rainy."

"So you will wear stockings."

"What are stockings?"

"Lord!" Kazimiera groaned. "Tights, then."

"Tights? I don't like tights. Feels like my legs are wrapped in bandages."

"You'll get used to that."

"Grandma...," Joanna enquired carefully. "Do you think this doctor will find a cure?"

"How am I supposed to know?!" The woman looked at Joanna with deep sympathy. "I'm constantly praying for that to happen. Everything is in the hands of God," said Kazimiera, putting her hands together as if she were praying.

"And the hands of the professor", Joanna added.

"He's merely...," Kazimiera waved her hand in the air, making the sign of the cross. "He's merely a tool of the Lord's will."

The door slammed shut and Zygmunt entered the lounge, confirming Kazimiera's assumptions. Using her own words, he was drunk like Marian the lush.

"I know, I know, I'm a little late, but...," he raised his finger, as though forcing the Earth to stop for a while because he would like to make an announcement. "I had to go over some serious matters with Banaszczyk. I would also like to calm down my blessed mother-in-law, whom I de... de... finitely do not deserve, that everything is going smoothly and we're off tomorrow at ten a.m. sharp. And now, if mama doesn't mind, I should have a nap. I swear I'd love to gossip with mama but Jo's father-in-law pumped me full of disgusting moonshine... and this irresponsible behavior disrupted my innate ability to consciously understand all the subtleties of mama's rhetoric. Anyhow..." he went silent, his mouth open.

"Do I look like Tweggy?" Joanna asked, instinctively feeling that he was staring at her, analyzing the sight of the dress in his intoxicated mind.

"What? Tweggy? Twiggy... no, not like Twiggy, but like...," he loudly swallowed and closed his mouth.

"Zygmunt...," Kazimiera took a step towards him. "I thought that she doesn't have any dress and she should look decent at that appointment. She just can't go there in these worn-out pants."

A silence ensued, with the sound of distant, mournful wailing of an ambulance carrying someone's life hanging in the balance, overpowering the slow ticking of a wall clock.

"Dad, if you want to, I can wear pants."

"What?... No, no!" Zygmunt seemingly woke up from a deep sleep and sobered up in seconds. "Grandma is right," he admitted, touched his temple and then left the room, rubbing his stubbly cheek. "Good night!"

Joanna wanted to follow him and say something good, reassuring and uplifting; deep down, however, she felt it was this particular moment when her father had to be alone with his thoughts, as any attempt to take his mind off them would violate something that made him the most human – the yearning for his wife.

Midnight came when Joanna was standing by the open window – silent, sleepily engrossed in her thoughts. "Come to me, don't let me go without saying goodbye", she whispered.

He came, took her hand and pulled her towards the unknown. They found themselves among the bustling crowd that attempted to be discreet and remain barely audible. As long as the man held her hand tight, ensuring safety and encouraging her, Joanna was not afraid. But when he let go of her palm, she felt somewhat perplexed, as though she were removed and separated from everything she knew. A gentle breeze carried the scent of musty leaves and burning wood. A bonfire, Joanna thought. With her heart racing, she stood still, waiting for something that was bound to happen, every single particle of her body sensing that it would be something extraordinary.

Meanwhile, the man, standing by her side and carefully looking at Joanna – glowing in the halo of sparkling flames, noble, silent and unsettled – recalled his school trip to Metropolitan Museum of Art in New York City. Getting lost in winding corridors of the massive building, he stumbled upon an ancient sculpture. Making little of the voices of the teacher, the guide and finally his friends telling him it was time to leave and that he would end up locked in, he was standing in front of her and wondering – almost obsessively – why people consider her beautiful. He did not like anything – not even a single thing about her: a marble body with eyes expressing "nothing" in particular. Why so beautiful, then…? He gazed upon her naked stomach, arms, breasts, neck… and nothing. Harmony, ideal, almost perfect proportions. Is this enough to embody beauty? No. Because he couldn't feel any connection to this sculpture. There was no deeper thought that would stick to his mind, one of these that suddenly pop up and irritate your brain, constantly reminding: *Hey, remember me?* That's when his beliefs came into focus; the idea everything but music is futile, and nothing in his life will shake him to the core. Only music, only violin.

He couldn't have been more wrong!

How much can you learn about someone by spending a dozen or so hours in their company? A lot. Just four weeks ago such a question wouldn't even come to his mind. People in general did not evoke in him such enthusiasm or sentimentalism. But then he met her and everything changed. Suddenly he saw beauty not external and superficial, but so internal and pure; beauty that matured him and made him like himself. He was drawn to her like a moth to a flame, while her aura tickled him with otherworldly pleasure. Was it normal that he would think about her in such an intensive, frantic, almost obsessive way? Over and over again? Despite everything that divided them? Apart from music – literally everything?

"What's going on?" Joanna's question brought him back to reality. "Is...," she did not finish, as he covered her mouth with his hand. Softly, gently, not evoking any fear.

He took off his sweater and covered her arms with it. Then he motioned for the instrument to be passed to him.

Suddenly the buzz of the voices faded away and silence ensued, like a gray cloud hovering over a bonfire, ready for a downpour at any moment. The man relaxed his shoulders, body and neck, brought the violin to his chin and propped the instrument upon his shoulder. He brought the bow to the strings stretched over the ebony fretboard. Pushing and sliding it, he pierced heavy silence with breathtaking sounds of frantic adventure hiding within the pieces brimming with upliftment, contrasts and winding paths.

It was the most magnificent night in Joanna's life. She was startled by the music, bonfire, the bustle of the crowd and everything that happened then. She explored his face and felt his heart when he held her hand tightly against his chest. But she had no idea how torn the boy was and how painful these heartbeats were as he knew he had to leave, thinking it would be for forever.

Her neighbor, Kramer, walked her home, insisting she does not ask about anything.

"Don't ask, Jo. Neither me nor you need to get in any trouble, right? I just did just what I was asked to. I was supposed to put out the bonfire and walk you from this clearing. Well...," the man sighed and kindly patted her on the shoulder, "we will see what this important American professor will do for your eyes."

"And the man, what about him?"

"He asked me to tell you he's not coming back."

"Not coming back? Asked you to tell me...? But he doesn't speak."

"He does, just not the way we do."

Sphinx would always sense Joanna's presence even before she actually entered the house. Now, with its tail high up in the air, the cat wandered towards the doorway and waited for her. *Asked me to tell you he's not coming back* – it couldn't end like this! She focused all her thoughts on it so much it physically hurt her. Then she sent this thought somewhere far, far away, desperately longing for someone to seize it – *Please, don't let it be the last time!*

Days passed and weeks faded away, the fall rolled in. After that night of the violin concert, quite a few important things happened in Joanna's life.

First, she went to the clinic. Having undergone numerous examinations she learned that her blindness is inoperable, irreversible and bound to last forever. While this brutal diagnosis crushed Kazimiera and Zygmunt, Joanna took it with surprising humility.

Her engagement with Roman was another important milestone. This unfortunate and sad experience made Joanna realize that disability is not the worst thing that could happen to a person. Living without a heart that one once had at their fingertips, however, definitely was.

The wedding was planned for next summer. Up until that moment, the fiancés were allowed to see each other only in the presence of their families. Kazimiera requested such behavior, as she believed both in God and the idea that the bride should be as pure as the white veil on her head. Unsatisfied Roman approached the situation with pain in his heart and loins, while Joanna felt a quiet relief and inexpressible gratitude towards her wise grandmother. Especially given that the perspective of future life and intimacy with Roman loomed on the horizon like a harsh sentence that she could not appeal and definitely had done nothing to deserve. With her face lackluster and devoid of any dreams, she roamed the corners of the room looking for traces of that soothing presence.

Time passed inexorably, crushing her youth and everything she had like a flood wave... Winter passed, spring arrived and the day came when church bells, silent since the Maundy Thursday, announced to the people on Earth that Christ has risen.

Barefoot Joanna went downstairs, and moving her fingers along the wall, anxiously entered grandma's room. Already half an hour ago Kazimiera should have left for the morning mass resurrection and experience the return of the blessed sacrament to the high altar.

"Grandma?", using her hands, Joanna found a familiar shape in the bedding. "Grandma? Did you sleep in?"

A stroke took away Kazimiera's mobility and independence, and turned her speech into incomprehensible jabber. The elderly lady was so weak, that soon she fell into complete numbness. Joanna, who took turns at the bedside with her father, almost experienced physically her great suffering, which awakened her from her own apathy. She feared for grandma. Feared she would die. The face of that fear lifted her, like a kite, above all other troubles and worries that she had experienced in profound silence.

For Joanna, caring for grandma was neither exhausting nor burdensome. After all, it came down to a few simple steps, such as propping up a pillow or applying a moisturizer on her back to prevent painful bedsores. Joanna would grab her Gospel and read out loud, carefully listening to her patient's reaction. It seemed as though the tips on how to live, suffer and die, written down in the holy book, brought grandma noticeable relief. Then it was like a miracle happened. The heavy, labored breathing would become even and calm; grandma would try to hum some holy melodies and the bitter scent of illness would drift away into the unknown. All of this filled Joanna's sorrowful heart with quiet hope. Hope for a miraculous recovery. On the other hand, both Joanna and Jesus Christ, looking at them from the wall above the headboard, where he was hanging in the majesty of his suffering on an ebony cross, witnessed one more miracle that happened, day by day, right before them. The miracle of her father's transformation. A grumpy and grouchy man, devoid of any tendency to express his feelings, slowly started to show certain signs of sensitivity – which, as Joanna suspected, he had always carried within. On the day when he buried his wife, he hid it from the whole world, even his daughter. Now Zygmunt behaved as if he found a new obsession in caring for his mother-in-law's health. In these moments spent by her side, he radiated concern, maybe even tenderness. Hearing the soft, calm and extraordinarily patient way that her father talked to Kazimiera, Joanna could even imagine how gently would he turn her limp body. He fed and even bathed her. After a few weeks, Zygmunt was visibly tired, often falling asleep in an armchair right next to the patient's bed. While he didn't complain, Joanna sensed that he had reached the end of his strength. In this case, she proposed that she would take all the night shifts so that he could have proper sleep after an exhausting day at the carpentry shop and by grandma's side. Surprisingly, he also stopped drinking. Joanna felt as though some long, closed door opened within her, the new circumstances giving her sudden courage to fight for herself and her life. She just hoped her father would understand.

Joanna was in grandma's bedroom, awaiting her father's arrival from the carpentry shop. He returned slightly later than he should have. She heard him open the door, take off the shoes and wash his hands. Finally, Zygmunt stood before her and touched her shoulder.

"I'm late, but I had errands to run. Roman told me to hug you. So...? How was she today? What's up with grandma?"

"Nothing happened, it appears she's sleeping. Dad...," Joanna held the Gospel tight against her chest. "I don't want to marry. I don't want Roman. He's a bad person."

"What?" Zygmunt plopped on a chair. "How do you know he's a bad person?" he gazed at Joanna in astonishment.

"I don't know. I don't like him."

"You think he's bad because you don't like him? You don't go around judging people like that. It's really immature."

"I know, I'm not judging him. I just... I'm afraid of him, that's all!"

"Afraid?" Zygmunt looked at her, his glance suspicious and fearful at the same time. "Why? Has he ever done anything to make you think like this? Did he ever... I don't know... hurt you... or something?"

"I don't think so. He's never hurt me but there is something in him that bothers me."

"Hey, my dear," Zygmunt crouched down and took her hand which was resting on her knee. "If I had even the slightest doubt that he would hurt you, he'd be dead by now."

"Dad, stop! I'm serious."

He got up and approached the window, leaned his hips against the window sill and looked at the elderly woman. Anemic light from a brass sconce hanging above the ebony cross flowed down on an unmoving face, dramatically bringing out the suffering that she had humbly accepted.

"I'm serious too," he spoke finally, moving his tired gaze towards Joanna. "Grandma looks in this bed like a... corpse on a catafalque. You don't see with your eyes, but you've got wits. You can think, foresee, plan... you're wise."

"She looks the way she looks. She's sick, after all. I don't understand where you're going. What does Roman have to do with all of this... with grandma's sickness?"

"You will marry Roman and live in his house," her father's kind and soothing tone turned firm and straightforward.

"In his house?" Joanna's mouth dropped wide open. "But... how? Dad! My home is here!"

"This house... is not the right place for you two. Roman is

setting up a room at his parents' home. Big, beautiful, south-facing, so there's a perfect amount of sunlight. You will have a separate kitchen, so your mother-in-law won't be sticking her nose in your business. That's what matters in marriage."

Suddenly she experienced a peculiar feeling, as though she were sitting on a strange chair in a foreign home. This anxious thought moved down to her stomach, causing a nauseating commotion. *This house is not the right place for you two.* Joanna kept processing her father's words in her mind as they suddenly became a painful vision of possible consequences.

"No!" she protested, her mouth dry. "No!" the woman repeated, stressing her words even more.

"Excuse me?"

"Dad...," Joanna got up from the chair, "there's a box in the attic, with all my dolls that you have bought me. Do you remember the first one, a rag doll? I called her Joan because that's what you called me back then... There's my piano in my room that I inherited from my grandpa." She took an uncertain step forward in his direction, clutching the Gospel ever so tightly. "Dad, do you remember the first piece I played on it?" Joanna fought back tears, puckering up her mouth. "You were so moved, so moved because it was *Happy birthday* for you, on your birthday. I was three years old at the time. Remember...?". He was listening to her intently, his face focused, furrowing the brows. "You don't remember," disappointed Joanna concluded when he remained silent. "And in the garden, near the gazebo, lies my old rusty bike that you used to teach me how to ride. Remember how you were teaching me how to cycle...? When you let go of the stick and shouted *clear the way, for my sweet blue jay!* We carved MDJ on the kitchen table using a fork. Mom. Dad. Jo. Don't make me leave this house! It's my home..."

"I have to take care of grandma," he passed Joanna and approached the bed. "Go to your room now," Zygmunt stated over his shoulder. "Get some sleep. You will sit by her side at night."

Two hours later he knocked on the door of Joanna's bedroom and asked her to play *Happy birthday* for him.

"No, I won't do it."

"Why?"

"Because I don't play the piano anymore, I don't know how."

"You don't know how…," he whispered, as he sat on the edge of the bed and lowered his head.

"Dad, it's your birthday today."

"I guess so…? You remembered?"

"I always remember. Happy birthday, dad."

The following days were atrocious, filled with the necessary care for grandma and the crushing silence that ensued between them. It's so sad when two people that live together have nothing to say to each other, just passing by and trying not to get in each other's way. They wouldn't eat meals or sit by grandma's bed together, doing everything alone. When she was taking care of grandma, he was either at work or sleeping. When he was the caregiver, she was trying to sleep off the all-nighters. But she couldn't get a good rest. She would often wake up, hearing her father walk around the room and talk to himself. In such cases, Joanna would wonder what was bugging him.

Zygmunt was first to extend the olive branch, starting with small gestures, a few words here and there, irrelevant messages, a cup of tea brought to her room. Oh. And he also baked a loaf of bread.

It was May. On this sunny day, the chestnut tree flowers were beautifully whitened against the lush, green leaves, as some of them – a whole lot of upright clusters – covered the ground underneath the tree. Zygmunt climbed down the ladder, picked up all the flowers into a wicker basket and brought them into the kitchen.

"Well, Jo…," he pulled out the chair, fished a pack of cigarettes out of his pocket, sat down and lit up one of them. "In July and August, we will pick some young chestnuts. In September we will harvest all the ripe ones and pour some spirit over them so you can rub it on grandma's back. This year we will make lots of this tincture, way more than usual."

"Why more? We've got plenty from the last year," Joanna said, plucking the flowers from the stem. Later on, she would spread them on brown paper and leave them to dry, subsequently mixing the blossoms with yarrow and nettle and storing the herbal blend in glass jars. She would make tea from it – one of these wonderful infusions that cure every ailment.

"Old Banaszczyk has some leg problems, he's constantly complaining about varicose veins. You will surely win the heart of your future father-in-law if you give him a few bottles."

"And what will he do to win my heart?"

"What's wrong with you?" Zygmunt eyed her up and down. "You've become so defiant. It's completely unnecessary," the man inhaled the smoke and slowly exhaled it. "Delicacy suits you better."

"One does not exclude the other. You can be both defiant and delicate."

"You're talking like your grandma," Zygmunt put the cigarette out in the ashtray. "Speaking of her, I'll check on her."

"As soon as I'm done with these flowers I'll go to the cemetery and then I will take over."

"There's no hurry, sit with mom for a little bit longer if you wish."

She arrived at the cemetery in the afternoon. The funeral of their neighbor down the road – Eugeniusz Latkowski – was taking place near the alley on the right. Apart from his name and surname, as well as the fact that he was the oldest neighbor in the area (people were talking he was over 100 but remained in good health), Joanna knew nothing about the man. Sadness overcame her when they started to sing *We shall gather at the river* and she heard the thud of dirt falling on the wooden coffin. Sadness that she never had a chance to speak to this man, never even said *good morning* to him, and there's nothing she can do about it right now. The story is over without even a single *good morning*.

"Goodbye, Mr. Latkowski…," Joanna said her quiet goodbye to the neighbor. She had this peculiar belief that she owed this to the man who lived a dozen or so homes down the road. Suddenly, Roman sat on the bench next to her. Without saying a word, he was just sitting and sitting there, the sweet fragrance of his aftershave wafting in the air.

"I want to be alone," Joanna said, slightly irritated, turning towards him. "Could you respect it? I haven't visited her in a while."

"Why do you spend so much time with your grandma? She's bedridden, it's not like she's going to hurt herself."

"You wouldn't do the same?"

"Well," Roman murmured, shoving his hands in his pockets. "I don't have to deal with this problem, my grandma lives in Gdansk."

"Roman," Joanna broke the long silence upon realizing he's in no hurry to leave her alone, "why are you doing this?"

"Doing what?"

"Why me? Why do you want me in particular? There are other girls. Normal, ordinary... you know, with me it's not going to be easy for you."

"Seriously?" Roman crossed his ankles. "I'm madly in love with you."

"I don't love you, though."

"So what? I know that."

"And it doesn't bother you? You'll be miserable because of me."

"We should see, darling. I've got a feeling you will love me in the future," Roman suddenly jumped up from the bench. "You will love me, you'll see!"

Like a barometer predicting bad weather, Joanna was able to sense the incoming change in his mood. From mellow, reflective spirit to sudden rage. And that's what scared her the most about him.

One month later Kazimiera's body resembled a skeleton. Apart from the sickly-sweet scent of illness and mothballs, Joanna started to sense the irrevocable death creeping up in the corners of the house.

One night she took her blanket and pillow to make herself comfortable in the chair right next to grandma's bed, but it was too hot. She sat on the floor, leaning her back against the side of the bed, and started praying for her. Joanna was so afraid that grandma would die. She was also afraid about her fate, as she would be completely alone in this world – with her father and Roman in tow, but still alone. Joanna lost everyone that she was comfortable around, everyone that she felt important to. Please, don't let her die! God, don't let her die! She longed for a miracle so much, so that the good Lord would fix grandma on the inside and erase whatever had happened in her brain. She was the only one that could stand up to her father. Maybe she could convince him and then he would go back on his word to Banaszczyk? God, how much she missed their quarrels! Insults. Making each other angry. And if the good Lord has no intention to fix her, he could just keep her in this sleepy state. But not take her away, not yet. Joanna wiped away the tears and felt a sudden wave of emotions towards her grandma. She laid next to the fragile, elderly woman and embraced her, realizing that the only thing she could do for her right now is let her go. To mom, to grandpa, who were definitely waiting for this petite woman that she wrapped in the cocoon of her selfish reasons, keeping her on this side of life.

The day came where neither sickness nor mothballs could be sensed in the air. The room was filled with the presence of loved ones that left the earth long ago and now came back to take their mother, wife, daughter… Joanna whispered into her ear the words of her gratitude and love for all the care and everything she did for her.

"I love you. You can go now." Grandma's soul finally escaped the aching body, headed towards what she would call the Kingdom of God, and what her son-in-law would call the Nothingness.

Even though Joanna had no idea where her grandma's soul went – to Heaven or the Nothingness – one thing was certain: she passed away calmly, in sympathetic company.

Joanna's inclination for solitude made her leave the bedroom less and less. She felt abandoned by her father and the whole world; not that the latter understood her anyway. Maybe because her vulnerability matured her more than other young people her age. She was no prisoner to vanity; standing for hours in front of a mirror, carefully investigating the defects of her appearance or delving into self-love was not for her. There was no sulking or blaming the unfair destiny; strength and sensitivity overpowered her character. Anyways, she had other worries. An alcoholic father and an unwanted fiancé. It must have been also tough to find a fortunate side to the coincidence of two events, so starkly different in their nature: her grandma's death and the upcoming wedding. There was one, as due to Joanna being in mourning, the nuptials were postponed. On the other hand, her father again took to measuring the pain following his wife's passing and the uncertainty regarding his blind daughter's fate in glasses of vodka.

The days went by unnoticed, and then fall came with the leaves of the chestnut tree changing colors and the nights setting in earlier, spreading fearful silence that tormented Joanna and overwhelmed her with sadness. It was true that since she gave up playing the piano she would go to bed earlier – but had trouble falling asleep and thus gained a few night hours that she couldn't, just wasn't able to fill. She was exhausted by tossing and turning in her bed or roaming the house like a ghost. Sometimes she would drape a shawl over her shoulders, cover Sphinx with it and venture into the garden.

That October night, pushed by the high winds, the branches of the chestnut tree knocked strongly on the window, as though they were attempting to get inside. Annoyed, Sphinx was wandering around the corners of the room.

"Here, kitty, kitty, where are you?"

Joanna found him on the piano, licking his paw.

"Oh, here… here is my kitty," she picked up and hugged him, "let's go to bed, I'll read saint Matthew's tales, as our godless father calls them."

Sphinx wasn't in the mood for tales, as he gracefully slipped out from under the covers and ran away.

"Kitty, kitty, where are you? Huh?… Oh, forget it!" Joanna scolded him, as he sat on the piano again. "I don't play it anymore. Decide, kitty: the tales or we're sleeping apart tonight!"

Apparently, some people experience a glimpse of certain feelings; the ability to predict specific events, capture moments, times that can forcefully impact their whole life or entirely change it. This phenomenon of subconsciousness was carving into Joanna's mind. For some time, she would suffer from vivid dreams and wake unable to tell whether it was day or night. Last night she dreamed that everything around her dematerialized and was swallowed by her eyes. The whole room. No shapes, no colors. Apart from bewildered Sphinx who had no idea what to do. It was similar this night; he was anxious and uneasy, his mood contagious and slowly starting to affect Joanna. She didn't feel like sleeping, resting, sitting, reading, overwhelmed by the sounds of the outdoors – the sounds of intensifying rain. The woman approached the window and when she opened it, a waft of chilly air sprinkled her face with raindrops, awakening the suppressed desire to play the piano.

Her fingers danced on the familiar surface of the keyboard, releasing the sounds into the space of the night. The music, traveling through the pouring rain, warmed someone's heart, clearing doubts and uncertainty, giving hope.

He stood in the rain for a while and started to fumble

around in the dark, touching the rough bark of the tree. When he finally found a familiar peg, he pulled himself up and grabbed one branch, then another. Heavy drops hit his face and arms, but he did not stop and kept on climbing.

A few minutes passed before Joanna started sensing that she wasn't alone in the room anymore. Something similar had happened to her that summer, when he suddenly abandoned her; back at the time this sensation would be so strong, she would reach her hands out just to make sure he wasn't standing in front of her. She did it this time as well but in a completely different direction.

"God, this is madness…," she whispered to herself.

He looked at her, completely astonished, and then – whether he wanted it or not –had to smile.

"Is that you?" she asked just in case, quickly scolding herself that apart from her sight, apparently she also lost her senses. "If you leave me again…," Joanna suddenly turned in his direction, "…my heart will break into thousands of pieces." She put it all into a few passionate words and blew air on his face. "Do you understand?!"

He did not understand a thing, but he pulled her towards his body with all the strength, depriving her of all doubts and air. Joanna felt the pressure of his body, raindrops on the lips and his tongue, boldly attempting to make its way into her mouth. How disappointing it must have been to him when she broke off. But before the devastated man managed to think with utter despair that there was only one thing to do now - tear this love from his heart - Joanna overcame her fleeting embarrassment caused by the closeness of someone else's body, throwing herself into his arms. Despite being so petite, she managed to knock him over to the floor. He was so pleasant to touch, had curious hands and prolific imagination.

The fading sound of the waning rain could be heard outside the window, dark clouds were giving way to the stars in the sky as the two of them explored love in its full form.

The hands of the clock traveled around the dial several times and a new dawn seeped through the night; dawn so different to the one that came a day, two, and any other day before. It brought Joanna joy and plans for the future. And then, the next night came and she spent it waiting by the open window. He, however, did not come.

Winter came in full force at the beginning of December, bringing the season of freezing cold and snowfall. Suddenly, something started happening. Something that drew Zygmunt's attention to Joanna. It all began with morning sickness.

"What's the matter with you? Did you eat some expired food?"

"I don't know," Joanna admitted, fighting a noticeable wave of nausea.

"Take some herbs."

So she got them. For three weeks she would season her food with ginger, drink mint, lemon balm, chamomile; and when her digestion problems seemingly faded away, other symptoms occurred: dizziness, a heightened sense of smell and tender breasts. Zygmunt started feeling uneasy, but Joanna did not panic. She was just waiting patiently for the unpleasant illness to pass.

One day Joanna was bustling around the kitchen, looking for something to eat and deal with her insatiable hunger. Zygmunt was sitting with his hands on the table, carefully looking at his daughter. *And what if she's...?* He shook his head, trying to clear his mind of these thoughts, looked out into the garden wrapped in the depressing darkness of winter, and sighed.

Like an inflating balloon, the shadow of suspicion grew when Zygmunt noticed that Joanna avoided certain smells that she had never minded before – such as his aftershave, *Przemysławka*. On the other hand, different aromas would bring a blissful expression to her face. One day he was polishing his shoes before seeing Banaszczyk for a meeting during which they were supposed to arrange the most convenient date for their children's wedding. Joanna grabbed the can with black shoe polish and brought it to her nose.

"Ohhh, it smells so beautiful," she stated. "This one must be black. Where's the brown one, I'd like to compare them."

She even found his wood glues interesting and he hid them before her so effectively that later when he needed them, he couldn't find them, so he had to buy new ones.

"Jo...?" A surprising gentleness sounded in his voice. "Did you and Roman... did Roman do something to you?"

"What do you mean, dad? Harm me?"

"Harm, not harm, call it whatever you like... I'm asking if he's done to you something you wouldn't want, something against your will, forced you... or maybe didn't force you?"

"Dad, you're hurting me the most! By wanting me to marry him."

"Oh, girl, you don't understand a thing!" Zygmunt lost his temper, but upon seeing Joanna's miserable face, immediately regretted his tone.

"I'm not stupid."

"But you're naïve."

"And defiant. Remember? You called me that yourself.

Defiant. And I will never be okay with the fact you want me to move out of this house. My home, your home. Dad, why are you doing this to me?"

"One day, you will understand."

"I want to understand now. I want to wrap my head around this and acknowledge why you were allowed to love and I am not?!"

He remained silent.

"You still keep it, either in your breast pocket or behind your ear."

"What are you talking about?"

"The pencil. Yellow, whatever that means. That you used to draw mom's portraits with. This way, she's still with you. Right? Do you still draw her? Tell me! Do you sit somewhere in a corner and look into her... her paper face? No, not paper. Because for you these are not just a few skillfully drawn, flat lines, but... but something more than that. Right? It's her presence. You feel her, you still sense her; the scent, the touch... Paralyzed with happiness, you gaze at every tiniest detail: her mouth, eyes... carefully investigating your own feelings towards her. Dad, I understand it. I know, what you're going through. I can't see emotions, but I feel them, in this extremely profound way. God, can you even imagine me having any such memorabilia of Roman? Caressing it like a poor substitute of moments gone by? I won't be able to feel with him... after all. I will be miserable."

"What are you talking about?" he grew suspicious. "Explain everything to me. Tell me what you want to convey."

"Oh, dad... You haven't got the slightest idea. My heart is broken. Into a million pieces."

He would disappear for entire days, and whenever he came back, he reeked of alcohol. Finally, one day, he packed some things and left the house in hurry, loudly closing the door as if it were a manifesto of his desperation. Joanna, frightened, ran after him.

"Dad, where are you going?"

"I'm going to Warsaw!"

"Warsaw?!" Joanna stopped in her tracks, her mouth open. "When are you coming back?"

"In a few days." Zygmunt looked at his daughter.

"Dad, don't leave me alone. Take me with you."

"No way," he snapped. "Go back, you'll freeze. And close the door!"

Joanna obediently returned to the house and entered the kitchen, where she circled the table and settled behind it. And what now? Something was bothering her. Sphinx! By now, he should have been kneading her lap. She grabbed her cane and started to frantically look for him around the house.

"Kitty, kitty! Where are you?"

Silence.

Joanna gave up after two hours. Tired, with her soul torn, she pressed her head against the cold window glass, suddenly hearing birds take off as if something scared them. *Must have been Sphinx*, the woman thought; the poor thing must have hurriedly followed father the way she did, and then found himself locked out in the freezing garden. She ran downstairs, tripped over the threshold and lost a slipper; ignoring that she soon felt the cold, piercing wind on her body, her body trembling with emotions.

About an hour later Marian Kramer drew the curtain in his kitchen window, alarmed by someone's distressed wailing. Blowing away a plume of cigarette smoke that obscured his vision, he finally saw his young neighbor. Wearing a pullover sweater and one slipper, she was frantically dashing in front of her house. The man crushed the cigarette and ran to her.

"Jo, for God's sake. What are you doing here?"

"I'm looking for Sphinx, I must have lost him somewhere. Have you seen him?"

"No, I haven't. Jesus Christ, barefoot in this snow. And your father? Where's your father? Does he know you're outside?"

"Dad?" Joanna hesitated. "He had to leave for a while, but he's going to be back real soon." She didn't like this feeling: whenever she was lying, she had a feeling everyone around her immediately knew about it and would call her bluff.

"Alright, girl. Let's go back home," he put his arm around her. "Don't worry about Sphinx. It's a cat, after all, he will wander around other people's gardens and come back."

Seven long days had passed. Joanna was standing by the window in the kitchen, her cheek pressed against the glass covered by a thin layer of ice. The monotonous hum of an old fridge could be heard, while on the other side of the cold glass snow was falling slowly, wrapping the sleepy neighborhood in swelling silence.

Joanna missed Sphinx and was hungry. She ate leftover preserves made by grandma – salad mixes, pickled cucumbers, fruit compote – and everything she could find in the kitchen. Fear and uncertainty regarding the destiny of her father and cat scared her to the marrow. She imagined hungry, cold and confused Sphinx wandering around the neighborhood or having already fallen prey to some atrocity. Meanwhile, her father, presumably blackout drunk, must have fallen into a ditch where he subsequently froze to death with hungry crows circling above his dead body.

Joanna felt a painful hunger pang. There was neither enough

strength nor desire to whip up something warm. She found some canned food in the pantry, probably with meat, as dad liked them so much. Looking for a can opener, the woman grabbed the knob and realized the drawer was stuck. She pulled again, but something was clearly blocking it, so Joanna pulled another drawer, taking out a large kitchen knife. The blade slipped at the smooth metal surface of the can and she felt a sharp pain in her hand, followed by warmth spreading around the cut. Blood. The woman reached for the home first aid kit (the small cabinet by the window), found some bandage and did her best to wrap it around her injured hand. *Dad, where are you? Sphinx, please, come back. You know the way home.*

The sound of a key turning in the lock, followed by a creek of opening door resounded inside her with a feeling of deep relief. She immediately recognized that light, energetic walk. This could have been only her dad. That was a huge burden off her head, she wanted to come up and hug him. But as soon as he entered the kitchen, he didn't speak a word to her. He was just walking to and fro, breathing heavily, anxious and mad. At whom?

"Dad," she started, shyly. "So good that you're back. Sphinx…"

"What have you done!" Zygmunt shouted at her, despair blending with fury. "Who did that to you?! How on earth did this happen? How? Who, the fuck, did this, huh?!"

He looked around the kitchen like a beaten dog, when some magical force caught his eye and directed his sight onto the tree growing outside the window.

"The window! I'll kill that motherfucker! Was he coming through the window? Tell me, did he come through the window? And then broke your heart, right? Didn't you say you were heartbroken?"

"Yes! But it's over now!"

"Over?! How could this be over, what are you talking about?! Well, he left you a souvenir! You wanted it, you got it!"

He couldn't have been more surprised when he saw a smile emerge on her face; one of these that reminded him of Hanna so much.

"Where?" Joanna hopefully enquired.

At that moment, he broke down, put his arm around her and hugged her tight.

"Dear Lord! Jo..."

Two packed suitcases were waiting in the hall. Joanna had no idea where her father would send her with them, but before setting off he had taken her to the cemetery, asking her to say goodbye to all the loved ones. At that very moment, the woman felt as though she were about to travel into space or at least somewhere very far away. She called Sphinx one last time, to no avail.

The long journey felt like a symphony of horror and unrest. As if the train was running over her head. The clickety-clack of train wheels, the whistle and the brakes made her lose control over her own body. Immediately after leaving the train, they were thrown into the bustle of a rushing crowd. She could hear the sounds of the city when the earth shook, followed by a loud noise. Joanna covered her ears.

"No worries," her father said, trying to calm her down. "It's just a tram."

She enjoyed a few tramway rides when she was a child,

but somehow managed to forget about them. The thudding echo of its noise kept ricocheting in her head when they passed the windows of trendy coffee houses and elegant stores. Passersby bustled like a swarm of bees, absent-mindedly pushing her around. They reached a tall tenement house; her father opened the door so heavy it seemed to be made of iron and let her in first. Mad, sharp and high-pitched dog barks resounded at the staircase. *Must be a Pekingese*, Joanna assumed. Her father put a hand on her shoulder, letting her know she should stop. Something clanked and screeched, resembling a machine falling from a height.

"Don't be afraid, it's an elevator."

Elevator? She didn't know what an elevator was. They entered a cramped room, maybe a cage; it felt smaller than the pantry next to their kitchen. God, will she sit at the kitchen table ever again? Or go to the pantry to grab a bottle of chestnut syrup? Suddenly the cage moved and Joanna felt her whole body sink into the floor as if attempting to break through the surface. The elevator started moving upwards, eventually stopping three floors above. Either these were particularly high or the elevator was exceptionally slow.

Joanna's father rang the doorbell, which resounded with a piercing, hysterical sound. A man answered the door, at first opening the door ajar, and then wide open.

"Welcome," he said, taking a few steps back. "Please, come in."

He led them to a dark hall, where he immediately took Joanna's hand.

"I'm Wiktor," his handshake was firm and pleasant, his hands delicate. He was seventy, but he certainly didn't look his age – most people assumed he was sixty or younger.

Wiktor was an elegant, elderly man with a quiff hairstyle sprinkled with gray hair. He limped and used a cane. Well-preserved men like him supported themselves with their second (or maybe even third) wife or a mistress instead of a cane, but he was alone. As in making a conscious choice to be alone, because that's what he wanted. The profession of a watchmaker seemed to be tailored to his character; calmness, patience, meticulousness, manual skills and the ability to think logically. Moreover, his sight and hearing were still decent. The apartment that he invited them into resembled the owner: it was clean, neat, elegant, very much vintage and had high ceilings. Leaning on the cane, he kindly gestured them towards the largest of three rooms. Judging by the furniture, it was used as a living room as well as a place where the owner would spend most of his time at home. First of all, a corner fireplace. Tiled, with a fire burning throughout the whole winter. An antique Gustav Becker clock was standing on a hanging shelf by the fireplace, next to the only photograph in the whole house – a black and white photo in a decorative frame. On the colorful Arabic carpet stood an art-deco couch and two armchairs with a tiny coffee table in between, all covered with some papers; the whole scene seemed as though someone has just left them to go and, for example, make a cup of tea or coffee.

"Well…," Wiktor approached his guests. "I'll leave you two alone for a moment."

Joanna felt her father give her a tight embrace, for the second time in these last few days. He buried his face in her hair, inhaling its scent as if wanting to take it with him. All of his ignorance and indifference disappeared. He was shaking.

"Dad. Daddy, I love you, don't push me away. Don't push me away."

He pulled away from her and she heard his footsteps grow distant. Joanna ran after him to the staircase, moving as if she were trapped in a dangerous maze. One step to the left, two steps to the right, taking a left again.

"Dad, wait!"

The heavy door slammed shut. Her father did not wait. As soon as he was outside, his thoughts caught up with him and he acknowledged what had just happened – as though the realization of his loss and the burning pain in his chest that followed it required larger space.

"He's not coming back, is he?" Joanna desperately asked.

Wiktor embraced her, giving her enough time to cry with her face against his slightly worn-out jacket.

Zygmunt felt out of breath. He reached underneath the bed and pulled a tin box closed with a padlock. The man opened it and took out an old gun, a war memorabilia and the only souvenir of his father, a soldier from the People's Army. Kneeling by the bed, he put the barrel of the pistol in his mouth, took off the safety and closed his eyes. And then he saw them. Both.

(Little Jo carefully looking at a snowman, then standing on her tiptoes and trying to reach for the carrot nose. Amused, Hanna trying to break free from his embrace, shouting "Jo, leave it!"

"Why, will it huwt him?" Jo's chin would begin to tremble. That's when he would run towards her, put his arms around her and pick the girl up.

"And does my 'lil bundle of joy love 'er papa?" he would mimic his little one, twirl her around underneath the chestnut tree, all of them bursting into contagious laughter.)

A wave of nausea came over him. He held the gun with both hands, then slowly put the gun down. "Yes, daddy, I love you. So, so much."

～

"You probably smile only four times a year?"

All tense, with her knees together, Joanna was sitting on a stylish sofa in a spacious room with a fireplace. An elderly man was seated in an armchair opposite her. She realized she should somehow react to his question.

"Definitely more often," she responded after a lengthy silence. "But this year I simply didn't have a reason to smile."

"Um," the man cleared his throat and shifted in his chair. "I heard that you play the piano wonderfully."

"I've never played the piano."

"Nooo?"

"I play, I mean, I used to play a grand piano."

"Ah! Right! Graaand piano!", Wiktor raised his brows and nodded his head. "What's the difference between these two?"

"And what is a stone thinking when you throw it…? I don't know," Joanna shrugged. "I don't even remember what an upright piano looks like."

"I see that you're a bit annoyed. Please, forgive me. I'm not the best companion for such a young person."

"I think it has something to do with the sound."

"The sound? Am I speaking too loud?"

"The sound of the grand piano is loud, the upright one is quieter."

"Right!" Wiktor smacked his forehead. "Um… Funny I haven't thought about it before. Forte means loud, piano equals quiet. Would that be correct?"

"Well, what you said makes perfect sense."

"Sometimes I happen to say something that makes sense. Oh! Here comes the first of these four!" Wiktor joked, seeing Joanna smile. "I'll do my best to ensure there's many of them."

"Right...," he broke the silence after a long moment. He clenched his hands between his knees and leaned forward. "What would you say to some tea?" As he looked at her, waiting for an answer, eight clear chimes resounded in the room.

"These strings have a beautiful sound." Joanna turned her head towards the place where the tones were coming from.

"Pardon? Oh, right! It's Gustav," he elaborated, finally understanding which item grasped her attention.

"This clock has a name?"

"And surname. It is named after its creator, Gustav Becker, a German watchmaker. Indeed, it has a very pleasant sound. The clock itself is beautiful too, with a wooden housing and a round sphere glass for the clock face, surrounded by a brass frame...," he bit his tongue right in time, before saying *such a shame you can't see it.*

"And you're a watchmaker. Or a collector."

"I have to admit I'm surprised. Why would you think so? It's a correct assumption, by the way. I am a watchmaker."

"I can sense it in your voice and the way you talk about it."

He pushed himself up and got out of his chair, leaning on his cane as if he were trying to resist the emotions that overwhelmed him.

"As usual, time pushes us forward: it's dinner. Ah!" he motioned upwards with his index finger. "Milk. Warm milk with honey and garlic, that's what you need. You've got to be starving, I'm sure you haven't eaten anything in hours and well, now, as they say, you should be eating for two," the man added kindly.

"Why for two?" his concern pleasantly perplexed her. "It's enough if I eat for myself."

"Um… I mean you and the baby."

And in that unusual way, Joanna learned she was pregnant.

"I thought, I didn't suspect…" he blinked nervously. "…I mean I didn't think you could not know."

"Pregnant?" her face went limp. "But… but it's impossible! I don't have a husband."

Facing such decisive ignorance, Wiktor could only nod understandingly, frown, and then attempt to gently explain that there's no need to tie the knot for a man and woman to create a child. All it takes is physical love. Joanna somehow trusted this man with a wise voice; that's how she imagined her grandfather's voice sounded like. Soon, sparing him all the intimate details, she told him about the *ghost*. That's how she named this mysterious form that would visit her every now and then to disappear completely. Because what else had it been, this form, if merely a touch, scent, music. Gently as he could, Wiktor added that the fact she was expecting was absolute proof that the *ghost* most certainly had a material form made of flesh, bones and something else, just devoid of heart and reason. He advised her to stop making pointless assumptions as to why he never showed up again, carefully presenting his opinion on the matter.

"Well, it's easier to contribute to the growth of world population than to pass any exam. And then it sometimes happens that these pathetic daddies make innocent tiny human beings unhappy, ruining their mother's lives on the way. So, my dear, if he had run away, there's no use mourning him. He's not worth you and the baby. You're going to make it through, you look like someone who can do it. As they say, if God blessed you with a child, he's going to help you with it too. I will, for sure. So?" he looked into her eyes, his brows raised. "All good now?"

Joanna, still uncertain, nodded her head. From that moment on, she slowly started closing the chapter of her life that featured the *ghost*. Still, she hoped that he was out there, looking for her – and if he indeed was, he would surely find her one day. The woman immediately thought of Sphinx, whom she did not manage to find despite frantic searching.

For ten years, Sphinx had been her companion for better and worse. The bond between them could not be compared to any connection between two people. At night he would fall asleep curled up on her neck, during the day he would bring her tiny gifts from the garden that unfortunately had to be killed beforehand: small mice, birds. They were alike, had their respective worlds and followed their own paths that often crossed. His sudden departure hurt like incurable heart disease.

During the next few days, Joanna would suddenly wake up and walk around, touching unknown walls with both hands, finally sitting down in the armchair and thinking about her father's whereabouts. Probably he was whipping up some breakfast or drinking sour milk. And Sphinx? Did he come back home? She was imagining him, meowing and scratching her bedroom door, waiting for someone to open it so that he could make himself comfortable on the bed or hop on the piano.

Every single time, before heading to his studio, Wiktor would stand in the doorway and gaze at this somber situation. Wouldn't it be better if he sat down next to Joanna and held her hand? This situation overwhelmed him. Finally, to bring her out of this stupor, he got an idea.

"Everything okay?" he asked, furrowing his brows.

"Yes, thank you."

"I'm going to leave now. If you need anything… you know, don't hesitate. Ah," Wiktor turned towards her as if he suddenly remembered something. "I was wondering, maybe you would like to see my watchmaker studio? I think you would like it."

"Gladly, but I think it's impossible."

"Well," he cleared his throat. "I know what you mean. But there was neither a mistake nor any language mishap in my question. By saying *to see*, I meant senses far more sensitive than sight. The view our eyes present to us is merely an optical effect, oftentimes nothing more than an illusion. Our senses of hearing and touch make us sensitive. These let us see things deeper, with our soul and heart. What an experience it is to hear a few clocks at the same time. I'm sure you have never heard something this resonant before. You have no idea how amazing this is. Sometimes, once I repair them, there are six or eight resurrected patients in my studio, with their tick-tock sound, whirs, chimes and clangs. With a choir like this, you can easily forget that there's another life outside these walls, not always the one we would appreciate. So? And you, as far as I know, appreciate various sounds."

"How long am I going to stay here?"

The question perplexed Wiktor.

"Joanna…," he sighed and placed his hands on the knob of the cane. Finally, he sat down in the armchair in front of her. "I'm going to be honest with you. Your father brought you here to stay."

"Forever?" her mouth dropped open.

"Oh, this house will be your home for as long as you want it to be."

"Really? Is there anything that depends on my choice?" she inquired, a tone of irony in her voice.

"Everything, every single thing that regards your person depends solely on you. Undoubtedly, if you were stubborn enough, your father would come and bring you back home. But just think about it, Joanna. Do you really want it? Huh?... Just give it a second. Don't think about your father, he's going to be fine. Think about yourself. In hopeless situations, our fate likes to present us with a chance that can turn our life upside down, but it is us who have to make the decision," he studied her face, trying to recognize what effect the words had on her.

"So?" He said after a moment of silence and got up from the armchair. "Would you like to see the watchmaker's studio?"

"I do, even now."

"Now?" Surprised, he sat down again. "I've got a better idea. Visit me next week. On your own."

"On my own?" she said awkwardly. "But I... I don't know the address!"

It's a shame she couldn't see Wiktor's face. Instead of *I won't find it because I'm blind*, he was served with *I don't know the address*. He immediately thought that this girl is going to make it.

"Don't worry, my dear, Rome wasn't built in a day. We'll rehearse it for a few times and when you will be ready, I will be waiting at the studio, more than happy to show you around."

The next day, each of them with their cane in hand, they took the elevator and ventured onto the street. Wiktor was following Joanna, previously asking her to count the steps.

"Go straight ahead and I will follow right behind you. I'll

warn you about crosswalks, the studio is only two blocks away. Ready? Alright, let's go."

With her cane extended, Joanna walked with a slight uncertainty, bombarded on all sides by the overwhelming symphony of sounds and smells of a busy street. The clamor, squeak, bells, horns, the howl of a rushing ambulance, human voices, car fumes, fresh bread and fragrant flowers. She was unwittingly prodded and pushed. An adventure of one thousand steps to regain her independence and pride. There were thousands of times when she just wanted to scream *Enough! I won't make it!*. But she did! And she did it three times a day over the next five days. So far, she didn't enter the WATCHMAKER studio. She just symbolically touched the door handle, a sign of *I made it!*. Day seven, however, seemed to unravel in an entirely different direction. The journey of one thousand steps awaited her, just without the support of Wiktor following her – he was supposed to be waiting in the studio, accompanied by the ticking mechanisms that he had resurrected; forgetting that outside these walls there was a different life; not always the one she would appreciate.

Joanna took the elevator and uncertainly started moving ahead. A hunched figure emerged from the gateway and followed her like a shadow, leaning on his cane.

Having reached her destination, Joanna hesitated. Before pushing the door handle under the WATCHMAKER sign, she stated over her shoulder, seemingly towards no one in particular:

"Dear Wiktor, have a bit of faith in me!"

"When did you realize?"

"As soon as I rode down the elevator."

Over the numerous days that came after that, Joanna infallibly followed the same path on her own. As she covered the two blocks, she would inhale familiar smells and listen to well-known sounds, as passersby moved around her. On the way there, she would stop by the bakery and buy Wiktor's favorite pretzels to bring to the studio.

She knew the route so well, she was able to suddenly stop in front of a curb just because she felt an unfamiliar air current. Slowly, gradually, step by step, overcoming the fear of a big city, she was getting used to Warsaw. It was surprisingly pleasant to find oneself amid the rush of other people's affairs. The new scents, voices and sounds weren't scary anymore. They were exciting.

⌁

Before the arrival of the first day of spring in March, sand trucks and plows were forced to set off to roads again and fight the snowfall. This Saturday morning the snow was falling slowly, discreetly, quietly, as though it didn't want to wake sleeping Joanna. Wiktor was standing by the window, awaiting the sunrise. He hoped that the rising day would bring him some answers. Taking a few steps back from the window, he was certain that his elderly soul would be forced to bear the whole burden of a decision that had been slowly emerging since yesterday. He's decided to do his best to create a home for Joanna and her baby. A tolerant and safe one.

Before he set off to the studio, as he would do every single morning, he told Joanna that he will take her to dinner tonight.

"Oh, but where? I've never been to a restaurant or a bar."

"It's high time you explored these places."

"I don't want to. Not yet."

"No worries," he added immediately, trying to calm her down. "We've got plenty of time to catch up on all that. Alright, then I assume we could spend this evening at home, having a nice candlelight supper in our own kitchen. What about that, huh?"

"Candlelight? As in during a pastoral visit?"

"Why would you think it's going to be like this?" He looked at her, fairly amused.

"The scent of the flame," Joanna responded quickly.

"Oh, that's interesting. So?" he spread his arms, pretending to be hopeless. "I don't know anymore, should there be candles or not?"

It was seven o'clock in the evening. Underneath the light of an electric lamp hanging over the kitchen table, trying to hide her confusion, Joanna precariously sat on a chair that Wiktor had cleaned, nonchalantly wiping it with a kitchen towel.

"Have you already thought about a name for the baby?"

"There are a few that I like," Joanna responded, sipping tea from a porcelain cup adorned with roses. "For a boy and a girl. I guess it's too early to decide, don't you think?"

"You're right. But if you would need any, you know, advice, help, I'll be happy to assist."

"I'm not sure...," Joanna hesitated and put the cup down. "I don't think it's the most important thing right now."

"And what is more important now?"

"What's more important? The future. I'm afraid I won't be able to provide a good future for my child. Or myself."

"No need to worry. As long as you're here, in this house, you and your little one won't miss anything," Wiktor ensured, taking a swig.

"Why? Why are you doing this for me? Why did my dad decide to leave me here, at your place?"

"Alright, enough, enough." The man got up from the chair.

"It was supposed to be a nice evening. Let's leave some topics for another time."

"It's not going to work," she shook her head skeptically. "This evening won't be nice because I will be thinking about something else all the time. I can't pretend," Joanna continued, "and neither tea served in a fine porcelain cup nor this delicious salad won't change it. It might turn out your efforts will be futile. I want honesty."

"Honesty, you say? Alright then, I will be completely honest." Wiktor rubbed his eyes, as he sat in the chair again. "I will never tell you why your father had decided that the best way out of the predicament that you… pardon my rather inappropriate words, fell into, would be to bring you here, to me. All that I can tell you about it is that your father did the right thing. Maybe it was the best thing he has ever done for his own daughter so far. I can ensure you that you will find answers to all your doubts and questions, you just need a little time and patience. Everything will fall into its place, like in a puzzle. You can be sure of that. But now I would like you to think about a certain proposition. But before I tell you about it, and for you to understand me correctly, I mean, understand my intentions, I need to tell you something about me. Dear Lord," he sighed, looking upwards, "give me the strength!"

Certain circumstances forced Wiktor to experience his first love in secret. The love that affected all the remaining years of his life, with nothing similar to it happening ever again. Love destined for social ostracism and damnation; one that was worth being born, and, if needed, dying for.

Suddenly he fell silent.

"It might be hard both for me and for you, Joanna. Do you want me to continue?"

"Well if I am supposed to learn about your intentions...,"
she smiled, encouraging him, "that's what you said."

"I'll start from the top, then. I think that back at the time
when I was a kid, my survival instinct kicked in. I felt like I had
to hide, I couldn't trust and believe anyone. That's why I avoided
looking people in the eye; for the fear they would decode and
then damn me. I lived as if there was a life sentence hanging
above, fully aware I will never be happy. But I was wrong. Happiness embraced me. One day I went to the restaurant where my
mother was working, I think I was supposed to tell her something. I don't even remember what it was, it was so long ago...
before the war, we lived in Lviv at the time..."

"In Lviv? My grandfather... my grandparents," Joanna
corrected. "They came from Lviv, that's where my mom was
born too."

"Really? We have common roots then. I guess we would
have a lot to say to each other, like me and your grandparents. We, the people of the Recovered Territories, resemble one
large family, there are so many memories that we share... tastes,
scents, homes... songs."

"And what happened next? You entered the restaurant and..."

"...and I saw a boy. Well, maybe not really a boy anymore,
but a man. Much older than me. He was playing the piano, so
wonderfully, not showing off by any means. The aim of his playing was simply playing. I don't know what tempted me, maybe
it was intuition, some feeling, maybe destiny, but I looked him
in the eye. With so much bravery, courage, not even fearing
that I was doing something inappropriate. Actually, I stared
into his eyes, completely intentionally, because I wanted him to
notice me in the group of people surrounding him. They were
astonished, enchanted by his piano skills. But I was amazed by

something else: his long fingers, arms underneath the rolled sleeves of his white shirt, hunched silhouette, that sly smile on his face and the fuming cigarette in the corner of his mouth… My heart was out of control," he stopped and hesitated. "Before I move on, please tell me whether it's not embarrassing for you. It might be incomprehensible or offensive to someone like you."

"Dear Wiktor, I might be an adult but I was raised in such a way that I know nothing about the world around me. Whatever offends other people might not seem offensive to me at all."

"You think?" Wiktor took a deep breath and smiled. "He responded with a gaze, in the same way: intentionally and intriguingly. At first, it seemed to be an ordinary relation. We both pretended to be unaware of how good it felt to be together and how much we liked each other. One day he dragged me to a photographer's studio and we had a photo taken together. I still have it, it's standing on the shelf next to Gustav. The only thing I have left of him," his voice started breaking. "Two years. Two years of happiness."

"And that's it? These two years? Were the two years of your happiness a misery to other people?"

"No, not at all," Wiktor vigorously denied. "Nobody suffered because of us, or at least that's what it seems. At the time we were both free people. But it could have happened that someone would get hurt had I not decided to end it."

"End?! Why?"

"Why? His career was blooming."

"Was he a pianist?"

"An amateur one. It wasn't his profession, music was his free love – and that's why it gave him so much pleasure and joy. He was making a career, well," Wiktor cleared his throat, "in a different area. I don't even remember what it was, so many years have passed. He couldn't appear in public with me, he would have been finished. So he got married."

"Does it mean he abandoned you?"

"Not really. She was a good girl, very young, seventeen at the time. A daughter of his nanny who brought up both him and his little brother. Anyway, they were like siblings too, knowing everything about each other. She drew a veil over his *otherness*, hiding it from the rest of the world, putting an end to all the rumors. It cut various suspicions short and he provided her with a comfortable life and a higher social status. It was supposed to be a white marriage that granted them mutual freedom – but it ended far from that. One day I was informed he was going to be a father. He ensured me nothing would change between us and it will all stay the same, but at the very same moment, we both knew it wasn't true. Underneath the thin veil of proper upbringing and discretion, the world can sometimes be promiscuous and cruel. Adults are always covering up their second lives. What was the fault of that innocent, unborn child? So I had to leave. I knew that sooner or later our conscience would kill this affection."

"And he? What did he say to that?"

"He just acknowledged it."

"*Acknowledged* it… it's so ruthless."

"Joanna, I didn't want you to cry. I had no idea this story would move you this much, oh dear! Girl, there's no use crying." He was so hopeless about her tears that he stared down at the plates and cutlery set on the table in front of them. "You barely ate, come on, eat something. I did my best to prepare the food. Please, eat," Wiktor moved the salad towards her and placed a cotton napkin in her hand. "Food always lifts one's mood."

That evening Wiktor asked Joanna to marry him. Her face

showed astonishment so huge, he couldn't help and had to heartily laugh despite the whole significance of the moment. And
then he started convincing her. It will be a white marriage, but
oh! The benefits! The child will never be stigmatized by the lack
of a father figure in their life, she won't hear a bad word for
being an unwed mother. And so on, and so on... He kept on
talking, as if he wanted to justify something, all smothered with
remorse. Joanna was listening to him in silence, and when he
finally presented all of his arguments and his tired voice turned
into a whisper, she eventually spoke.

"I'm not sure if I understand you correctly... are you trying
to convince me that I should become your wife because otherwise both me and my child are going to be unhappy?"

"I didn't say that but it's highly possible, especially given
some people's nasty mentality."

"And what do you expect in return?" Joanna asked cautiously.

"Friendship."

"Friendship? I have never been friends with anyone. I don't
know if I will be able to become friends with you. You're old,
I'm young."

"Friendship doesn't fall under any age category."

"I can't accept this proposition. It's going to be easier for
you and me."

"Listen, child, I thought it over and I would like you to do
the same. Think it through."

Joanna was firmly convinced she had made the right decision – maybe a spur-of-the-moment one, but at least with clear
intentions. At first, she didn't intend to consider in detail all the
pros and cons as Wiktor had asked her – as such further elabo-
ration seemed wildly inappropriate to her. But something was
clearly bothering her. She discovered that deep inside she was

still hoping that the *ghost* would find her, and then she could tell him about the baby. But then the doubts came: and what if that never happens? What is going to happen to her baby? Joanna was frightened of those deeply rooted human prejudices that made Wiktor hide his affection before the whole world. Prejudices that will affect the life of her child, as it will not only be illegitimate; it will also have a blind mother. And then other fears came: will she be able to keep the baby safe? And if not? Will they take it away from her? She tried to remain calm in front of Wiktor, but inside her soul was torn.

One afternoon, when Wiktor was still in his studio, Joanna fell asleep in the fireplace room, wrapped in a blanket on a couch. She had a nightmare that she wanted to forget as soon as possible. And then she felt something in her stomach. The baby's first moves! This gentle kick that resonated inside her like the flutter of butterfly wings was like a mighty punch directed precisely at her common sense.

Barbara and Tadeusz, a couple of friendly neighbors who dropped by Wiktor's place from time to time – whether to have a refreshing cup of tea or talk some things over – became the witnesses during their short marriage ceremony at the city clerk office. Wiktor polished his best, though admittedly quite old shoes, and put on a tie, while Joanna wore a new, loose dress and a charming little hat borrowed from Barbara.

When the official asked Joanna to repeat the vows: "Aware of the rights and obligations...", the woman suddenly felt sick and Barbara, all concerned, led her into the bathroom where Joanna threw up. When they returned, the bride looked horrible, pale as a ghost – but it did not interrupt the further course of the ceremony, after which the newlyweds went back home, inviting their kind neighbors for a glass of champagne and some cheesecake.

Oh, people talking! While the wedding was supposed to protect Joanna and her baby against ostracism and provide stability, it did not protect her against one thing: people's chattering. Sometimes, just before breakfast, Barbara would drop by and bring her home-made jam and share some rumors flying around the tenement house. Who would have thought, a young woman and an old man? Some people would delve deeper and perceive it as Wiktor's act of mercy; he chose a cripple for a wife, but God rewarded him, as what could be already seen, with children. Under the guise of these words, some "kind" souls could have had some rather dirty thoughts. He may be quite up in his years, but he's surely enjoying it! He even impregnated her!

Wiktor not only opened before Joanna the door to his house; he even bought an upright piano for her. In order for it to fit, he got rid of some furniture from the room with a tile stove.

"Thank you, Wiktor. What would I have done without you?"

"Mistakes only, that's for sure!" The man joked kindly, impatiently tapping his fingers on the fallboard of the brown *Calisia*. "Try it out, please."

"Oh, I'm not sure, really… I haven't played for so long," Joanna cradled her bump. "Exactly as long as this little one is old."

"Oh," he nodded his head. "So how old is the little one?"

"Almost six months."

"Okay, my dear, no excuses. It doesn't explain anything," Wiktor touched her arms and sat her down on a little stool. "Come on, play something."

"But I have never played any upright piano…"

"Joanna!" he was almost shuffling his feet.

With some uncertainty, she tickled the ivories. Then she extended her neck and started playing. Her old husband sat down in an armchair, tears streaming down his wrinkled face.

Joanna quickly noticed other differences between a grand and upright piano, such as its size or placement of strings or resonance chambers. And, first and foremost, the sound. It wasn't possible to change the tone with an upright one. But given the circumstances in which she became the owner of the instrument, it was nothing short of a magnificent concert grand piano.

The sixth month of the pregnancy fell in the full bloom of spring. Cradling her stomach, Joanna could feel the outline of a tiny body. She was wondering how the *ghost* would react to the news about the child; and then, for that fleeting moment, just one moment, she felt the way she used to. When happiness would sit on her chest, ensuring her that he would be back.

Despite her prominent belly, Joanna felt light and energetic. Every day, moving with grace and ease, she ran errands and stopped by Wiktor's studio, always greatly surprising him with her visit. One day Wiktor asked if she's ever been to the seaside.

"No."

"Noooo?!"

"Well, no!"

Wiktor closed the studio for a week and traveled with her to the Baltic Sea.

The roar! She felt the mighty power of the sea and found herself among sounds she's never heard before. First of all, the rustle that came forward and went away, rose and fell down.

"These are waves," Wiktor explained. "Take off your shoes."

"Why?"

"You have to feel this."

When she was walking, she felt her feet sink in the wet, cold sand. The strange, screeching of birds could be heard from above. Joanna raised her head.

"It's seagulls," Wiktor said, took her hand and led her further into the sea. The waves washed over her legs up to her knees and wet her dress.

"Brr, so cold."

"Alright, let's get out of water."

"No!" Joanna objected. "It's cold, but I like it!"

"Dear Lord, you will catch a cold!" Wiktor scolded her.

"Just a little while," attempting to splash him, Joanna raised her leg and wobbled.

"You crazy woman!" he shouted, saving her from the fall. "Christ, think about the baby!" He kept on pushing her gently, but decidedly towards the shore.

They strolled along the tideline. Joanna reveled in everything that the wild wind and salty, humid air did to her.

"Put out your hand," Wiktor said.

"What's this? Feels like parts of crushed eggshells."

"These are the treasures of the sea... shells!"

"Shells..," Joanna marveled. "They're so fragile."

"Some of them are, some of them are not."

Feeling slightly tired, they rested in a roofed wicker beach chair, the sea roaring behind them.

"Wiktor, when you were young...," Joanna enquired, lazily flexing her bare foot in the sun and burying the other in the sand.

"What are you asking me about?" He looked at her. "I'm still young!"

Joanna smiled.

"Obviously. I'm sorry. What I meant to say was, when you were younger... so just some fifty years ago," Joanna joked and he responded with a gentle chuckle. "Did you ever like any woman?"

"Well, of course, I could easily notice beautiful women. But ever since I can remember, I never fancied them, if you know what I mean. Maybe I was even slightly afraid of them, so I kept them at distance. Is it... wrong?"

"Not at all!"

"You really think so?" He took a deep breath and smiled.

"Sure, I even think it's... fascinating."

"You don't say?! Nobody has ever phrased it like that."

"Is it wrong?"

"Wrong?! Of course not! It's fascinating! You know what, my dear?" Wiktor broke the silence after a while, suddenly serious. "There are so many parallel worlds, and that's what is really fascinating. Your world is one of them, all innocent, sensitive, honest, sensual, spontaneous... and there's this world of mine..." the man fell into a pensive mood, his gaze fixed at some distant point before him. "Unfortunately, people like me have to be invisible, fighting ignorance, disdain, and judgment..."

Her feet would swell extremely during the ninth month of pregnancy, which made her stay at home more and play the piano or sleep for hours. Wiktor would tenderly tuck her in with a blanket.

Soon Adam was born and their home was a place where they were dynamically learning about family relations. A mother, a father and a child. There was only no physical relationship between a husband and wife.

Joanna and Wiktor, lost, restless and sleepy, were adjusting to the son's needs, making all of the mistakes that young parents would do, holding on tight to certain legends and myths while taking care of a newborn. They swaddled him "to his teeth" in a lace-adorned, thick sleeping bag and would take off his hat for bath only. Adam, however, would dismiss their ignorance and quickly adapt to the circumstances in which he was growing healthy and secure, for he was surrounded by love. From time to time he would let them know, his voice mighty and powerful, that they took it a bit too far this time.

Marriage was no tedious chore for them. They based it on friendship, cemented with trust and unity, and Adam's upbringing remained the priority. He was destined to have both mom and dad, even if the latter were to be one hundred years old because age did not play an important role here. It was love that mattered the most. Wiktor acted as if Adam were his own son; parenthood made him feel younger and invigorated him. Still, there were moments when he felt completely helpless about the little one – especially when the boy cried. He tried everything that every new father would do in such a situation – make silly faces. But usually, it did not work. With his loud cry, Adam let him know that he's not buying it and Joanna would step into action. Rocked in her arms, the baby would immediately calm down and fall asleep.

"Sometimes I wonder how is it that a newborn baby can perfectly sense the moment when its parents fall asleep. They always choose precisely that second to terrorize them with crying," Wiktor once noticed.

"I guess we all used to be like this," Joanna responded.

"Maybe you! I wasn't like this, never in my life!"

"You know, Wiktor, I've been thinking a lot lately."

"Thank God, Jo."

"You keep on joking and I'm serious. I mean, I could do something else, not just take care of our home."

"Do you want to work?"

"I know it's stupid, because…"

"Wait, wait… why stupid? It's a brilliant idea."

"Oh! Do you really think so? What do you think, what could I do?"

"You tell me what you would like to do."

"I don't know. I can only take care of home and Adam. Barbara told me about a disabled workers cooperative for people like me."

"Housekeeping and bringing up Adam is a lot. But you can do much more. Joanna, you're a pianist."

After a long hesitation, resisting Wiktor's persevering insistence, Joanna finally gave in and agreed to give a sample piano lesson to a red-haired, eight-year-old Kasia – the unruly granddaughter of their neighbor, Barbara. Years later, the girl admitted that she went to that class with great defiance. Had it not been for the curiosity of the pretty blind woman, she would have never let her headstrong grandma take her to plonk away on that piano. At the time, music did not enthuse her at all – they might as well have enrolled her into a boxing or go-carting class. However, time would tell how important that first meeting by the old Calisia was for both Joanna and Katarzyna. Twenty years later, Joanna, clad in an evening gown, would sit straight in the first row of the Vienna Philharmonic, clutching an invitation. She heard the audience adjust in their seats. Then the ovation, and when it faded away, silence filled the concert hall. The pianist hung over the keyboard; when she finally touched the keys, the storm of her fiery red hair fell on her face, the notes came into life. People were enchanted. After the concerto, hearing the bits of amazing conversations and flattering comments towards the pianist, Joanna smiled. *That's my Kasia. My first student.*

For the next years, up until his death, Wiktor would patiently listen to monotonous exercises of future pianists. Some of them were quick learners, the other... well, it would be hard to describe it.

"I wonder...," Wiktor would sometimes think out loud. "How many of them will make a career by playing with orchestras, on stages, in concert halls, and how many will end up in restaurants and pubs, playing to the table for an audience that does not expect anything of them."

Two months earlier, Joanna first noticed worrying symptoms in Wiktor. A cough. Fatigue. These first signs resembled the flu or severe cold. But then he started shuffling his feet and lost appetite. He also started using the elevator more often than the stairs, and he always considered his daily climb upstairs to be a great exercise keeping him in shape. Now he could barely walk the stairs, frantically clutching onto the handrail. Joanna asked him multiple times to see the doctor, but he just didn't listen.

It was a late, summer afternoon. Gustav the clock, with its noble tone, reminded Joanna that it was precisely the time for Wiktor to pick up his Zorka camera in a leather brown case and go with Adam to the park to snap some pictures of trees and squirrels running up and down them. She could then prepare for the lessons, spread the sheets and wait for the students. This time, Wiktor was late.

"Sorry," he said upon entering the house and closing the

door. "I did what you wanted me to do so much. I went to the clinic."

"And what did the doctor say?"

"Oh," he waved her off. "Nothing new. When you're as old as I am there are basically no illnesses that we shouldn't suspect I could be having. Thank God he didn't mention any mental disorders. He gave me a referral for some blood tests and so on."

"What do you mean, *and so on*?"

"He asked me to have an X-Ray done and to quit smoking. Can you imagine? I don't smoke! Sure, when I was young I used to smoke but now...?"

Now Wiktor was severely ill. Joanna realized they don't have much time left, which made her somber, anxious and unhappy, but she did not fall into despair. That's not what he would have wanted. Thanks to him she understood that despite the past or the present, there is always a future. She still had plans and dreams, but her realistic approach to life protected her against those unlikely to fulfill. Joanna was as determined to learn the world as she wanted to pass her musical knowledge to her students. This world, though complicated, was not scary. The hardships of everyday life and daily duties slowly erased the resentment towards her father for abandoning her.

The moment she left her home, she got back on her feet by the side of a husband who could as well be her grandfather.

Their marriage was not typical, given the significant age difference and no consummation; still, they loved each other the way few couples do. Their affection was the love of best friends. She protected him against old age's worst nightmare: loneliness. He, on the other hand, helped her find herself as a teacher of young pianists and a mother. Motherhood, which initially brought Joanna so many fears, anxiety, even despair, turned out to be the most indestructible and stable element of her life. Adam was a brilliant, kind boy. He had his mother's character, for whom he was the whole world... and eyes. While Joanna was preparing meals or cleaning up afterward, he was sitting in his chair and swinging his legs, describing everything she could not see herself – always employing his childish fantasy and spicing it up for a better effect. Joanna listened to all of this smiling, but there were also moments when her face went blank.

"Mommy, why do you sleep in my bedroom, and not with dad? Jacek, Anka, even Beata's parents who constantly yell at each other sleep in one bed. Is this because dad is old?"

"Umm... I have to go to our dear neighbor, Barbara, she promised me some eggs. Dad will explain everything to you. Wiktor!"

Fortunately Wiktor, with his watchmaker's precision and educated voice, attempted to satisfy his son's curiosity. But sometimes, as it was the case in that situation, for the sake of the family's wellbeing, he convincingly deceived his son.

After school, Adam would rush into the studio to watch his old father work. With such an assistant Wiktor would gladly grab his tools, stumps, hammers, openers, reamers and files of all sizes and shapes, and fiddle with complicated movements. He approached his watches the way a doctor treats his patients, diagnosing the disease, determining the treatment and cure: fixing, adjusting or renovating.

"Dad, what does transplantation mean?" Adam asked when one autumn day the radio broadcasted the news that in a hospital in Zabrze a professor named Zbigniew Religa conducted a pioneer heart transplantation.

"See this little gearwheel?" hunched over, a loupe in his

eye, Wiktor was fixing a French pendulum mounted inside a porcelain figurine of a ballerina. "Here... right here? It's worn out now. To make this beautiful clock work again, pleasing the eyes and ears of its owners, and maybe even their heirs...," the man reached for spare parts that he collected over the years and that allowed saving the life of many beautiful items, "...we will replace them with this, exactly this healthy gearwheel that I saved from another broken watch that resembled this one and could not be revived. Oh! See? Beautiful! Fits like a glove. That's what a transplantation is," Wiktor concluded proudly.

"So for one man to live another has to give him his heart?"

"Kinda. Though he did not exactly *give* it."

"Understandable, he was already dead. But if he were dead, then how come his heart was still beating so that they could take it out and place inside a living man without a heart, but then...," Adam ruffled his fair hair, "how come he was still alive?"

Wiktor noticed early that Adam was a sharp boy who caught everything without a hitch. He was pleased to welcome a thought that with his intelligence, the boy certainly didn't take after his biological father, as only a complete idiot could leave a woman like Joanna.

"It's complicated, but it can be explained, for sure," he dodged the question and for a few seconds imagined Adam, eight years old at the time, as a future heir to his profession or at least a successful surgeon.

At that moment he couldn't even suspect that his apprentice will choose an entirely different profession. One that was rooted deep in his genes. But before little Adam became whoever his adult version would be, his passion – definitely under the heavy influence of Wiktor – revolved around collecting various items. Broken watches, rust-covered keys, nails, butterflies and wildflowers that he thoroughly investigated using a magnifying glass and then placed in a thick encyclopedia to dry them out.

One day he stopped by the music store. He saw a violin, pressed his nose against the window and fell in love.

⌇

During these years when Wiktor accompanied her, Joanna overcame her fears and anxieties, learned to move around in open space and go beyond the stiff way of perceiving people and the world. Because, as her old friend-husband would say, there are more colorful worlds parallel to the accepted reality, which is not even fascinating – it is thoroughly humane. Before Wiktor passed away, he shared with Joanna a little secret. Or, rather, gave her the key to unlock it.

"I'm dying. You know that." Wiktor, resting in a sea of white sheets, extended his hand, inviting Joanna to hold it. Sitting by his hospital bed, she always infallibly sensed this expectant waiting of an open hand; with every passing day his grip grew weaker, faded, softened.

"I know, Wiktor, I know. Oh… it's so tough and I can't find words to talk about it. Thank you for everything. Everything…"

"My dear, no problem. You were a perfect wife."

"I have to admit," Joanna tried to smile, "that you did your best too. I admire you, you know that. I would like to grow old with you so, so much."

"What are you talking about? I would have to live at least to one hundred and fifty. Do you realize what would I look like?"

"Of course," Joanna smiled solemnly. "A cane on one side and me on the other, also with a cane."

"Well… a strong, solid and stable construction. Yes…," he

sighed and turned his head towards the wall. "You supported me more than a whole army of canes," the man said quietly. "Joanna," he started and settled in his bed, "do me a favor. Or maybe it's more of advice. You see… secrets, mysteries, avoiding conversation, all of this casts a shadow on every relationship. Particularly in love, because love is like a plant; it's flexing towards the sun, looking for the light that it needs to grow. You know that as good as I do, right? Listen…," he tried to get up on his elbows, "…send Adam to Pawłowice. His grandfather would like to know him. He deserves a second chance."

"You surprised me, Wiktor. Where did this idea come from?… How do you know my father would like to know Adam? He had hated him before he was even born! He kicked me out! Do you remember? You can't," Joanna shook her head, "you can't demand this from me, Wiktor!"

"Joanna, I'm not demanding. I just want you to be sure."

"Sure? Sure of what, Wiktor, what should I be sure of?"

"That you're doing the right thing."

"It's just allusions. Secrets, mysteries, avoiding conversation… you told me that a minute ago. Don't talk to me like this. Explain to me! I deserve it."

"You deserve the best. If I knew how to love women, I wouldn't leave you here." He held her hand tight with both hands. "I would take you with me wherever I am going right now."

So he left. And she closed his eyes.

Almost 250 miles away, south-west of Warsaw, lies the tiny town of Pawłowice. And there, a man who had finally accepted his fate, was reading a letter about his daughter and a grandson that he knew only from photographs; a blonde tot running around the park between plenty of trees and squirrels. Having finished reading, he slowly and carefully folded the letter, opened a chest of drawers and put the envelope away, next to the rest of them. Just like he used to do for the past eight years. Then he relished the silence and thought, with a dash of uncertainty, about his own fatherhood. Maybe it wasn't that lousy after all.

Two months later he met Adam, his grandson.

The old house with a copper roof impressed the boy. He was wandering around the rooms as if it were a museum, carefully examining all the furniture, bric-a-brac and paintings, like they were valuable items. He climbed the sofa, opened a clock's closet doors and took a peek at its movement.

"Nice, it still works," he said, his voice sounding like that of a professional.

With noticeable interest, he flipped through a pile of sheet music, and then, slightly less fascinated, went through a box with glass figurines; two blue dolphins playing ball, swans connected by a heart, tiny angels, fish, colorful balls.

"It's all stuff for girls," Adam claimed.

Finally, the weary boy fell onto a cat-scratched armchair. He looked around, his gaze unfixed, as if searching for something.

"Can I go upstairs?" he enquired his grandpa, who was leaning against a chest of drawers with his arms crossed over, carefully looking at him. "So, can I?", he asked again.

"No!"

Confused, the boy smiled uncertainly, unsure whether his grandpa was joking or not. There was childish hope that over the month of his vacation he would explore every corner of the home where his mom used to live, following the traces of her childhood and discovering the reason he learned about his grandfather so late. It was supposed to be so fascinating!

Slightly disappointed – though keeping a straight face– he adjusted himself in the armchair and looked to the side.

"Oh! I know this picture!" he extended his hand towards the coffee table nearby and grabbed the old photograph. "It's a photo of my dad when he was very young and lived in Lviv. The same picture stands on a shelf in the piano room at our home."

"Do you know who the second man is, the one standing next to your dad?"

"I do. It's his old friend from Lviv."

"He wasn't only his friend."

"No? Who was he as well?"

"Hopefully, one day your mom will explain it to you. If she finally learns the truth…," he murmured quietly, as if talking to himself only; then he added louder: "his name was Józef Lubczyński and he was your great-grandfather," Zygmunt explained, gazing at the black and white photograph of two men in a friendly embrace. Adam was not listening to him anymore, already on the stairs.

"Can I go to the room upstairs?"

"No!"

"Why not?"

"Because I said so!" Zygmunt returned impatiently, though happily. This kid was not the one to use *yes* and *no* only when conversing with adults. He was like his mother, curious and headstrong. "Your mom wrote that you like working with watches, is that right?"

"Yes. Why are you asking?"

"Just because. Have you ever had a hammer and nails in hand?"

"No. Why are you asking?"

"That's a pity. I've got a few shelves in the attic that need to be put together. I could use an assistant."

"I'm a quick learner!"

PART II

HERACLES

HIS NAME WAS Heracles. He was conceived on land but born in heaven. More specifically, on a plane, during a flight from the New York International Airport, destined to arrive in his parents' homeland. The land of gods, thousands of islands and a stunning sea: Greece. One of the passengers, a nun who fortunately graduated a nursing school years ago, delivered him. Thanks to that, the whole process was uneventful and smooth. According to the Ius soli law, every person born either *in* or *above* the territory of the United States receives American citizenship, the newborn named Heracles – to honor the captain of the flight – became a citizen of two countries: mythical Greece and the multicultural United States of America. The idea of returning to the old homeland flourished in the mind of the baby's mother. She wanted her firstborn to grow surrounded by stunning views, ancient culture and wise philosophical thought.

Heracles' father, a recognized guitarist, was not that fond of the idea. He departed Boston, where they spent five wonderful years, with a heavy heart, leaving behind quite a bunch of aficionados of his guitar virtuosity.

Upon turning 18, Heracles left his Greek family home and returned to America to take up studies at the renowned Harvard University, where he crammed like crazy. Not that it was particularly challenging for him; it was just that everyone at Harvard kept on cramming, as studying was basically worshipped at the university. During his time there he lived in one of those red brick dormitories with a shared dining and common rooms full of Victorian furniture.

When he wasn't studying, he would be either swimming or working at the university library. Anyway, at Harvard, these two – swimming and the Harry Elkins Widener Memorial Library – were somehow connected. The monumental library building, supported on marble columns, was founded by the mother of Harry Elkins Widener. A Harvard graduate himself, Widener passed away in 1912 at the age of 27, during the tragic Titanic voyage. Among the many myths of Harvard, one is rooted in this story: a generous founder demanded a swimming-proficiency requirement for all students.

Initially, Heracles studied history, then chose musicology, and then... well, then completely lost his way and was unable to decide which scientific discipline was worth exploring. While in a predicament, he would lay down underneath one of the many trees of Harvard Yard, pick a blade of grass and chew it philosophically while observing students spilling out of red brick buildings; this peculiar group consisting of high IQ, painstaking work and ambition to reach for the stars. All of them cheerful, light-hearted, looking like they've always been friends. He would mutter, "What the heck am I even doing here!"

Work at the library brought him tremendous satisfaction. In the fall he developed a habit of spending hours there, wandering through all the wisdom found in the rich literary collection and then taking a nap on one of the desks.

On that day, however, there was no time for a nap. With finals looming on the horizon, the library was particularly busy.

"*Kurwa*, you're such a jerk!" someone inappropriately broke the silence in the reading room.

Heracles turned around to see who it was. It was a young man, not too tall, yet well built, who addressed the student in horn-rimmed glasses sitting next to him. The first word of his statement, clearly not in English, intrigued Heracles and resulted in close observation of the student. He had dark skin, black hair combed into a ducktail and a humped nose. The well-worn elbows of his tweed jacket, neatly hidden underneath leather patches, along with stretched material at the knees in his gray trousers proved that his complexion was not a result of a tan on a European ski tour with his rich father, but rather his natural feature.

The stranger approached the counter.

"Do you happen to have any of these?" the reading list for mathematics students was slid towards Heracles. "Um" the man looked pensive as he leaned over the sheet of paper, "I would be most interested in number two and... oh, this! Number six" he tapped his finger on a six written in roman numerals.

Heracles gazed lazily at him.

"I'm in a hurry!" the man tapped his fingers at the desktop and raised his brow peculiarly high. Not even knowing why, at this very moment, maybe due to this spectacular brow trick, Herakles felt sympathy for this student that seemed crude, slightly hot-headed and straightforward. Without hesitation, he turned around and approached the shelves to collect indicated books.

"Here you go," he said, placing three large tomes on the counter, "I'm adding number five to two and six."

"Five?" The stranger looked at the list again. "It's a book on art! Dude, I appreciate your good intentions but it's probably the least interesting one for me right now. I've got a test in two days, I have to go through two and six."

"Knowledge of fine arts deepens the understanding of exact science."

The stranger looked up at him with slightly more respect than before.

"Alright, Mr. library man, maybe you're right, but it's mathematics that deepens the rational outlook on all the phenomena that occur in our lovely and somewhat chaotic world. It provides a universal method to develop the ability to make connections and think logically. One that is comprehensible to everyone."

"That was an interesting lecture," Heracles concluded, thinking that intelligence was truly a common element at Harvard.

"I could gladly elaborate," the stranger proposed, raising his brow. "Not necessarily over tea," he added with a suggestive smile.

"I'm not so sure, are you going to yell at me? Look at that poor guy," Herakles nodded towards the young man in horn-rimmed glasses, "he's still shaky."

"Trust me, it was well deserved."

"How come?"

"Well, he has an annoying talent for telling bad jokes."

"Ah, right!" Herakles pushed his hands into his pockets and nodded his head, "that explains everything."

This was the beginning of a lifelong friendship between these two. One of them pretended to be someone else, hiding in the shadow of the *American dream* archetype, wanting to escape his past.

Their friendship resembled a peculiar duet, like a combination of black and white, an alliance of order and chaos, the natural ability to interact in society and acquired politeness. Even their appearance highlighted the stark difference between them. Vlad was a well-built, brunette man of average height, with a tan complexion and a piercing, dark glance. His hands were extraordinarily delicate, with carefully manicured nails. Just like most of the Ivy League community, Vlad embraced the preppy style; a blend of elegance and casual, timeless pieces and high-quality fabric. Neither his jacket nor his trousers, however, were made of the highest quality materials. With clothes stretched here and there, he was more of a poor relation among a flock of students hanging around Harvard Yard. None of this made him insecure. His constant cheerful disposition only confirmed that he took to the Ivy League environment like a fish to water. Interestingly, despite his dark eyes, olive complexion, raven hair and hooked nose, he had Slavic roots. The ability to blend perfectly into any society, along with an impeccable Boston accent, confirmed his deep immersion in the American culture. He seemed to be someone who was at ease not only living in this extraordinary country but also with himself.

Heracles was a slim man, over 6 feet tall. There were two distinct features of his appearance; a scar on his left cheek and silver hair tied into a ponytail. It seemed that the hair must have turned gray as a result of stress or shock; this color certainly did not match the black, mysterious gaze, the olive skin, the name Heracles, and – most certainly – it did not go well with his age. At that, he resembled a cross between an angel and the devil. He dressed in black suits and white, starched shirts. There would rarely be a smile on his face, and even when one appeared, it was one of those nonchalant, casual and lazy grins. Unapproachable as he might have seemed, the girls seemed to like his aura of mystery. However, he either ignored the attention or was completely unaware of it.

Soon, Heracles' life took a substantial turn, as a simple coincidence enabled him to decide which discipline would he like to explore more. While at the library, he stumbled upon *The Republic*, perhaps Plato's most famous work. He opened it, read it, started having doubts and that was it. He was lost. A perfect being and the real world reflected in it, except that there was an abundance of vices and sins. Thousands of questions ran through his head, and he wanted answers to all of them. Not at once; slowly, taking delight in following the path to truth and wisdom. And so he chose philosophy.

Heracles and Vlad did not want to be like all these people standing at the window and staring at the vibrant life bustling outside. They would rather be where the said life was happening, at the center of events. While living on campus, getting on with people was not a problem – but it was the integration with the city rather than with university society that they both desired, and so they packed up their stuff and rented an apartment outside the campus. They lived on the first floor of an old house. There were spacious rooms and hardwood flooring, white walls and furniture, maybe worn-out, but still of superior quality. Time was divided between studying – always a priority – and taking short breaks to relax. They would roam the streets of Boston, making the most of its excitements and charming nooks. There was their favorite bar, where ritual drinks accompanied the broadening of thought horizons and lengthy conversations with friends. The group included both students and their cherished lecturers; the friendly atmosphere helped them lose cultural constraints and turn into great companions. Apart from being a brilliant mathematician, Vlad was also a competent storyteller and planned to become a writer after graduation. Hence, he gladly voiced his opinion during conversations or listened intently to captivating stories, treating them as a base upon which his future novels would be built. Heracles, on the other hand, followed Epictetus' thought that we have two ears and one mouth so that we can listen twice as much as we speak – so he was the listener type. But not the one who constantly nods their head, murmuring *mhmhm* under their breath; quite the opposite – whenever the speaker would start talking nonsense, he would ostentatiously rub his chin, lean back on the chair and fold his arms, making a face as if he were about to say: *it's all bullshit*. An interesting discussion, however, encouraged him to ask questions to understand the situation better. All of this gave him a reputation as a person, who despite being quiet, earned the respect and authority that could easily be the envy of many long-time lecturers.

It was late autumn when one Sunday they sat down at their favorite bench in Boston Common. Staring at birds and pretty girls, they were breaking away from the city life. Vlad reminisced about Poland and his passionate, yet gentle summer fling. The feelings that came over him when he was visiting his parents' homeland to meet his aunt left him broken-hearted. Silent, Heracles both listened and not listened to him, observing a pair of tiny birds pecking at the grass. There was some surreality to it, as if he were longing for something he could not experience himself.

"I have a dream…", he said suddenly.

"What are you talking about?" Vlad enquired, taking the last sips of coffee from a paper cup.

"Nothing, it's just… I'm quoting Luther King. He spoke at this park."

"Correct, but he talked about his dreams a bit earlier and somewhere else," Vlad noted, crushing the empty cup and aiming it at the trash can without moving an inch from his spot, "Score!", he marveled at his shot and added: "he said it in '63 at the Lincoln Memorial in Washington, D.C."

"He clearly had a way with words," Heracles concluded, crossing his feet.

"Can you imagine? The emotions? Quarter a million people listening to him! Their mouths wide open, tears in their eyes. And do you know why? Because apart from emotions, there was truth in his words. Do you understand? Truth, dude. Pure truth, with no mask of hypocrisy.

"When I listen to what you say, I hear who you are."

"Emerson?"

"Emerson."

"And you, Heracles? Who are you? And what's your dream?"

"What dream?" Heracles shifted on the bench. "Are you serious?"

"Serious as hell!"

"Dude, what do you need that for?"

"What for? I've been living with a Greek god for two years and I don't even know the name of his father. Your personality is so fucking enigmatic."

"Zeus."

"What Zeus?"

"It's my father's name."

"Screw you."

"Come on, I'm serious. My father's name is Zeus."

"Christ! And your mother is Alcmene?"

"No. Aphrodite."

"Aphrodite?! Hah!" Vlad's particularly animate brow has risen. "That's what I thought. So you are truly a deity, not just a demi-god. Oh, look! Chicks!" Two girls that passed by, one of them looking like a confident tennis player and the other resembling a timid librarian, both gave them a quick glance.

"Nice, right?" Vlad quickly assessed the situation.

Heracles followed them with his eyes.

"Yeah, not so bad."

"I'm gonna go and talk to them."

"Hold your horses, Casanova …," Heracles glanced at his watch, "…it's getting late. Time to go back! Stevenson can't wait for you to submit your paper."

"Sssh, you're going to scare them away!" Vlad responded. "Sit and watch!"

Heracles leaned forward, elbows on his knees, his head low.

"Jerk," the man murmured, staring at his shoes.

Three hours later, all four crashed the boys' place and were eating reheated mac and cheese over a few bottles of wine and beer. Later on, Vlad grabbed the hand of Jenny – the one who resembled an athletic tennis player – and led her into his room. Betty, the epitome of a library chic, stayed with Heracles and spent quite a while over the last glass of wine.

"Will you walk me home?" the girl asked, getting up from the chair.

"You sure you want that?" Heracles looked at her so intensely that she felt a thrill travel up her spine.

"I'm sure," she muttered, putting a red beanie on her perfectly black hair.

As they were leaving the apartment, he briefly touched her back and felt how she stiffened up upon his touch. Seemingly unfazed, Betty nonchalantly fixed her glasses on her nose.

The night was cold. The slender crescent of the new moon hung above them when they stopped in front of her home. At a certain point, Heracles made a step forward, removed her beanie and kissed her on the forehead.

"Goodnight," he said.

"That was nice," Betty responded, her hand caressing the place where his lips were seconds ago. "Goodnight," the woman said, and after she ran upstairs, one of the windows of a red brick brownstone lit up with a dimmed light.

The cold wind picked up and Heracles turned his collar up. Accompanied by a street busker on a guitar who nobody listened to and a siren of a wailing ambulance, he walked the empty street. *That was nice*, he kept on reminiscing. Home was three blocks away and as soon as he reached it, he laid down on the bed, not even bothering to take off his clothes and shoes. Resting with arms under his head, he stared blankly at the light from a street lamp flooding the ceiling, the warm buzz of beer and red wine warming him from the inside. A gust of cold wind danced with the curtains, directing his gaze towards the open window. Unwittingly, his mind wandered to these fleeting moments of that life. The life he left behind and was forced to forget, even though he couldn't make himself. Or maybe he just didn't want to.

When in the morning Heracles suddenly woke up and sat

on the edge of his bed, the clock was showing ten to eight. *Damn, I slept in!* The man stroked the stubble on his cheek and went to the bathroom to freshen up and shave. A quick glance in the mirror showed him what he feared: dull skin, bags under eyes, the worst case of bed-head imaginable and morning breath that characteristically reeked of digested alcohol. *Crap, what do I look like?* As he was standing with his legs slightly apart in front of the toilet, he unzipped his pants and suddenly remembered he had an appointment with professor Johnson at eight. Heracles cursed again.

"Hello, Adonis!" he heard behind his back and twitched.

Leaning against the doorframe was Jenny, sending his way a charming smile.

"Hi! You look beautiful," he lied, zipping up his pants. Clad in Vlad's dirty T-shirt, with her make-up smudged, she finally broke away from the door and, entirely unfazed, marched towards the sink.

"No kidding!" the woman said, rolling her eyes in the mirror. "Christ, look at me!" She brushed her blonde, messy curls with red fingernails. "Tell me, where did you get that color hair? Were you always gray? Or was it stress? You know, they say Marie Antoinette's hair turned white overnight before her execution, poor thing. Betty told me that. One time we saw you at a hockey game and when you took your helmet off, your gray locks flowed out. Gosh, Betty was so impressed, it's a pity you didn't see that."

"So we know each other by sight?"

"Sure thing, you often go to the park and sit on the same bench. We would always hang around nearby, but..." Jenny moved closer to the mirror and scraped her tooth with a fingernail, "but you did not notice us until now. Betty didn't tell you about it?"

"No, she didn't mention it. Is that why you went to the game?"

"That was a coincidence, but it was the first time Betty noticed you in the crowd of these hunky barbarians on ice. My brother took us there. He's a hockey fan and even played on the school team at Dartmouth. Well, I like it too, you all look cool. Chunks packed in protective gear that resembles inflatable biceps, all chasing a small puck and ruthlessly knocking down their opponents. Blood, sweat and tears. And you, among all those barbarians. I appreciate a good show when I see it."

"It's just a thing of the past. I don't play anymore, now I'm swimming."

"I know…," she turned around to look at him. "Betty told me, obviously."

"Alright, I've got to go," he said, raised his hand and got a strand of hair out of her eye, almost tenderly. She might have been hungover, but she was still sexy. "The bathroom is yours," he said and rushed towards the door.

"Adonis!" she shouted after him.

"Heracles," the man corrected.

"Come on, I know. Heracles. Quite an original name."

"It's from Greek."

"I know that too, Adonis." The mistake was deliberate, but this time he dismissed it with a smile. "Maybe I'm not as smart as Betty, the fount of all wisdom…," she inspected her profile in the mirror and smiled with satisfaction. "But I'm not dumb either. Each of us has some good sides. By the way, where is she? Still asleep?"

"Who?"

"Who, who! Betty!"

"I don't know. Check on her once you get home."

"She didn't stay the night?" Jenny turned towards him.

"Right. Typical. Chickened out again, that immaculate virgin. Did you at least get to walk her home?"

"Have a nice day, Jenny, I'm late for class."

"So long, Adonis! Ah, almost forgot. Please check on Vlad, he asked about you."

"Listen, I'm leaving him in your hands."

"No, wait! I'm serious, he asked for you to see him."

Vlad's room was a mess: it reeked of cigarettes and alcohol, the floor was littered with bottles and scattered clothes. On the desk, among books on mathematic successes of Gauss and Riemann, there was a pair of pink undies. Vlad was resting in his bed with a hot water bottle on his head. Upon seeing his friend, he perked up.

"Hey, dude!"

"Hello. You alive?"

"Well, hard to say. But since I can see you, that probably means yes. Christ…," he winced, "look at you!"

"Have you seen yourself today?"

"Get lost!"

"Do you need anything? There's some more beer in the fridge."

"What? Ah… no, no. Thanks! Jenny already took good care of me. Listen," he adjusted the hot water bottle. "I think I'm gonna give up on today, I'm not going to uni. Could you do something for me? I should submit this paper on Riemann to Stevens."

"I know, told ya about it, Casanova."

"Okay, okay, stop pretending to be a saint. Don't know

about you, but I have no regrets... last night I was busy with something way better than that. But if you would be so nice, save my ass and come up with something... dude, I'd be eternally grateful."

"What am I supposed to come up with, huh?"

"What? I don't know! Maybe that I'm sick...? Or that I was hit by a car...? Damn...," he propped himself up on his elbows, "...not gonna lie, that's what I feel right now. As if I got run over by a fucking huge truck. But you know... I'd like to be still in shape. Did you see Jenny? Those luscious lips?"

"Okay, I'll think of something."

It so happened that Heracles did not come up with anything to save Vlad's ass. He did not only fail to visit professor Stevenson, he didn't even show up at the university. That day, hands deep in his pockets, he wandered aimlessly about the city amid the frenzy of cars, skyscrapers and Victorian houses. Somewhere between the Boston Revolt, the Boston Massacre and the Boston Tea Party, he was going through some sort of trial by fire, engrossing himself in that sense of purpose that drew him to Boston so many years ago. He was supposed to forget. Instead, he kept on remembering. This memory was the source of his torture and frustration, evoking the uninhibited desire to love a woman he cannot have. There was not a chance in hell he would see her again, anytime and anywhere. Despite this torment, he was constantly on the lookout, searching for her in the streets and in the crowd. It's been a few years now... Though he could sleep just fine, sometimes even through the entire night, he would always wake up wondering whether the history of their extraordinary meetings was just a dream – or maybe not. This obsession ruined his life. Today, before going on the campus, he made a certain decision. Though it seemed conscious and irrevocable, he realized that making it happen would be equally painful as removing a limb that would radiate with phantom pains for years to come. But he wanted to live! No matter how flawed it was, he seemed to appreciate this world more and more. Maybe it was thanks to professor Johnson, who straightforwardly fixed his wicked life? Or maybe thanks to the education? Delving into the biographies and works of ancient thinkers, exploring their hypotheses, theorems, formulas and paradoxes, seeking answers to questions that they had asked centuries ago: regarding the essence of time, space, matter, thinking what love is. He felt really good among his fellow university brethren, this nationally diversified melting pot where nearly every person spoke English with a different accent. Maybe it was the friendship with Vlad that gave him good energy, forcing his lungs to breathe again and making the blood flow to all the organs. And maybe it was Betty – the girl he met yesterday – and her *That was nice* that made his heart skip a beat again. Anyway, he wanted to forget once and for all, no matter what the cost.

Even if it were to be equally painful as it is for a wild, wounded animal that is ready to bite its paw off before the spreading gangrene destroys its whole body. He had to finally clear his mind of all the tragic events of that life and that girl whom he loved and then... he didn't know what happened to her next, but he could be sure of one thing: he broke her heart into millions of pieces.

It was already late and he was standing at the bus stop when he noticed a peculiar couple intently watching him. The woman was a long-haired hippie in flowing, floral robes, while the man was elegantly clad in tweed. The two shared a smoke. The girl quietly muttered something to her companion, and he burst into laughter. Then Heracles remembered the morning face that looked at him in the mirror and shot them a glance that could easily mean *Christ, what are you two staring at?!* At the same moment, their forgiving smile put his outrage to a stop, so he even smiled back. There was something uplifting about this moment; something that made him think about Betty again, wishing he were with her.

Heracles stood in front of her house for a minute or two before he mustered up enough courage to ring the doorbell. When she opened the door, he was leaning against the doorframe and gazing at her. Only at that moment did he notice her charm; ethereal beauty imperceptible to a passing observer. With her mouth half-open she looked so lovely surprised; Betty squinted her eyes, fixed her glasses and asked: "Did something happen, Heracles?"

"Yes!"

"Yes?"

"I want to make love with you."

"Oh!" Betty adorably blinked her eyes. "When?"

"Now."

"You're more than welcome, Heracles," the woman stated, swinging the door wide open.

They made love all through the night, slowly and gently. It was starkly different from all his previous flings with other girls. Maybe because for the very first time he wasn't thinking about the past. He was in the very moment, with a smart, yet an extraordinarily tender woman. With Betty.

The memory of these joyful months, when he was rushing through the city after his classes, showering her with passionate kisses right after closing the door and hurriedly removing the clothes, throwing them on the floor, would warm him up during lonely evenings that awaited him after graduation. But that's something he was yet about to learn.

When the semester finished and the overwhelming frenzy of the finals faded away – as all the papers had already been submitted – most of the students packed up their stuff and returned to their hometowns. Vlad invited Heracles to his parents' place in the countryside. It was a Victorian villa with a charming porch, where one spends hours with cookies and tea, relishing the views stretching for miles over the local area. Vlad's father, John Kovalski, resembling an older matrix used to mold subsequent Vlads, was a bank owner. Prior to that, he dabbled in real estate, purchasing homes and apartments from impoverished people and flipping them. His determination and perseverance in building a family business resulted in the creation of a Chicago-based investment corporation. His next step involved buying a failing bank from one of his fellow countrymen. In less than two years, he managed to revive the bank, and John Kovalski had made a name for himself in particular circles. Vlad's father was not only a skilled businessman; along with his wife Magdalena, a wide-smiled blonde, they were known as generous donors to charities, especially among Poles living in the States.

Mr. and Mrs. Kovalski wanted to meet their only son's friend. Having accepted their kind invitation, Heracles finally stood on the porch of their Plainfield house, savoring the beautiful view over the countryside and the wild joy of being in the outdoors – and then the interrogation regarding his past and plans for the nearest future started.

"Why philosophy?" Heracles responded, scratching the back of his neck, when Vlad's father, a cigar in his hand, enquired about the reason behind the choice of his major. "I just like it," he admitted, bluntly honest.

John ostentatiously flicked the embers from his cigar and served Heracles a lengthy gaze that could say *Bullshit, my son!* He made the effort to phrase it differently, though.

"Alright! Forgive me, young man, I wouldn't like to offend you, but I find it hard to believe that a normal, healthy guy would like to study philosophy. And well, you know, if you're thinking about providing yourself and your future family with an appropriate standard of living... this *I just like it* thing is not a fortunate life stance, it's just an empty phrase."

Heracles, slightly confused, fixed his gaze on his drink.

"That depends on what the term *appropriate standard of living* refers to", he responded after a while.

"Oh! Everything, my boy!" John spread his arms. "Everything! Every single thing that satisfies our basic needs: a roof over our head and a sense of security. Anything else, such as spiritual development, is merely a fantasy for dissatisfied intellectuals. You've got a sharp look and my intuition tells me you know very well what I'm talking about. A man has to be a man: strong, resourceful, madly in love with his only lady, always following his common sense. Do you understand?" he looked searchingly at Heracles and added: "Let's not forget that this huge country isn't very tolerant of human weaknesses." The man leaned back in his chair and wondered for a moment. "Let me tell you a story...," he put out the cigar in an ashtray, "...about myself. On September fifth, nineteen..."

"John, for God's sake! Again?!" The voice of his wife Magda, coming from inside the house, interrupted his anecdote.

"What is it, darling?" He opened his mouth slightly and listened intently. As only silence resounded, he continued his story. "As I was telling you, on September fifth, nineteen thirty-nine, after nine days of sailing, I disembarked the M.S. Batory.

All I had were my dreams and an old haversack. This ship was supposed to liberate me from the poverty that I left behind in my hometown in Kuyavia." His gaze showed the determination that he engaged to overcome all the great obstacles on his way to this country. "When I stepped on American soil, the war was raging around the world. But I had a mission to complete, and that gave me the courage I needed. I promised myself I will survive, I owed it to my parents. They raised me with all the means they had, doing everything they could, and then helped me collect money for a ticket to board this ship. I was barely seventeen, I had strong hands," he raised his clenched fist, "and I wanted to survive so much to help them. But," his hand fell limply, "I didn't make it on time. My father died in Auschwitz, my mother succumbed to typhus. After the war, I found my sister in an orphanage, but she didn't want to come here to the States. She's doing quite well in Poland, such a brave soul. We sent Vlad to visit her, he was absolutely delighted and brushed up on his language skills... We do our best to make sure he doesn't forget his roots. It's very important to us," he reached again for the cigar resting in the ashtray the size of a dinner plate and then lit it up. "Yes. Life had kicked my ass for long enough to make me realize what really matters. Well..," he pointed the cigar at Heracles, "my young friend, an avid fan of Plato and Socrates, here's my advice for you: think it through."

Magda, wearing a cute cardigan adorned with a row of tiny buttons, appeared on the porch clutching a crystal glass, one third filled with a drink.

"Am I interrupting you?"

"Oh, no. Have a seat, honey."

"Darling, aren't you boring our guest a little bit?" Magda

sat down on the arm of her husband's chair and smiled politely at Heracles.

"No, not at all, the gentleman here…"

"Oh, stop with the gentleman thing. John, Heracles. Call me John, that's what my friends call me."

"So…," Heracles hesitated, "John gave me some valuable advice and I learned about the incredible history of your family."

"Alright, so just like I thought: he bored you to death." She bowed down and kindly kissed John on the forehead. Then she reached out her hand with a glass towards Vlad, who was standing in the doorway, asking him to fill up her drink. "Maybe you would play something for us?" she addressed her husband again.

Heracles showed noticeable interest: "Play?"

"That's right," Vlad tilted the bottle and filled up his mother's glass. "Dad is truly a violin virtuoso. You know, a getaway from the constant fight for the family's prosperity," he winked at him. "In other words," the man took a sip of scotch and wiped his mouth with his hand, "it's a sort of his spiritual development. Though he won't admit it."

"Everything okay?" Magda asked, noticing that all of a sudden, Heracles became sullen. Vlad already got used to these periods of prolonged, silent pondering that bordered on sadness, but for those who didn't know Heracles quite well, these could be a sign of unpleasant disposition and gloominess.

"Oh, of course, sure!" he responded, as if suddenly woken from a dream.

As they headed to the dining room, where a table that would easily seat thirty people was set for the family and their guest, Heracles discreetly looked around the rooms. All of them oozed rich luxury, every single thing being beautiful; mirrors in extraordinary frames, mahogany wood, a sparkly chandelier dripping with crystals. As he peeked into the office, Heracles quickly glanced at a leather sofa, a snuggle chair and a massive desk with black leather inlay. With his hands clasped behind his back, he approached a walnut bookcase packed to the brim with thousands of pages of words – some of them bound in calfskin, spines adorned with the title and author's name in gold letters. Suddenly he stopped in his tracks: in a glass cabinet, there was an old violin covered in gold varnish displayed.

"Oh! And that's actually proof that my old man happens to be a hypocrite," Vlad, with his hands in his pockets, rocked on his feet.

"What do you mean?"

"Oh, you know! His critical stance towards any kind of spiritual activity... fantasies for dissatisfied intellectuals, artists and so on... all the while keeping this," he nodded his head forward, opened the glass door and took the violin out.

"It's beautiful, isn't it? A very valuable instrument. Stradivarius. Golden varnish... top made of spruce wood... a sycamore scroll... and the rhythm of the curvature..."

"Are you sure it's genuine?"

"Why would you doubt it?" he grimaced. "Are you an expert?"

"No, but you know... a Stradivarius? I guess there aren't that many out there. It's so beautiful..."

"...and genuine," Vlad added quickly. "You'd like to touch it, wouldn't you? Watch your hands," he jokingly slapped his palm. "Here you go. Just be careful."

"Someone's been using it."

"Geez," Vlad rolled his eyes. "Obviously it's not new. Stradivarius is, like, eighteenth century."

"No, that's not what I mean," Heracles tenderly caressed

the top of the violin and closed his eyes for a while. "Someone is still playing it."

"Correct, it's my father. And me... I used to play."

"You?"

"What? Are you surprised?"

"Come on, prove it!"

"Screw you! Play something yourself."

"I don't know how."

"Because you need actual talent for that, you dumbass!"

"Alright, Mr. maestro, and you've got what it takes?"

"Well, there was a time when I would play for hours. Day after day. For a week."

"A week? And? What was the effect?"

"Sounded like someone was being murdered. But the passion was there. Remember that girl I once told you about? The one from Poland? It's because of her that my enthusiasm just faded away."

"Really? And what now?"

"Nothing. I don't play. Another waste of talent. But my father can play, and boy, he plays good! But he practices a lot."

"It shows," Heracles admitted unexpectedly.

"It shows? How would you know that? Is it one of these divine powers of yours?"

"Well... the fiddler's neck says everything," he scratched his own neck.

"What is fiddler's neck?"

"It's like... a hickey. But it has nothing to do with sex, loverboy. It's a kind of a reddish mark on the left side of the neck, where the violin is held."

"You know quite a lot for an amateur," said John, settling down in the armchair and lighting up his cigar. "The story of how we ended up owning this violin is remarkable. It's a result of a mature decision made years ago by some young man," he glanced at Vlad. "His choice between love and honor."

"Dad, let it go."

"Wait, I'm actually very much into this incredible story," Heracles admitted and gave Vlad a meaningful look.

"Oh well, it's five o'clock!" Vlad announced it loudly when the clock chimed, trying to dodge the bullet. "Let's go to the dining room!" He took the violin from Heracles, placed it in the cabinet and politely gestured them towards the door. "This way. Let's go before it comes out who really calls the shots here. Mom doesn't appreciate us being late for dinner."

"Mhm," John murmured. "Let me satisfy our guest's curiosity. It's very much an informative story."

"I like being informed," Heracles clasped his hands behind his back, rocking from his toes to his heels. "I'm all ears."

John got up from the armchair and approached them, holding the cigar between his fingers.

"I have already mentioned Anna, my sister from Poland, right?" he ensured.

Heracles nodded.

"So after the war she ended up living in Masuria."

"Masuria? Is it a city?"

"No, you idiot," Vlad returned. "It's a Polish Lakeland district."

"Oh! Something like our Great Lakes?"

"Well... not really. I mean, not that big," John explained, his tone expressing understanding towards his guest's justified ignorance. "But believe me: it's equally charming. So my sister and her husband used to live in a tenement house. Judging by what survived, their apartment most probably belonged to wealthy townspeople. They found this violin in the attic, not that it was anything extraordinary, such things happened back then. My brother-in-law made some repairs, glued it together, bought a bow, a case, and wanted to sell it for a few bucks to some hustler. In the meantime, I sent Vlad to visit my sister. He was allowed to play this violin for days. How old were you?" he asked Vlad.

"I don't really remember, father. Five?"

"Ha! Liar." The man pointed his hand with a cigar at his son. "Old enough to French kiss. You were fifteen."

"I like this story more with every minute," Heracles crossed his arms.

"Keep on listening. As an American, he was a phenomenon among all the kids from the communist backyard. One pretty girl, slightly older than him, particularly liked Vlad."

"If you want to spill the beans, get your facts straight. She wasn't pretty, she was stunning. I was fifteen, and she was... maybe a few months older."

"Seventeen. She was seventeen years old."

"Really? She never told me that. We were meeting at an old cemetery... for educational purposes. I taught her English. You know, *how do you say niebo? Sky. And gwiazdy? Stars. Chłopak? A boy. Dziewczyna? A girl. And is it true that I love you means kocham cię? The truest of truths!* After that lesson, I dared to hold her hand and then kissed her."

"Was it a French kiss?"

"Shut up!"

"One day...," John continued, "he, well, as we would say it, podpierdolił..."

"What does *podpierdolił* mean?" Heracles immediately expressed interest.

"It's Polish for *steal*. So he stole the violin from his aunt, and uncle…"

"I didn't steal it, not at all. I just borrowed it."

"Wanting to impress the girl even more, he borrowed the violin from his aunt and uncle without asking them for permission, intending to show off his skills. Except that instead of the girl, someone else appeared at the old cemetery. Her ex-fiancé with his friends from ZMS."

"What is ZMS?"

"An organization of young people believing in socialist ideology. Not only did they take his violin away and gave him a beating, they left him with a moral dilemma: *leave the girl alone or else you won't ever see the violin, you lousy bastard from the rotten west!*"

"Yeah, it's all laughs now but I was far from amused back then," Vlad interrupted. "I wanted to kill myself. I spent three days wondering what to do. I was pretty sure this shitty violin was not worth my sacrifice, my grand love. She was such a nice girl! But I chose the violin. Somehow my aunt learned about everything and instead of selling it, generously gifted it to me. I politely accepted the present, but I couldn't even look at it for years. You know, memories."

"Was your aunt aware of its value?"

"Not at all. I didn't know either. Had I known, I wouldn't have accepted it."

"When Vlad returned with the violin," John chimed in, "I obviously took a close look at it. Inside I noticed this inscription: Antonius Stradivarius Cremonensis Faciebat Anno 1714. My heart was in my mouth, I immediately wrote to my sister, but she didn't even want to hear about accepting it back. *Stradivarius* did not ring a bell at all, she's a simple woman. When

I started explaining it, she doubted its authenticity. Anyway, making her aware that it is truly a treasure is a whole other story. This is neither the time nor the place to discuss it all.

"Excuse my curiosity, but have you had it checked by a reliable expert?"

"Well, one time it nearly happened. But I changed my mind at the last minute. You know, Heracles...," the man embraced Heracles' shoulders and guided him towards the dining room. "Every discovery, every treasure covered in the dust of history, causes a sensation and evokes hope that it is, indeed, a genuine artifact. When it happens to be true, the lives of many a man are turned upside down. I don't want that. I don't want to change anything. I just want to have hope."

The dinner was served in a relaxed, pleasant atmosphere. John Kovalski proved to be a great host and storyteller. Employing a hearty and crude manner – though sometimes adding a dash of caution and subtlety – he would entertain his guests with anecdotes and stories from his time in Poland. When the main course was served, roasted turkey, a specialty of the lady of the house, Heracles felt as if he were among his old friends. And as soon as the dessert – a truly spectacular apple pie – landed on the table, Heracles managed to open up and share quite a lot about himself, a thing rather uncommon for a person so unforthcoming, maybe even reserved as he was. The man was particularly fond on describing his family home set in the heart of an olive grove on top of a hill, with breathtaking views over the Schiza and Sapientza bays.

"Heracles, and your father...," John wiped the corners of his mouth with a cotton napkin and grabbed a glass of water. "What does he do?"

"Oh, and it's a wrap when it comes to the dinner. Mom...,"

Vlad suddenly got up from his chair and gracefully kissed her on the top of her head, "…everything was delicious, as usual. Come on, dude!" he addressed Heracles.

"Why are you two in such a rush?" John reacted quickly. "I thought we would go to the study and have a glass of scotch."

"Excuse us, dad, but I promised to show Heracles the area."

"If you don't mind, Mr. Kov… I mean, John, if you don't mind, we could obviously make quick amendments to our plan and finish the night with some scotch," Heracles added kindly.

"No way…," Vlad shook his head. "Forget it, dude! Wanting to get away with it, huh? Mom, dad, Heracles bragged that he's great at riding horses. I don't believe him."

"Alright. If it's a matter of honor, I'm not going to insist."

"Just Vlad, for heaven's sake," Magda wagged her finger at them, "leave Spaniard alone."

The walk towards a small stable in the western part of the estate resembled one giant attempt to keep the conversation alive. Heracles, clearly absorbed in his thoughts, replied with monosyllables to parts of Vlad's stories and information, asking questions that he actually managed to hear. After a few minutes of this awkward, absurd situation where they both pretended everything was okay, Heracles kicked a pebble and, out of the blue, revealed what really bothered him.

"I don't remember ever telling you that I'm riding horses. Was that supposed to be some kind of an excuse? Is that it? Are you embarrassed in front of John that he's hosting under his roof the son of an ordinary fiddler? You didn't want me to tell your father what does my father do to support his family? That's what's bothering you, right?"

"Listen, dude, no offense but in his case, it's not easy to

win him over. I mean, don't get me wrong. He likes people in general but needs a bit more time to let someone join the tribe. You know: sniff, check, challenge… And I see that he liked you. Right away. It suits me," Vlad nudged him gently.

"It doesn't suit me to hide the truth about my own father as if he were a criminal of some sort."

"Damn, Hera! You've climbed that mount Olympus of yours and don't understand the lives of normal people at all."

"Enlighten me, then."

"Listen, it's not about how you feel. It's about how my father feels. See, if you told him that you were raised in a family of musicians, where free thoughts and an artistic spirit reign, all the…," Vlad paused.

"All the what?"

"All the sparks I noticed in his eyes ever since you appeared at our house would disappear. You must have noticed how he fawns over you. *Call me John, that's what my friends call me.* Instead of these sparks, there would be uncertainty, pretense, avoiding certain topics, a stiff atmosphere. He might get the impression that you look down on him."

"Me? Looking down on him?! It's rubbish! What nonsense!"

"Not really. See, he has reasons to think like that. People like your father, artists, writers… are destined for leftism. As if humanity inflicted upon them a moral obligation to stigmatize people like my father – rich, unethical motherfuckers, bloodsuckers that made fortunes from someone else's pain. You heard how he reacted to your *I chose philosophy because I just like it.*"

"Vlad, it's ridiculous. Just because I deal with philosophy and my father is a musician… No way," he shook his head. "It's nothing more but ludicrous stigmatizing. I have no problem talking with him about it."

"It's not going to change anything, let it go. You will be explaining yourself like a guilty man in court. Trust me, it's harder than you can imagine, I know my father well. When he fixates on something... ah," Vlad waved his hand dismissively. "It's a waste of words, believe me. Anyway, it's one of the reasons I didn't tell him I want to be a writer."

"Why do you make such a mystery of it? I think it's a mistake. You should admit what your plans are."

"Exactly! Can you hear yourself?! Admit! You can admit to being guilty, being a criminal... and that's precisely how I would feel. As if I were guilty of betraying the hope he placed in me. And yeah, he has high hopes... very high. Listen, when I was... maybe five, I don't know... I was playing with toy soldiers. Suddenly my dad stood in a doorway and kindly informed me that I am going to be a banker because I've got brains. You know, rumor had it I was a child prodigy, some bullshit about a little mathematical genius. My aunts would pinch my cheeks and then ask: Vladi, what is two thousand six hundred fifty-three plus six thousand seventeen? What's six hundred and five times twenty-nine?"

"Did you know?"

"Not at all! I would tell them a whopper. I put on a wise face and blurted out random numbers that I didn't have the faintest idea about. After all, being a genius brings great responsibility, so I had to improvise and make a certain impression. And back then, when my father came into the room and informed me that I would become a banker, I held a mad Apache with a rifle on a horse in one hand and a good-hearted cowboy with two colts in the other. My mouth dropped open and then, tears streaming down my cheeks, I told him – dad, I don't want to be a banker, I want to be a fireman, or maybe a brave cowboy. *No, son*, he

protested. *I know better who you should become when you grow up.*
God, how I didn't want to grow up at the time, I'm telling you!"

"Yeah, nice stories. Still, I think you're a bit too rough on your father."

"Hera, I want you to understand me correctly: my father is stubborn, he forces his will upon other people and thinks he has a monopoly on knowledge about the world. He could discuss human nature with Freud himself if he were alive. I know he's not a bad person, I don't judge him harshly. He's been building his business from scratch, for years, working his ass off. And yet somehow he's never forgotten about his family, friends, he's a kind-hearted, good guy. And that's why seeing people treat those like him as ruthless swindlers capitalizing on someone else's misfortune just hurts him."

"And it hurts you because he sees you as the only heir to his business empire. And he doesn't even accept the thought that he might have raised a future Steinbeck or Hemingway."

"Oh, he actually likes Hemingway. Honestly, though, everything you've said is spot-on. As his only son, I am supposed to be the successor of his heritage. Remorsefully, I have to admit that for some reason I grew accustomed to the thought of it... I'm no rebellious Antigone, rather a freaking cowardly Oedipus. That places me in a rather unenviable position, doesn't it?"

"Meh... I'm not so sure. I think I sort of envy you, though."

"The money?"

"No, dumbass! I'm jealous of your father. You see, whether you agree with him or not, he still cares about you. He instilled some values in you, taught you about responsibility... on his own example. See, my father never gave me any advice. He didn't even ask who I wanted to be when I grow up. It's not like

I'm blaming him now, that's just who he is. A rolling stone, a careless soul surrounded by a magical aura, Zeus with a guitar."

"Are you trying to tell me he's never showed you a way, a path, never set boundaries?"

"Well, no. He's got other virtues, though."

"Really? And which is the most valuable to you?"

"He loves horses and plays the violin."

"Like a Gypsy, huh? Wait, wait... doesn't he play the guitar?"

"The guitar, right."

"And that's Spaniard," Vlad nodded his head towards the third stall from the entrance, when they entered a neat stable, still jokingly pushing each other. A characteristic smell of hay and sweaty horse skin hit their nostrils.

"Such a beauty," Heracles said and boldly approached the horse. He patted her on the neck and then stroked the animal's head, right above the muzzle.

"Careful, she tolerates only me and her keeper."

"Fierce Spanish blood, right? You're a kicker, aren't you?"

"How do you know that?"

"There's a red ribbon in her tail."

"Do you want me to saddle her up?"

"That won't be necessary."

"What, are you suddenly afraid?"

"There's no need to saddle her up. I prefer bareback riding," Heracles admitted.

Standing by Spaniard's side right by her shoulder blade, he looked over his shoulder at Vlad and seeing his face – surprised, yet uplifting, warm and kind – he couldn't help but smile, as if to himself. He couldn't believe how easy it was to blend a part of his life story into their conversation – the genuine one, not the version he used to satisfy the curiosity of strangers. Still, he wasn't ready to open up to him. Maybe one day. But not now.

Few hundred noble luminaries – the president in academic regalia, professors, lecturers – were all seated in chairs on the adorned stairs of the chapel and listened to the graduates' speeches. There was not a hint of pompousness in them nor were they boring; they were a perfect blend of effortless nonchalance, class and humor.

Globe balloons, smiling paper jaws, wooden gavels and other symbolic attributes of various departments swirled in the air to the sound of untamed joy that rose like a wild roar from a few thousand graduates.

Before the paths of Heracles and Vlad parted, so both of them could face the unavoidable clash of hopes and expectations with reality, they managed to hit a few of these eccentric parties, where wild dancing, music and alcohol help the students cut the cord with their respected university.

On the last Saturday of July, they were saying their goodbyes in a restaurant. An old waiter, with a kitchen towel on his shoulder, was pouring their drinks. Sitting at the bar, they were ritually swirling scotch in low ball glasses, discussing the future and coming up with more or less possible scenarios on where and with whom they will be in ten or twenty years.

"Let me know once you're done writing that book of yours," Heracles enquired.

"Sure thing," Vlad responded, leaning with his forearms on the counter, and taking a hearty swig of his drink. "Don't expect it to happen anytime soon, though. Because you know, the creative process is not just...," he waved his hand in the air, "...fun and games!"

"Mhm. Obviously, there's no rush, but you were born with a talent to convey emotions. Especially when it comes to women," Vlad nudged him. "You will find a theme and it's gonna be easy, you'll see."

"Women..., girls... it isn't a rewarding theme," he smiled at the empty glass in his hands.

"Find another one. Look around. There's plenty of great literary themes that would make a wonderful story."

"Sure, but I need a theme, a history that will stand out from *plenty*. One that will crush the reader, enrich them or maybe even damage them. And you...," he turned towards Heracles, his head propped up on his hand. "What do you want to do with your life? Do you want to delve deeper into philosophy, follow the ancient paths or spend it with Betty?"

"One does not exclude the other, but... well, I'd like to teach. More than that, I would like to learn."

"Washington, then?" Vlad asked and leaned towards the barman to ask for a refill.

"Los Angeles, University of California."

"Did Johnson's recommendation work?"

"I didn't use it."

"Oh, right! How could I have thought that! It's not like the son of a mighty Zeus could need any help. Not even the opinion of famed professor Johnson. And Betty? What about her? Are you going to take her with you?"

"To Betty!" Heracles raised his glass and downed it.

"Hey, what's going on...? Are you avoiding the answer or the responsibility?"

"I don't feel responsible for her," Heracles pushed a strand of his gray hair back. "She's an adult woman."

"She's a good girl above all else."

"I know."

"So don't hurt her."

"What? Why would you assume that? I'm not hurting her. And I don't intend to do so."

"So take her with you and then marry her."

"You think she would like to come with me?"

"I don't think. I just know it."

"And you and Jenny? She's a good one too."

"Really? She's hiding it very well then. But I must admit one thing," Vlad finished his scotch and wiped his mouth. "She's pleasant to touch."

A few tranquil years had passed since the moment when they – both newly graduated from Harvard – sat at the bar in a crowded room, thinking out loud about their future. Everything went according to their predictions, though not always in line with the dreams. Vlad was working at his father's bank. To his own surprise, as time passed the profession of a banker started giving him a sense of satisfaction and he soon became the CEO. His charming persona and outstanding communication skills also helped.

His father taught his business partners his *no punches pulled* attitude. Moreover, he had an annoying manner of pointing his nervously chewed Hawaiian cigar at them, conveying a clear non-verbal message; *Shut up – I call the shots here!* Vlad's behavior was a pleasant antithesis to his father's antics. His eloquence, impeccable manners, as well as extraordinary intuition

– a characteristic so desirable in business – endeared not only a host of other clients but also his ever-growing circle of friends. The family business thrived and while the patriarch remained silent, he must have been bursting with pride. This seemingly comfortable stability that provided Vlad with a quite good life missed one thing: satisfaction. At night, he would lay in his enormous, ten thousand dollar bed and stare at the shadows on the ceiling, constantly fantasizing. No, not about women. About the book. He had a feeling his life wouldn't be complete until he writes it, that it would resemble an incomplete text. And so he was waiting for a spurt, some sign that would unchain his long-dormant creativity and fully unleash his innate – as Heracles once remarked – the ability to convey human emotions. Obviously, his father went about his life completely unaware of it, deeply convinced that the only thing keeping his son awake at night were stock market fluctuations.

In the meantime, Heracles earned his doctoral degree and followed the path of wisdom, adamantly exploring the realms of philosophy. He inspired his students who liked and appreciated him, especially for employing simple, comprehensible language to present intricate, oftentimes complex philosophical ideas. At this stage of his life, he spent more and more time reminiscing about Betty. These memories awakened emotions in him – emotions that he finally allowed to flow freely. And soon he realized that he was missing her.

"You look beautiful," he was sitting right opposite Betty's brown eyes. Leaning with his elbows on the tabletop, he propped his chin on his hands, his gaze following her movements. She was holding the menu, wondering what to choose.

His colleagues from the university recommended this

white-tablecloth restaurant to him. A few of them celebrated some joyous life milestones here, three even proposed to their future wives. Though he had no intention to put a ring on Betty's finger, he wanted to get the lay of the land before asking her to move in with him; see, whether there were even trace amounts of the feelings she once had for him. Granted, they regularly corresponded, but these were only letters. As they say, paper endures all, even if it were nothing but an extraordinary lie.

"Hello, beautiful!" Heracles gently kicked the woman with his foot under the table. "Did you hear what I was saying?"

She slowly moved her gaze from the menu to him and adjusted her glasses.

"Sorry, Heracles. I was wondering what should I order. They have a great selection here."

"You're not the best at pretending."

"I don't understand," Betty blinked quickly.

"I said you look terrible today."

"Liar!" Betty scoffed and laughed heartily.

"Oh, so you were listening to me after all. You're still beautiful, you know?"

"I've always listened to you, Heracles." Betty neatly put the menu on the table and stared at him intently. "Always. With utmost attention. And that's how I know when you're lying."

He wanted to give a witty comeback, but the waiter arrived, a wide smile on his face, and asked about their orders. They both settled for steak with boiled vegetables.

Sitting opposite, they both gazed at each other in silence. Heracles was looking into her intelligent eyes and wondered whether he could fall asleep and wake up right next to her every single day. In her eyes, he saw that she wanted it. There was still chemistry between them, particularly noticeable in their gestures and voice tone.

"It's very pretty here." Betty looked around. "Do you come here often?"

"My friends recommended this place to me."

"Which friends?" The woman asked and took a sip of water.

"A rector, a dean, two Nobel prize winners and so on… they drop by this place because of the soft bread, I think it comes straight from the oven," he joked.

"A rector, a dean, Nobel prize winners… doc, what are you doing here with an ordinary librarian?"

He ignored her remark with a sly smile, thinking *What are we even talking about?*

"Listen," he started, leaning forward, his tone serious. "Are you seeing someone?" He tried to catch her gaze.

Surprised, she only managed to open her mouth before the waiter approached their table. The man opened a bottle of red wine with a sommelier corkscrew, offered Heracles a bit to taste and then poured it into their glasses.

"I am. I mean," she pushed her hair out of her eyes. "Oh, come on. You know I'm not. Why harass me with all these personal questions?"

"I want to make sure."

"Make sure? Of what? What do you want to be sure about, Heracles?" Betty grabbed her glass and brought it to her luscious, passionate lips.

"That after tonight, that we are bound to spend together, you will want to stay longer at my place."

"Well, that's surprising," her voice came to a whisper. "I don't know… dear Lord, I don't know…"

"We learn unexpectedly about things that are important to us. And don't drag God into this."

She looked down and smiled innocently, as if she still were a virgin awaiting a long wedding night. He took this gesture as approval.

After leaving the restaurant, he held her tightly next to him and led her through the city, not letting her out of his embrace. Then he led her onto the couch in his apartment, where they spent almost the entire night whispering a litany of incoherent words; both romantic and naughty, deriving from the bliss that they both succumbed to. In the morning, Heracles overslept for work.

There was still space for this tiny woman in Heracles' small bachelor pad furnished with bookshelves full of philosophical books.

Soon they got to know each other's characters, desires and flaws very well. Betty's presence brought order to Heracles' life. Day after day, night after night, sharing with her one pillow, one bathroom and a place at the kitchen table, to him resembled the routine of wedded bliss. Even though Betty was an important figure in his life and he felt he needed her, Heracles did not care for formalizing their union.

For some time it seemed that Betty herself got used to his thoughts on the matter. But after two years she became impatient. She loved him with all her heart and explored all the nuances of physical love with him. Betty was spontaneous in bed, even more so given that she wanted to conceive. Heracles, completely unaware of that fact, believed that Betty controlled the whole situation. Small pills and a glass of water were always on her nightstand, except she never took them. Whenever her cycle was off, she would hopefully wait for morning sickness or lock herself in the bathroom and, standing in front of the mirror, check whether her breasts were tender.

◌

Since Vlad's twenty-fifth birthday, he became subject to constant remarks on the possible birth of an heir to the family fortune – sophisticated innuendos courtesy of his mother and far less subtle blows that came from his father. The problem was, he still hadn't met the right woman that he could intentionally have a son with.

"Helena Modrzejewska," John said loudly, pacing the floor of the huge living room. He finally stopped by the window.

"Who?" asked Vlad.

"Helena Modrzejewska," the man repeated in a tired voice, removing a cigar from his mouth. He stared at the snowflakes flurrying outside.

Vlad settled in an armchair, a glass of whisky in hand, and tried to remember which person should he connect with the name.

"The actress? She's not even my type! And she's dead by the way."

His father turned towards him.

"Stop with the jokes. I'm talking about the eldest daughter of Juliusz Modrzejewski. Yes, right. This Modrzejewski."

"So what? Do you want me to marry her? Like it's some freaking *raison d'etat* and we should combine our estates and give you a grandchild? That's what it's about?"

"And what are you, a dolphin? And I'm a king? Let it go. Before you two give me a grandchild, I suggest you get to know each other. You should go to the movies. I bought the tickets already."

"Dad, you've got to be kidding."

Magdalena quietly entered the living room. She always stepped in – gracefully, gently, but effectively – when the discussion among her two men became more heated.

"No, son. I couldn't be more serious."

"And I'm an adult. That's enough to let me decide about my life."

"And that's why you should share this adult life…"

"Alright, boys!" Magda chirped, her voice fake-nice. She approached Vlad and took his half-empty whisky glass, leaned over him and kissed him on the forehead. Then she moved towards her husband, alluringly took the cigar out of his mouth, stood on her tippy toes and kissed him on the forehead too. Then she added: "Let's go, it's time for dessert!"

Right before the entrance to the dining room, she grabbed Vlad's wrist and discretely took him to the side.

"Dad's right. You should have a girlfriend."

"Mom, I have a girlfriend."

"I know, son. A new one each week. It's time to settle down."

"But…"

"Quiet! I'm talking now." Heracles was stunned. It was the first time she addressed him like this. "You've had enough time to be wild and free. And I hope you took advantage of it. If not, you're just plain stupid."

"Mom…"

"I'm not done yet!" She fiercely raised her hand. "You will meet Helena! And go with her to the movies! And then, if she likes you, because I don't have any doubts you're going to adore her, you will be seeing her! Regularly! Do you understand?!" her determination was clearly visible.

"Love you, mom. You're wonderful."

Her motherly intuition did not fail her. Vlad fell for Helena the first time he laid his eyes upon her. She was stunning; her raven hair and big, cobalt eyes created an eccentric combination with her fair skin and a few freckles sprinkled over her perky nose. Helena had this aura of extraordinary sensitivity and benevolence; making Vlad laugh was one of her favorite pastimes. Right. She was too good for him. And it was this benevolence that destined their promising relationship for failure. A particularly painful one, especially for John.

Accompanied by helpful waiters in red vests, Heracles and Betty were toasting their next anniversary. They were at the very same restaurant where a few years ago just a few breezy words on spending a night together launched their relationship that took on more and more characteristics typical for marriage: one roof over their heads, a bed they shared, maintaining a budget together. There were no children though, and there was still this question: was it even love?

In the candlelight, they unhurriedly relished the delicacies of the sophisticated world.

"Hey, sweetheart," Heracles interrupted, rubbing his finger along the rim of the wine glass. "Where are you?"

"Where you can always find me. Wherever you are. Alright, sorry. I got lost in my thoughts."

Betty spent a good fifteen minutes daydreaming. Another glass of champagne livened her up.

"Heracles?"

"What is it, honey?"

"I love you."

"You're wonderful."

"Heracles."

"Yes, sweetheart?"

Betty reached for the glass with her trembling hand and brought it to her lips, seemingly wanting to take a sip. Instead, she just smelled it.

"Tell me you love me."

Silence ensued and grew bigger as if it were a balloon. They both knew it was about to burst.

"Heracles, why won't you marry me?"

He looked at her quizzically.

"I didn't know it's so important to you."

"Well, it is. You told me once that we learn unexpectedly about things that are important to us. Do you remember?"

"I do."

"Except I don't think it's true. We learn about important things by listening carefully. Processing the information that bombards us every single day, day by day, even at night. How could you not notice all the signals I've been sending? Oh, stop looking at me like that, will you? You think it's nothing more but empty words? That I'm blabbering here about some demanding insinuations?

"Come on, you know me. I would have never thought something like this about you."

"Exactly, you would have never thought," Betty looked down on her plate and pushed her salad around it. "And what do you think when you look at me? Because I never really noticed your eyes sparkle as if you had too much love for me."

"Betty," he covered her palm with his hand and looked her in the eye, his own gaze full of raw remorse. "You are the most important person to me. And I want you to be happy."

"Oh, Heracles!" Betty took her hand away. "You know

Greek, you speak fluent Latin, you delve into the whole glitz of
the wise men of this world but you cannot just jump out of the
ocean of your own reason and simply say *I love you* to a woman
who is head over heels in love with you?"

Heracles' gaze ran across the glass of wine he held in his
hand. He tightened his grip.

"Forgive me... I'm not pretending when I'm with you."

"I know, Heracles. I know you're not pretending when
you're with me. And that's why I'm never going to hear *I love
you*, right?" Her gaze swelled with pain, sorrow, but also arguments. "You're hiding something from me. Am I wrong? You're
silent, right. For me, this conversation is just painful. And for
you, it's slowly reaching the level of banality." Betty looked down
at her lap, finishing the conversation and their night out. "It's
time to go back home."

They stepped out onto a sidewalk covered by colorful leaves,
into the chilly air, the faint light of the streetlamp glistening over
them. As they walked together, Betty looped her arm into his.
Seemingly the two of them looked like a perfect married couple:
pure love with no calculation involved, a relation deeply rooted
in friendship, seasoned with tender passion. But it wasn't like
that. As they walked a few blocks towards the nearest subway
station, not a word was uttered. It was that kind of silence that
felt tangibly heavy. What was supposed to be an unforgettable
evening was overtaken by a brutally honest conversation. Overwhelmed by the sense of absurdity of their situation, they both
knew that this evening was, indeed, remarkable; just not in the
way they had expected. That it will either leave a deep scar on
their relationship or will be the end of it. Betty and Heracles
both suffered in silence. Suddenly, out of the blue, one of the
taxis rapidly changed lanes and came to a halt so close that

Heracles spontaneously grabbed Betty closer, as if he wanted to protect her against potential danger.

The passenger door cracked open, revealing Vlad's joyful face.

"Heracles! What a surprise!"

"Vlad?" Suddenly, they found themselves locked in a heartfelt embrace. "What are you doing in the city?"

Vlad did not respond. He was just standing there, looking at Betty who seemed a bit flustered.

"Oh, sorry. Betty, here, let me introduce... wait, you two actually know each other."

"That's right." Betty put her hand out. "Good evening, Vlad. Nice to meet you. After all these years..."

"Betty? You are Betty?! Forgive me, I didn't recognize you. Wow, you look fabulous! Well, Hera, I see that you followed your friend's advice." Vlad patted him friendly on the back. "Listen, we're not going to stand here like idiots. It calls for a celebration! What about we go to the Biltmore Hotel? It's on me."

"I'm sorry to say we can't make it. Not here, not now." Betty reacted. When she looked at Heracles, all bewildered, he embraced her – as if wanting to confirm her words.

"We're having a little celebration tonight," he added after a while.

"Alright, I get it." Vlad resigned. "But well, it's a pity since I'm leaving tomorrow. Oh damn!" The man wrapped his collar and looked into the sky. "It's going to rain in a second. Hop in, I'll give you a ride."

"No problem. I'll be fine," Betty rummaged through her handbag for a while and took out a small collapsible umbrella. "But Heracles, you should go! You haven't seen each other in ages. You can't just miss an opportunity like this, I bet you have so much to go over."

"No way," he responded rapidly. "You know I'm not going to leave you alone."

"I insist."

"Betty, come on!" Heracles responded impatiently and looked at her sternly.

"Alright, alright, my friends!" Vlad's gaze resembled that of a child looking at its quarreling parents. "Don't do this to me, my heart is torn. I don't want to be of any trouble to you…"

"Everything's fine, no need to lose your sleep over it," Betty reassured him and locked arms with Heracles. "If you are so keen on insisting, help me get back home and you're good to go. My head hurts, you know, must be the champagne that you kept on filling my glass with. It was delicious but now I just want to have a good night's sleep."

Two hours later, Heracles was looking around a hotel's spacious atrium. Marble columns, sophisticated furniture, thick tapestry, the ambiance of Victorian times. He marched towards a glass door and walked through it, finding himself in a spacious restaurant.

That unexpected meeting with Vlad made him genuinely happy. The second he saw his friend's face emerge from the taxi, his memory – at the speed of a huge, strong lorry that wipes out everything on its way – started bringing up the frames of these crazy days and restless nights when they shared all their youthful doubts with such intensity. And he missed it all so much. He missed it all and he missed that Vlad.

But he felt that Betty shouldn't be alone at their home. There was an emotional hangover involved and he felt like an ungrateful bastard. But she insisted.

("No, thank you," Betty said, shaking off her umbrella. He offered her a hot drink to warm up. "Join him. He was your friend once. This meeting is important for the both of you."

"I don't want to leave you alone."

"Come on, you've done it thousands of times before."

"You know it's not about that."

"Oh, will you please leave already? I'm going to be fine." Betty quickly wiped away a stray tear from her cheek.

"Betty, listen, I…"

"Sorry, I'll be fine in a moment. Just give me a minute."

Heracles approached her and put his finger underneath her chin, forcing her to look at him. She looked desperate. The worst part though was that he couldn't do anything for her, and looking into her eyes, he realized she probably knows it.

"Listen, I want to be alone." While it might have been a quiet statement, there was a tone of determination in it.)

Heracles entered the hotel restaurant and ran his gaze across a luxuriously lit interior, looking for Vlad. He noticed him in the corner of the room. His tie nonchalantly loose, the top button of his shirt undone, he was trying to focus on the calculator in his hand. His frowned demeanor made it seem like it was a particularly demanding task.

"A calculator? So you keep on counting and multiplying. And I thought you would finally grab a pen and become a writer."

"Oh dear, I'm so happy to see you," they shook hands. "Sit down, please! Are you hungry? Because I definitely am."

"No, thanks. I've already eaten."

"Ah, right! With Betty! So, what do you fancy? Whisky? Cognac? Scotch? Or maybe champagne?"

"Vodka!"

"Great choice!" his eyes already seemed bleary.

The waiter brought two bottles of Polish vodka and set them down on the table.

"Alright. Now let's speak on equal terms. *Sto lat*," Vlad stated in Polish, clinking his shot glass with Heracles'.

They drank to their meeting. And then to their health.

"Who would have thought?" Vlad shook his head, as if in disbelief. "This librarian! Damn, she changed. You know what I'm gonna tell you? It's unfair that some women just bloom this late in life. Do you remember Jenny? Jenny the sex bomb?"

"I sure do."

"Well, she's not a sex bomb anymore."

"Really? She swept you off your feet real quick once. Quicker than vodka."

"Oh come on, you're overreacting. She was all over me and I... you know... I didn't want to make a fuss about it. I succumbed to her like a helpless child. You know what? I think I'm getting old. As the years go by, I'm more keen on wine. Do you know what I mean? Okay, so just one more," Vlad added, filling their glasses up. "To the meeting!"

"I know," Heracles downed the shot and responded. "Wine is tasty, classy... and lets you relish it for a longer time."

"Oh, you freaking debaucherous philosopher! To the point, as always. Come on, spill the beans. What's up with Betty? What's up with the two of you?"

"What's up with the two of us? Betty is still a librarian."

"I envy you. Do you know that I almost got married? Can you believe it?"

"Honestly? No!"

"And yet here we are. She was beautiful, kind… with her, the world seemed to be a… brighter place."

"Did she pass away? My condolences, dude."

"No, what's wrong with you?" He filled the glasses again and raised his own. "She's in great health."

"So why you two didn't marry?"

"Oh, *kurwa jego mać*, she didn't have a single flaw!"

"You still swear a lot," Heracles noted.

"And you still get it when I swear in Polish. Can you imagine it: she was just so sweet, fuck, just so unbearably sweet. Her angelic aura just blocked me. Whenever I looked into her cobalt eyes I didn't have any dirty thoughts about her divine body. And I should have. So fortunately my angel of common sense smacked me in the head with its caring wing and I understood that I wasn't the one for her and she wasn't the one for me. As far as I know, she lives in Monaco with some lovely bastard right now. Wait, and what about you? Why won't you marry Betty? And make some sweet demigods with her?"

"Mhm… someone already asked me about that today."

"And that's how it should be! You have some reasonable friends. Listen to them, they're offering you some good advice."

"The thing is, it wasn't my friend asking me about it. It was her."

"Betty? Betty asked you about sweet demigods?"

"Let's change the topic," Heracles scoffed and took a quick swig of vodka. "I don't want to talk about it." He looked intently into the empty glass. "I hurt her," he added after a while.

"Hurt her as in did what? You just brushed her off, right?"

"Something like that."

"You know what, Mr. philosopher? Maybe you can distinguish between Plotinus and Plato but you are fucking clueless when it comes to women. No shit! Marry her, I'm telling you. Before someone snatches her from you. She's the real deal. If you don't see it, you're either completely dumb... or..."

"Or?"

"Or you're running to her to get away from... I don't know... something you fear?"

"You're looking for things that aren't even there. Bro, you're smashed."

"Sure. I'm not denying that. But even drunk out of my mind I can see something's bugging you. You're running from something. What is it? The past? You're not saying a word. See! I got it! I'm right, yeah? Listen to the old friend and let it go. Just like I let go of some things from my past."

"Do you mean your Polish girlfriend?"

"What girlfriend? Ah, that one! It's all water under the bridge now," he waved him off. "I forgot about her. She's in my memories, these kind, joyful, refreshing, inspiring ones. But as a person, physically, she just doesn't exist anymore. I don't think about what she's doing, who is she sleeping with... she just doesn't inflict any pain upon me anymore. And you... just see: there's something in your philosophical head that brings so much fucking pain to you, but you just don't want to say a word about it. I'm telling you, stop running away from it because one day you will just fall flat on your face, completely exhausted. Deal with it, human fate is like a... like a snowball that one deity or another damn thing forms in their hands, kneads it and then just releases it from their almighty hands, and the snowball grows with everything it wipes out of its way. This is how memories are made. Without memories, there would be no snowball, there would be no us. Are you even listening to me?"

"Fragmentarily," Heracles dismissed him.

"Fragmentarily? What a pity," Vlad grabbed a bottle of vodka from the cooler and kissed it. "At today's meeting, this lovely companion is bringing out the whole depth of my spirit. Here's my good advice: don't run away from your past. Marry Betty, because that's the only way you can change your memories. Mr. philosopher, do you understand what I'm saying? Even just fragmentarily?"

"I'm doing my best but you're speaking too metaphorically today."

"And you're an asshole! Here's to you!"

Heracles, dead tired and reeking of alcohol, walked home. When he opened the door, the wall clock announced that it was three o'clock in the morning.

Quietly, alcoholic pangs of conscience kicking in, he wobbled into the kitchen. The first thing he noticed was the missing sweater. The red woolen sweater was an indispensable attribute of a funny chair that they purchased with Betty at a flea market last fall. The chair did not particularly stand out; it was just a wooden piece of furniture to sit on. But it had a particularly high back, which immediately drew their attention. Back then, Betty chuckled sweetly and stated that it was high time they started collecting furniture for purely decorative, not only utility purposes. While Heracles ignored this argument, he couldn't let go of another one that ignited his imagination.

"Honey, don't you think it would be a perfect place for my red sweater? Wham, bam, I get rid of it and hang it on the chair instead of throwing it on the floor or into the corner, and then I lay down on the table like a delicious dessert for you..."

"Please," Heracles placed his palm over her mouth. "Stop

here. Excuse me, how much is this chair?" he approached the amused seller clad in worn-out glossy shoes.

The funny chair with the high back stood in their kitchen, right by the fridge. And always hanging over it was the thick, red woolen sweater. The sweater was stretched out of proportion, its sleeves too long, but Heracles still adored watching Betty stretch in such a way that it raised with her arms, showing her shapely, firm thighs and pert bottom.

When all these memories with the chair, the sweater and smooth thighs ran through his head, he came to the fridge and opened it. There was everything but beer inside. Cold air wafted on his face and sobered him up; suddenly he felt anxious and went to the bedroom. The bed was empty. It wasn't until he returned to the kitchen that he noticed an envelope on the table. Heracles stared at the object for a long time before he mustered up enough courage to open it.

FORGIVE ME, BUT THE VAIN HOPE THAT ONE DAY YOU MIGHT LOVE ME CANNOT RUIN MY LIFE.
LESS AND LESS YOURS,
BETTY

Had it not been for the alcohol, he wouldn't be able to fall asleep. When he woke up, his gaze ran across the empty walls. He couldn't stand it. In his empty apartment, without Betty around, he felt like a squatter. Around midday, he finally dressed and went outside. He looked at the window, but this time there was no one behind the curtain to wave at him.

Heracles leaned against the post, reeling. The street was brimming with life; the bustle of people around him, the monotonous hum of the cars, the wail of police sirens. He felt cut off from this world. Everything around him resembled a scene design arranged for that one moment that was still on the back of his eyelids. Betty's face when she said *tell me you love me.*

"You sick? Did you have bwoccoli for dinner too?" A little girl was looking at him, purest childish empathy in her eyes.

"Come on, sweetie. Stop bothering strangers," rushing forward, her father pulled on her wrist.

The girl's words resembled a weak ray of sunshine on that cloudy day and brought him out of the comatose state he's been in since early morning. Instinctively, Heracles looked up to the sky and his eyes became wet. These weren't tears, it was raindrops falling straight into his eyes. Opposite the street, afraid of the downpour, a street artist was hurriedly packing up his paintings. A pensive elderly couple clad in raincoats passed him, followed by a group of girls in school uniforms that held books over their heads, protecting their curls from getting wet. Vanity versus wisdom. What bestiality!

And that's when the sky opened up. People started rushing, looking for shelter before the cold driving rain, as he stood there unfazed. An uncontrolled sob came out of his deepest memory, but he quickly suppressed it. He couldn't stop the memories that nearly choked him. Not even asking for permission, they stopped crawling out of all the corners of his mind like ghosts of mistakes made and loves lost. He spent the day wandering around the places he knew and then, soaked through, returned home to carry through the night with his eyes open.

Heracles spent these few first days without Betty alone, shunning his friends and wandering the streets at night, listening to the patter of his own shoes. Days and months passed by, and so a gray, damp fall turned into a gloomy winter, followed by a restorative breath of blooming spring. Then summer came, and he started meeting his students – those that weren't visiting their family homes during summer holidays, but rather kept busy patching up their leaky budgets by taking some odd jobs near the university. They would hang around gardens and parks, losing themselves in philosophical discussions to such an extent it seemed there was nothing in this world besides philosophy. One student was particularly ardent, and his name was Bond. John Bond. A dark-haired man with acne-prone pale skin, always wearing wire-rimmed glasses, walked on his stick-thin, long legs with the grace of a marionette. He was a stark antithesis to the cinematic hero that shared the same surname. Bond. But James. John Bond had every single feature that could make him look slightly nerdy. On the other hand, he could write intelligent poetry; more than that, he was able to pen poems in classical languages. His linguistic genius was a source of everlasting frustration for his stepfather. A Vietnam war veteran and an accomplished officer of the American Army found it embarrassing that his own stepson, a person raised by a real tough guy as he probably thought of himself, shows inclinations as useless as a passion for the Greek language.

"What in tarnation!" he reacted, when the then thirteen-year-old John translated one of his Greek romantic poems into English.

At that very moment, a tormented poet-linguist understood that he had to nurture his talent far from home. And so it happened. At the University of California, he not only acclimatized very quickly – he even became the leader of the philosophy club led by Heracles himself.

❧

Heracles grew to appreciate early wake-up calls, greeting the sun and quick showers. There was a small restaurant at the end of the road, where he would buy coffee and pastries. It was owned by a Turkish man that he had already befriended. He would then spend a few hours at work and later return briefly to the Turk's restaurant to look through the newspapers. On Mondays and Saturdays, he played basketball with his university friends.

During one of these friendly matches, he tore a ligament. Even though it put him on the sidelines when it came to sports, it became an unexpected opportunity to start a new relation.

She was a woman of exotic beauty (due to a Native American mother and Irish father) and no less exotic name, one that Heracles struggled to remember so he would just call her Pocahontas. At first, there was nothing beyond a professional patient-doctor relation between them, but it quickly turned into a fiery romance. Not one that would demand any declarations; it was more of a reciprocal fascination with no deeper feelings involved. Whenever they could spend time together, they holed up at Heracles' apartment. Pocahontas reveled in looking at him and listening as he read aloud Plato's dialogues. Even though these texts seemed entirely absurd to her, his face was so sexy and regal during these moments... not to mention his deep, slightly coarse voice.

Maybe their relationship would have lasted longer, had it not been for one peculiar coincidence. One day Heracles was sitting focused at his desk, going through his students' essays.

"Read something cool to me," Pocahontas asked.

He looked at her, puzzled. She was naked, lounging on the bed, a glass of wine in her hand.

"What??" the woman shrugged. "It's cold here. And you know how to warm me up."

Heracles hopped out of his chair and sat down by her side.

"What about we skip foreplay today. Hm?" He kissed her shoulder blade. "Let's get down to it."

"Oh no! No way."

"Okay, you naughty one."

He approached the bookshelf, took out a random book and noticed a sheet of paper fall on the floor. When he bent down to pick it up, his heart stopped beating for a split second. Betty. Heracles immediately recognized her writing; pretty, slightly right-slanted, with decorative initials.

CAN YOU HEAR IT?

A STRING IN MY HEART BROKE

TORN OUT OF THE VIOLIN OF HAPPINESS

SO

DON'T ASK FOR AN ENCORE, MY DEAR

WHEN THERE'S A FUNERAL MARCHING DOWN THE STREET

(He recollected that day. Betty wrote this in grave despair, when during a guest concert of the Boston Symphony Orchestra at Constitution Hall he got out of his chair, his gaze wild and absent, and left her and his coat in the cloakroom to wander the streets for the next three days as if he were a hobo. When he returned home, Betty was on the verge of a mental breakdown.

"Why, Heracles, why would you do this to me?"

"Because of the violin," he responded.

"What? What violin? What are you talking about?"

"Betty, don't ask, please. Just never ask me about that."

"That as in what? What am I supposed not to ask you about?" she inquired desperately.

"About the violin."

And so she never asked. But that evening she wrote a poem and placed it before Heracles on the desk, saying: "You can tie a string when it breaks. But no matter how hard you pluck it afterwards, it will never sing for you again.")

"Heracles?" he heard the voice of Pocahontas behind his back. "Honey, something wrong?"

Awoken from his catatonic state, he left the memories behind.

"What? No, no… sorry. I just got lost in my thoughts."

"Show it to me!" she ripped a sheet from his hand. "What is this poetic blabber about?"

His look was the only answer.

"God," she blinked quickly, "stop staring at me like this, I behaved like an idiot. I feel so dumb right now. So… no foreplay today… and nothing else to follow…," she concluded and started to pick up her clothes scattered on the floor. "Am I right?" She finally stood up, awaiting his reaction.

"I don't think it's the best moment."

She accepted it with neutral grace, got dressed and left without a word, quietly closing the door behind her. And she never came back. Maybe she didn't want to compete with melancholy triggered by an inconspicuous piece of paper lost among a collection of ancient thinkers' works.

Ever since that moment, his apartment started making him more and more distressed, and he finally began yearning for change. He pondered about returning to Boston – something professor Johnson has been convincing him to do for a while.

One of Harvard's most honored philosophers, professor William Johnson, was the epitome of clumsiness with a particular inclination to trip over his own shoes. Oh, how these apparent shortcomings could fool an outside observer! The professor was truly a remarkable person. A person with an open mind, always eager to share his sharp remarks; he was a magical speaker – everyone would leave his lectures feeling slightly overwhelmed. It was thanks to him that Heracles mastered to near perfection the challenging art of discussion and argumentation. But more on that later.

Finally, Heracles applied for the position of assistant professor at Harvard. Before he stood in front of the selection committee, he first went to the barber and regrettably asked to have his hair cut. A kind, chatty elderly man took to the scissors and transformed his eccentric, avant-garde silver ponytail into a meticulously trimmed hairstyle. Heracles looked neat and demure, but his aura of mystery, completed by an unsettling scar on his face, thick black brows and eyes that certainly held some secret, was still there. Then, he bought a white shirt and a tie.

"Welcome on board!" He was overjoyed to hear that.

Heracles packed up his clothes, books, notes, and took one last look around the apartment, contemplating whether the furniture meant anything to him. Probably not. He just smiled upon seeing the chair with the high back.

A suitcase in his hand, he was waiting for a taxi to drop him off at the railway station where he was supposed to take a train to Boston. He purposefully chose a long and exhausting trip over a comfortable flight. Heracles was the observing type, choosing to relish the views and landscapes instead of peeking at bits of sky or ground through a tiny window – given that he would get a place near a window to start with. Only when he was leaving this house did he take a closer look at it and came to a certain conclusion regarding his nature. No matter where he lived, where he spent time and with whom… he was always ready to get up and close all the doors behind him once and for all.

And it petrified him. Why? Why does he always find himself where he shouldn't be? So where is his place? Or maybe it was all because he was who he was before becoming who he is right now? There was one certain thing: like an apostle proclaiming the Gospel, he wanted to proclaim the praise of thinking. Thinking about important human matters, a natural part of which is questioning nearly everything, as well as trying to find the answers.

⁓

He entered the lecture hall to take a place on the other side of the lectern and then gazed around the familiar places. Not much had changed. A gathering of students welcomed him with both silence and curiosity that showed in their eyes. Heracles opened a thick briefcase and fished out a pile of hand-written notes, which by some miracle were even thicker than the briefcase itself. He took a few deep breaths and started reading.

"I'm Heracles Papadopoulos and this semester, I'll have fourteen lectures with you. I require my students to read ten classic must-read books, but I leave it to you to choose the titles. I require, however, that you know them by heart by the end of the semester. Or at least quote extensive passages from the books you decide to read," Heracles became quiet.

He took his eyes off the sheet of paper and moved his gaze across the rows. Recent curiosity turned into confusion. With some satisfaction, he could suspect what kind of a brainstorm was happening inside these wise heads: How?! Memorize them?! What kind of a person is this? What about a modern and attractive presentation? And the Harvard debate between a professor and a student, as equal partners? Jesus Christ, what a huge dose! Ten tomes! By heart?!

Alright, Heracles mused, *enough fooling around at the youngsters' expense.*

"Alright, that won't be necessary," he finally spoke and pushed aside the prepared notes. "Anyway, my memory is fine. And yours... I have no intention of testing it. Not in such an inhumane way, that is," he smiled slyly at the audience.

A muffled sigh of relief spread around the room. So he was bluffing.

"Regarding *memoria*... Let's devote our first meeting to it. Memory. So... what is memory?"

His question was met by silence, students meticulously staring at their yet unwritten notes.

"The human brain's predisposition to store," one brave girl said.

"Store what?" Heracles inquired, trying to encourage other students.

"Everything."

"Too vague," he assessed firmly.

"To store knowledge, experiences, images...," a young man in the third row added. "Things that shook, moved us or just drew our attention in the past."

"Memory is... complete the thought!"

"Sinful."

"Justify it."

"Because it's selective," a young man with the face of a fifteen-year-old seemed very proud of his answer.

"Prone to suggestion," a voice could be heard at the end of the hall.

"And biased as hell," another voice added.

"The most powerful memory triggers include..."

"Smell."

"Taste... and stink!" the response was met with a hearty laugh.

"Music." Someone leaned out from the second row. "It helps regain forgotten memories tangled in notes and lost moments of our lives. Recalls even those elusive bits of time that are suspended between the sounds."

The last statement caused Heracles to reflect. He stood there, pondering, for a good few minutes, leaving the students slightly bewildered.

"So, who wants to summarize everything that we discussed here?" He shook his thoughts off and addressed his students again.

"Me! Me!" The hand of the guy with the face of a teenager shot up into the air. "Memory is the power of senses. Engraved traces of the past that the imagination, the enemy of reason that revels in correcting and reigning it, brings up to the consciousness," the man was bursting with pride.

The thought of Blaise Pascal, intricately woven into the last response, regarding the commanding imagination, the enemy of reason, as well as the statement heard from the second row – the one about music that recalls everything that was seemingly irretrievably lost, just like these subtle moments of silence suspended between notes – ignited in Heracles the desire to face his own past. Like never before he wanted to ensure that it wasn't just his imagination bringing up distorted memories, impressions and elations that were with him in that room; the room he was drawn to like a moth to a flame, where he experienced everything that matters in life. If he were a convict awaiting his death penalty and a sergeant would ask him *Boy, what's your last wish?* – there would be no other answer than this: *I want to recreate those moments once again.*

The university, lectures, trips to Europe for various meetings, articles for journals on both philosophy and literature written in extinct languages (Latin, ancient Greek), as well as work on his own book about Plato. Constantly growing, Heracles found genuine pleasure in all of this. He would say that both work and people contributed to his feeling of satisfaction.

The other people living in the tenement house where he was renting an apartment appreciated privacy, silence and calm. It was particularly important to Heracles, as he could finally focus on writing his book and articles, though he would barely submit the latter ones on time. His upstairs neighbors in the last apartment in Los Angeles, which were incredibly loud and surprisingly hospitable, made it all so much tougher for him. Once, right after Betty left him, he succumbed to the pressure and accepted an invitation to a party. *Never again!* He thought the day after, right after waking up. A life that revolved around alcohol and marijuana was not his cup of tea anymore. He had simply left that behind.

After moving to Boston it seemed he finally found his place

on Earth. And then George White, a music aficionado, moved next door and turned Heracles' inner peace upside down. George owned probably every single record featuring piano, harpsichord and pipe organ music ever produced. From genuine classical music, both secular and sacred, to swinging jazz improvisations. At first, Heracles would kindly ask his new neighbor to turn down the volume of the record player, but the man remained deaf to his requests. Sometimes he would even turn the volume up, as if deliberately trying to annoy everyone living next door.

The neighborly war lasted for half a year, until one evening.

Over the last few weeks, Heracles had been working on three essays and one review. Even though he's been planning to do them for a long time, three unplanned lectures, two conferences in New York and two panel discussions in Europe got in the way. Pressured by the editors – *well, Heracles, we have deadlines, we have this and that*, he intended to complete them on that very evening. He set down the resources, books, journals, a pile of documents and notes on the kitchen table and lit it up with a weak ray of light from a small lamp that he brought from his office.

The light from the lamp was warm and relaxing, the kitchen was wrapped in silence, the clock showed a late fall hour. He leaned over the book to highlight an important passage, focused his gaze, Greek letters started to sway in a sleepy dance...

He had a dream...

(He was looking at the finest detail of her face. She looked exactly the same way he remembered her, even though he didn't want to so badly. Her refined, delicate facial features. And the eyes. Always still. Never giving away any thoughts, as if she kept them to herself. He blew on her long, exposed neck and felt on his body the tender shivers that shook her to the core.)

…which ended, when a metal pen fell out of his limp hand, echoing like a mighty gap in the memory. He felt confused and had no idea whether it was daytime or nighttime, and what was he dreaming about. Heracles took a deep breath and rubbed his face. In a flash of consciousness, he lazily took up the pen and indifferently highlighted a sentence on page one hundred and six. The sound of his neighbor's music penetrated the tranquility of his own space. He got up from the chair and left the apartment.

"What the heck?!" Heracles heard before George's impatient face, John Lennon-style glasses on his nose, appeared in the door opened as much as a door chain would allow.

"Hi, George, how is it going?!" the man greeted him, leaning against the doorframe and blocked the door with his foot.

"You've got to be kidding," George adjusted his glasses with his middle finger. "The music is so quiet I can barely hear it."

"Can I come in?"

"What for? Do you want to kick my ass again?"

"I never did that."

"But you wanted to. Admit it!"

"Well, I did. Many times. But today…," Heracles raised his hands in a peaceful gesture, "I have nothing against you. I'm serious. Let me in, George."

The man hesitated for a while.

"Alright, come in."

They went through a dark hall into a room, that upon a first glance was filled to the brim with good music. Two giant hi-fi systems, powerful speakers, hundreds of vinyl records, cassettes and music journals – all placed neat and spotless on the shelves.

"Whoa, dude!" Heracles reacted. "It's a real treat to see my torture chamber!"

"Don't be petty," George snapped, shoving his fists into the pockets of his bathrobe. He set off to the kitchen, where he spent a moment and returned with two bottles of beer in his hands. He offered one to Heracles, putting his hand out.

"Want a drink?"

"Gladly," Heracles responded. He took a sip and started browsing the vinyl records. "Listen, George, could you play this piece once again?"

"Which one?"

"You know… the one you played a moment ago? I think it was Dvorak's *Humoresque*."

"Do you even know who Dvorak was?" George asked, crossed the room and plopped on the armchair, and then added: "Not to mention his humoresque."

"You know what, George?" Heracles took a swig of beer, still rummaging through the shelves with records. "I think I'm going to kick your ass."

And that was the beginning of their friendship. It didn't last very long, for soon George got an editorial position at the ABOUT JAZZ journal and moved into New York five months later. Regarding the journals, though, on that memorable night, Heracles did not succeed with all the planned articles for the philosophical periodicals. He only managed to write a review of *A Treatise of Human Nature* by David Hume, an Enlightenment thinker who stated it was passions, not reason that governs human behavior. Heracles the philosopher did not completely agree with that statement, but as if echoing the bold opinion presented years ago by a great thinker, for months to come he would spend every evening settling into George's comfortable armchair, sip whisky and listen to his records, succumbing in silence to the absolute power of passion.

"Dude, what are you thinking about so intensely?"

"George, shut up. I've told you so many times it's none of your business, my friend."

"Alright. Want a refill?"

Soon after George left for New York, Heracles received a message from Vlad that they have to talk. This succinct message left a striking impression. It was more concerning than cheerful. The last time they spoke, they were in Plainfield. Heracles was spending another Thanksgiving in a row with the Kovalski family. John, Magda and Vlad were important to him. They were like family. Whenever he could afford such luxury, he would just throw on a backpack and visit them for a weekend to have some friendly talks, go horse riding or simply sit on the porch and laugh at Vlad's jokes. But suddenly everything was over and it's been a good few years since these joyful moments. All the while it was that type of friendship that was supposed to last a lifetime. Heracles knew very well that his old friend would visit Boston from time to time, if only for his business, but didn't call him, didn't stop by his place, didn't visit. Not even once. Something was clearly wrong. It didn't feel right and he was certain Vlad felt the same way.

They chose the small pub that they visited to broaden their horizons over favorite drinks, discussing various matters with their Harvard colleagues. The pub had changed and so did they.

Heracles had short hair now, while Vlad's hair was insanely slicked back.

"What's up with your father?"

"He's starting to slow down. Thinking about retirement. You know… slippers, grandchildren and so on."

"John the brave? Who would have thought?" Heracles shook his head in disbelief. "So, did you take his advice regarding grandchildren to heart?"

"I met Betty," Vlad dismissed his question and took a swig of beer.

"Really? How is she doing?"

"Everything's fine. She works at a school in Plainfield."

"Plainfield? Don't tell me you two are neighbors."

"I won't. You know," he loosened the collar of his shirt. "We bumped into each other once, it was completely unplanned. I was walking down the street and felt someone tugging me. So I turn back, and I see…"

"Betty?"

"Exactly! Can you imagine?"

"No."

"No?"

"No."

"Why not?" Vlad asked, leaning back to let the waiter know he would like another beer.

"She would never do that," Heracles explained.

"What do you mean?"

Heracles raised his brow and didn't answer the question.

"Jesus, Hera, what are you thinking about?"

"I don't believe she approached you first. It's not how she is!" He slightly raised his voice, as if expecting Vlad to interrupt him. He, on the other hand, kept staring at him, frowning.

"How long have you been looking for her?"

"What? Looking for? How did you know I was looking for her?"

"You always liked her."

Vlad rummaged in his pocket and took out a pack of cigarettes.

"Want a smoke?"

"I still don't smoke."

"I forgot about that."

"Did you seriously lose your mind?"

"What? Actually, I'm not seeing what are you getting at."

Heracles didn't answer. They always understood each other mid-sentence. He raised one of his brows and waited for his friend to spill the tea.

"I don't know where to start...," Vlad began. "Thanks," he said to the waiter who set a glass of beer before him. "You know, my survival instinct would always tell me to run away from this girl," he took a cigarette and added, before dragging on it, "because she's your friend's woman."

"And now... what is your instinct telling you? Has something changed?"

"Everything. Everything, Heracles. You're not together anymore," he flicked the ash into an ashtray and leaned back on his chair. "You're right, I looked for her. But I didn't succeed, so I hired a detective."

"You sure were determined."

"Like hell."

"Do you think she will want to date you?"

"We've been together for six months."

Heracles stared at him and remained silent.

"Well," he finally broke the silence, "now I understand why you were avoiding me."

"Don't flatter yourself. I wasn't afraid of you. I was scared for her. I feared that when you two would meet again, everything will come back. Do you understand? I don't want to lose her. I love her."

"And she?"

"She's never said that to me," his gaze followed the waiter who roamed the room from table to table, using his notepad and pen as if he were giving tickets. "But I think she does love me."

"Marry her. You yourself gave me this advice once."

"Lucky for me, you never gave a shit about my good advice. Seriously, though," he reached into his pocket for a small box. "Just look."

"What's it?"

"Open it."

There was a ring with a massive diamond that only Vlad could afford.

"Are you proposing to me?"

"Oh shut up, you old dumbass!" Vlad reacted with noticeable relief, as if the air pumped into him over the last twenty minutes finally found an outlet. He fished another box out of his pocket.

Heracles picked one of the emerald earrings from it and held it up to the light.

"Beautiful," he stated in amazement.

"What would you advise me?" Vlad enquired. "Ring or earrings?"

"If I were Betty, I would choose the earrings."

"Alright, ring it is."

Betty's parents, Bob and Merlin, threw an engagement party at their place. While they didn't boast an estate as massive as Vlad's family, since Bob was a taxi driver and Merlin worked as a preschool teacher, they emanated some elusive aura of honesty and happiness that made everyone simply feel comfortable around them.

Heracles stayed in the back. His hand in his pocket, he was sipping on his drink and looking outside the window. Two bubbly women were joyously chattering behind his back. He took the last sip and wanted to leave when Betty touched him.

"Heracles, I would like you to meet my mother." Which, honestly, was baffling, to say the least. When they were still an item, he would repeatedly hint that he would like to meet her parents, but somehow she always dodged the subject. He started doubting they even knew he exists.

A short blonde woman was embracing Betty in a way that only a mother and her daughter would. Merlin was slightly chubby, although not yet in a Rubens kind of way, her curves accentuated by a tight dress with a big floral pattern. She curiously gazed at his face.

"Oh, so it's you?" she extended her hand, still smiling. "I'm Merlin."

"I'm afraid that's correct. Please call me Heracles."

"Heracles, what an original name. Betty," Merlin turned to her daughter, "honey, look at Vlad. Seems like he's looking for someone, huh? I'm pretty sure he's searching for you. Join him while I borrow Heracles for a moment."

"Should I bring you two something?"

"Don't worry about us, we're fine. Come on, go to your fiancé."

When Betty left, Merlin directed her curious gaze at Heracles.

"So," she kindly addressed him, "I can see you could use a drink. So do I. What about we settle down in a corner, a drink in hand, and chat for a while? Hmm?"

"Of course." Heracles led her towards an empty chair. "Please, take a seat and I'll look around for..."

"champagne," Merlin kindly squeezed his hand tighter.

Surrounded by the sounds of chatter, bursts of laughter and clinking glasses, Heracles was making his way through dozens of guests whose faces were entirely unknown to him, stunned by how many people could be crammed into a house this small. Merlin was right, he needed a drink. Desperately. Betty's mother seemed friendly, straightforward, but deep inside he felt he was in for a tough conversation.

"Heracles! What are you looking for?" John appeared before him like a good angel. Wearing a double-breasted blazer, a kind expression on his face, he embraced Heracles with his arm.

"Something to drink," he responded, briefly looking at a cigarette pack that John took out of his pocket. "I thought you gave this thing up?"

"This thing?" John raised his hand, a cigarette between his fingers, and brought it to his eyes. "My doctor explicitly denied me the right to enjoy cigars. He said: *John, give this shit up or else you will wreck your heart.* So I took his advice to... to heart and with a stinging pain deep inside... my heart, I gave them up. But you know what?" He smiled and scoffed. "He did not say a word about cigarettes."

"You're impossible! What does Magda think about it?"

"Magda? She's pouty. But you know, you can't be henpecked.

You've got to be tough. Be a… you know: the alpha male in your group."

Smiling, Heracles shook his head and started looking for Betty's mom to ensure he didn't lose her somewhere. Suddenly, Magda emerged from the back of the room and was clearly heading towards them, gracefully smiling. For a moment, she chatted to a corpulent lady whose mouth was full of appetizers.

In one quick movement, Heracles took the cigarette out of John's mouth and discretely put it out between his fingers.

"There you are!" Magdalena, like a classy socialite, familiarly took their hands and stood on her tiptoes to kiss them both on their cheeks. It seemed she didn't notice anything and the alpha male sighed with deep relief. "Heracles, did you have a chance to talk to Betty's mom? Such a charming person. I think that the young couple will work out some good family relations and oh, dear Lord, it's so important. Anyway… Oh! There she is!" she subtly pointed her finger in the right direction. "Let's join her."

"It was me who left her there moments ago. I'm actually looking for some drinks for us. I'm not sure… champagne maybe?"

"Damn!" John moved his hand across his forehead. "I'm afraid champagne is already gone. Bob told me that minutes ago. And it seemed like there was plenty of it. Who would have thought that the hosts have so many friends?"

"Well," Heracles blinked. "I'm not that surprised."

"Me too!" John ardently confirmed, slightly embarrassed that someone could even suspect him of bad thoughts towards the widely respected, honorable hosts.

"Gentlemen…" Magda rushed them. "Merlin's waiting for her champagne. Instead of standing here, do something!"

"Come with me, Heracles," John said. "I'm taking you for

a walk. To my car, to be exact. I've got something extra there,"
he winked, "for special occasions."

A quiet, illuminated neighborhood with low-rise residential buildings soothed their minds after the commotion inside Betty's house. Both in good mood, they were leisurely strolling towards a red Cadillac parked a block away.

When they reached the car, John opened the trunk and reached for a leather bag inside.

"Ah! Just look, my dear friend!" Content as if he just won the lottery, he demonstrated an inconspicuous bottle with no label. "Vodka of my homeland, moonshine. I wanted to gift it to Bob, but Magda was not happy about it, telling me that my idea was not... classy and definitely not tactful. Actually, she judged my gift more harshly, bashing me that it's just plain rude and primitive to serve moonshine at an engagement party. Can you imagine? That's what she said. A woman of Polish heritage since time immemorial, married to a man of Polish heritage since time immemorial. But what could I do? I let it go. I think I'm being too good for this conceited woman. But... here's a reason – we're out of champagne. Look! What a pity!" John shook his head, not even hiding the sarcasm.

"I'm so sorry it took so long," Heracles excused himself, giving Merlin a full glass. He found her sitting in an armchair, looking blankly into a direction that was hard to define.

"Look at them," she motioned her head towards the fiancés. Sinatra's swing ballad, *I'll Never Smile Again*, raised the happy couple up over everything that was happening around them; embraced, smiling, engrossed in their thoughts, sheltered in a corner.

"Do you think…," she asked after a while, not taking her eyes off them, "she will be happy with him?"

"Will she be happy?" Heracles appeared to be surprised. "I assume you would like to hear that yes, she will. But… I don't know, Merlin. I don't know. I'm the last person you should be asking about that," he responded and realized in the very same moment that the conversation was undoubtedly headed towards the topic that he wanted to avoid so much.

"Why would you say that? Because of you and Betty? And whatever happened between the two of you?"

"You knew about is? I thought that for some reason she was hiding her relationship from you."

"How could I not have known? Mothers don't have to be told such things. Mothers feel it. Heracles, my daughter loved you. She loved you. And you didn't love her back."

"I'm sorry. I'm really, really sorry…"

"Sorry?" She sighed. "I don't think it's necessary. You know… I really feel sorry for you."

"Excuse me?"

"After all of this, my daughter picked up the pieces. You didn't. You minced her heart like a meat grinder, but just look at her, she made it through. Thanks to him, thanks to Vlad. Meanwhile, you are out there still haunted by the pangs of conscience."

"Is it really so noticeable?" He asked humbly.

"Of course! Here's good advice for you, Heracles. Stop blaming yourself. My motherly instinct is telling me that my daughter, once your lover, and your best friend are going to be happy together. Look at them. They already are." She closed her eyes and took a long whiff of air. "Can you feel it?"

"Chanel number five? Betty used it." He was perfectly aware she didn't mean the scent of perfume.

"Oh, no...," she laughed heartily. "In this room, love is in the air. As you can see, there are things in the world that even philosophers haven't dreamed of. Well, at least one of them," she added and smiled kindly. "Love is one of these things. When you two broke up, I prayed so much for my daughter to experience love. Yes, Heracles, experience. Because even though she loved you, she still did not have a chance to learn about this feeling. Love is nothing but providing services to each other. I know, I know, it doesn't sound very romantic, but that's what it is. Love is in reciprocity. Can you love fishing? You can, my husband is a great example of that. Sometimes I get mad at him over it, you know. These floats, fishing rods, landing nets, hours spent at the lake waiting for some naïve fish to finally fall for the worm bluff. Catching it only to throw it back into the water. You can lose your marbles! I'll never understand it, but I know one thing for sure. This is not love. Even though Bob loves that fishing rod with a worm inside the fish's mouth, you cannot assume that the rod loves Bob back. Correct me if I'm wrong..."

He didn't respond. The only thing he could do at the time was to look towards the door, where the fiancés, sensing his direct gaze, waved at him kindly.

"Oh dear, I bored you, didn't I!" Merlin said, finishing her drink. "Please excuse me, a simple woman, for this highly untactful attempt at educating you. I don't want to make excuses but I think it's this fantastic alcohol that affected me so much. Please, pour a bit more into my glass. What is this? I need to tell Bob to replenish our home bar. And you know... that remark about philosophers was definitely unnecessary. I'm sorry. I took it too far. Isn't it scandalous what this delicious alcohol does to a person?! But I want… it is my biggest wish for you to know that I really consider you to be a very, very wise person. And… oh no, no, no," the woman protested upon Heracles wanting to interrupt her. "I know what I'm saying! Though we are light years away when it comes to…"

"Dear Merlin," Heracles cut in, "my wisdom does not reach to the mountaintops. I would rather say it is wandering in the valleys. Knowledge is nothing but a futile hassle if we don't know how to make use of it."

Merlin looked at him with admiration.

"You know what, Aristotle?"

"Heracles," the man corrected her tenderly.

"You're a nice guy!" She smiled appreciatively, the moonshine igniting sparks in her eyes.

"To Betty and Vlad!" Heracles raised his glass.

It happened on Christmas Day. Heracles was spending it at the Plainfield estate. Everyone was thrilled, as it was at home, and not in a hospital, that Betty and Vlad's firstborn was to arrive – the little heir, as John would affectionately call his grandson. The whole family agreed that there was one more person that couldn't miss a moment this important – a person whose fate was intertwined with that of some family members. Heracles was that person.

Whenever he crossed the threshold of their home, he always felt as if he entered a whole different world. Surrounded by a loving, heartfelt atmosphere and respect for Polish culture, language and tradition, all preserved to be passed on to the next generations. Everything with respect to the country that gave them shelter during the dramatic years of their lives.

"Hera! Hello, man!" Vlad opened his arms upon seeing him as if he wanted to embrace all the air around him.

"Are you happy because of me or is it because of that tiny tot?"

"Damn, you have no idea how stressed I am. Come in, come in, everyone's upstairs. Near the bedroom. Me, mom, dad... you know, like the Three Magi waiting for the good news."

"If it's okay, I'll wait in John's study. Go, join Betty. By the way, how is she? How is she doing?"

"The midwife says everything is going according to the plan and the patient is cooperative, whatever that means. I'll send Leokadia to you in a minute."

"There's no need to do so," Heracles ensured him, patting Vlad on the back. "Don't worry about me. There's nothing in this world that would drag Leokadia away from Betty right now."

"That's right," Vlad smacked himself on the forehead. "Please grab something from the bar," he shouted, climbing the stairs.

"Alright, alright, I'll take care of myself! Go!"

When Heracles entered the study and stopped in the middle of the room, he didn't notice the painting in a decorative frame that hadn't been there before. It depicted a pair of poor countrymen, a man and his son staring at storks flying away in v-formation. It was hung over a massive walnut desk that dominated the whole space. Despite such a perfect exposition, Heracles couldn't have possibly noticed it, because he was captivated by another, familiar sight – a violin in the showcase. It disturbed him so much he couldn't be bothered to think of the reason for which artwork of Józef Marian Chełmoński of the Prawdzic family was hung behind a walnut desk of a Polish patriot. And the reason for it was nostalgic: the painting would move poor Janek in Poland, now it moved wealthy and very much adult John in the States.

"You know a thing or two about it, right?"

"Excuse me?" distracted, Heracles turned his head around. He didn't even notice the moment John appeared next to him.

"Every time you're here this sight never fails to amaze you."

"That's right. It's a beautiful instrument."

"A violin like any other," John responded. "Nothing special. The craftwork of a talented luthier, except that it has a soul. Until you take and play it, its beauty will remain to you an unfulfilled promise. I rarely reach for it, unfortunately. You know, I think it doesn't really like me. I once heard that a violin does not belong to the musician, it is the musician that belongs to a violin. What do you think about it?"

"It's true," Heracles admitted emphatically. "A violin that's not played is slowly dying, its voice fading away. You should persuade it to like you."

"You know a lot about this instrument," John stated and took one, lonely cigarette out of his jacket pocket, as if it was deposited there for a rainy day. The man lit it up. "You didn't learn all of this during your philosophy studies, right?" He blew a puff of smoke into the air. "For you, this violin brings back emotions. Emotions, it seems, you'd rather not talk about." Blinking in the tobacco haze, he was carefully looking at Heracles, as if trying to see what kind of impression did his words make.

And indeed... the impression was crushing. So much that Heracles felt ready to open up to this man. And maybe he would even have done so, had it not been for the cry of a newborn that traveled across the rooms of the residence, all tense with waiting.

Sometimes in life, there are moments of joy so blinding, one cannot see the coming storm. And so it was this Christmas Day, when a little girl arrived, causing a sudden contraction of her grandfather's heart. All of the delighted witnesses to her birth took it as a harmless, funny incident triggered by a joyful event.

The light from the street was flooding the room and casting dark shadows on the floor in a way that resembled a Chinese shadow play. Heracles was resting on the bed, his soul aching, struggling to wrap his mind around what had just happened. The news of John's death shook him to the core, bringing up the dust of thoughts and feelings that buried him underneath and kept him awake at night, accompanied by the quiet hum of the AC unit and fridge.

The illness has been lurking in the darkness for years with nobody realizing that. Even John himself. He ignored all the red flags that his concerned body raised. John believed that once you bother with making a fuss about one slightly worrying behavior of your heart, you won't make it through. And so it was, until Magda and her alertness finally dragged him to the doctor. After that, there was nothing more but her sacrifice and adamant fight with her husband's illness; ready to leave no stone unturned, except that there were no more stones left to turn. Following the diagnosis she always accompanied John to his appointments and remembered the dosing schedule, meticulously counting every drop of bitter medicine and dividing colorful tablets. These for this, those for that. She cared for his diet and prepared the meals on her own; all healthy, cooked according to her mother's recipes that the elderly lady scribbled back in Poland. And she talked to God, promising to give Him everything for just one day more with John, her Jasiek.

The funeral took place on a warm, spring, yet exceptionally

windy day. Heracles stood in the back, deep sorrow and guilt overwhelming him. A subtle, ethereal sympathy connected them; they were soulmates. For years he carried a painful secret, but there were moments in his life when a sudden urge to break away from it would overpower him. To shed it like a cumbersome weight that was bringing him down, to look back at his past that actually involved something else than just demons. And that's what he wanted to tell John on that December day, when he caught him staring at the fake Stradivarius, wondering: *who's more fake, this Stradivarius violin or me?*

You left knowing nothing about me, he thought, coming closer to the casket to throw a handful of soil onto it. And that's when he involuntarily looked at little Kate. Blazing wind was ripping away flower petals that surrounded her head like a flock of colorful bugs. She was so cute and looked so much like Vlad. A biological form of the continuity of the house of Kovalski. A deposit of their memory. All the while he, lonely and childless, will be blown into oblivion by a gust of forgetfulness like unwanted dust in the public space.

However! He had no idea how wrong he was in his philosophical musings!

※

The university, lectures, conference trips, both domestic and international. That's the life he lived, such was his bread and butter. Heracles cherished his colleagues, particularly professor Johnson, but he relished his contact with the youth the most. He didn't feel lonely, even though, to the delight of some of his female associates and even his students that with their heads propped on their hands would dive into sexual fantasies that featured him, he was still a bachelor.

"Dispute on democracy!" Heracles announced to his students when the lecture hall finally went silent. "Let's argue over that, shall we. Let it all start from the artwork of some poet. His extraordinary metaphors, myths, and stories originated not from the source of poetic epiphany, but first and foremost, from great wisdom. Ladies and gentleman, Plato! Influenced by his master, Socrates, he abandoned poetry for philosophy to ponder, in a remarkably poetic way, over the best form of society. I don't think I have to convince you how important it is to thoroughly know his dialogues, just as I don't have to persuade that the ability to interpret these works is equally substantial... as it allows us to understand them better."

"And you, professor. Do you know the dialogues by heart?" A question followed from the back of the hall. This student was probably not a regular at his lectures.

"I do. And you?"

"I do too."

"Alright, let's put our declarations to the test. Let's set the bar scandalously low: 'Until philosophers are kings (...) cities will never have rest from their evils'. The book number?"

"I don't have a clue."

Laughter rolled through the hall. And then...

And then it was just like usual. Keenly interested students sat there, enchanted, all ears. From time to time Heracles would stop speaking for a second to wait for the ovation to fade away. Before the students left their places to head towards the exit, they had asked plenty of questions that he will have to reconsider at home before their next meeting, so that they can argue for a while again.

Soon all the murmurs, conversations and comments

dispersed and everyone left the room – except for the one student who *didn't have a clue.*

"I guess you do not come to my class very often, do you?" Heracles inquired.

"Indeed."

"What's your name, if I may ask?"

"I'm not your student. I'm Mark Podolski," the man said, extending his hand. "We have met before. At the Polish Association in Chicago."

(It was a few years ago. The tie with the Windsor knot. A stunning suit. The man standing in front of him kept on shouting, *going, going, gone.* He also remembered that between the first and second *going* John raised his hand and declared some horrendous price for one old cup with a saucer, both adorned with red roses. The asking price itself could knock one off their feet.

"Beautiful, isn't it?" John was raving about the item. "Look, Heracles, so fragile, so delicate and yet so tough and resilient. Who knows what story it carries? Anyway, we will write a new chapter to it. The story of the Kovalski family on American soil.)

"Right, I remember you," Heracles said after a short retrospection. "I think you conducted a charity auction, the proceeds were donated to support the education of children of Polish immigrants. My friend won a remarkable porcelain cup there. It's hard to say what was more extraordinary about it: the beauty or the asking price."

"Riiight, John Kovalski was a generous man for sure! Especially when it was about our fellow countrymen. I'm glad you remember me."

"I wonder how did you find me? Last time we met I wasn't

living in Boston. Unless you truly are interested in philosophy? Or Vlad…"

"No, it's not about Vlad. He doesn't know about our meeting. And when it comes to philosophy… well. I think today's performance proves that I'm a total ignoramus on the matter."

"So?" Heracles looked at him quizzically.

"So our specialists had no problem tracking down your address."

"Well, I'm curious what kind of specialists were after me."

"We've got various professionals," his mysterious gaze ran across the hall before it settled on Heracles again. "But I won't mention all of them. You know, in the world of art collectors it is not unusual for antiquarians to accept items of unproven provenance. Some items might originate from theft. So we hire several specialists who check whether the item is not… defected."

"You mean a legal defect?"

"That too."

"So what is the connection between me and the world of treasures?"

"John Kovalski."

"John? Please elaborate and explain it to me."

"Of course, that's why I am here. It seems that by sheer coincidence, I was chosen to supervise the execution of his will."

"If you excuse me, I don't really understand."

"Let me explain. Vladyslav came to us after John's death. He brought a violin with him. It was the wish of his mother, John's widow, to donate it for an auction so that the proceeds could support talented children of our countrymen. Following an assessment, not even a very thorough one at that, our expert determined that the violin is not authentic. Its value stands in stark opposition to a genuine violin presented in a catalog. Seems like up until his passing John believed he owned an authentic Stradivarius. Not him only, his friends seemed to be certain of that too. Rumor has it he learned to play it, eliciting authentic admiration. Especially given the fact that people thought he was rather unlikely to engage in such hobbies. You were his close acquaintance, so I don't really have to explain why. Anyhow, we concluded that donating the violin to the auction could do more harm than good for his memory... do you understand?"

"Jeopardize it?"

"You know, it might seem petty but there's noble and... less noble people in our circles. So while we were fighting with our consciences about this, deciding what to do, what is the best way to handle it...," having said this, the man reached into the inside pocket of his jacket and took out a sheet of paper. He carefully investigated it before handing it to Heracles. "That's what I discovered in the violin case. You should see it yourself."

I, THE UNDERSIGNED JOHN KOVALSKI, HEREBY DECLARE THAT IT IS MY WILL TO GIVE THIS VIOLIN, REGARDLESS OF ITS VALUE AS DETERMINED BY AN APPRAISER, TO MY FRIEND, HERACLES PAPADOPOULOS.

Heracles closed his eyes and immediately opened them. He took one quick glance at the sheet of paper again and then looked at the man.

"Who else knows about this letter?"

"Only you and me."

"Where do you have the violin?"

"In the hotel. It's not a Stradivarius, but it's a perfect copy from the nineteenth century. Stradivarii are tracked and cataloged, so it is very unlikely that it would change owners without appropriate documentation."

"Please return it to Magdalena and Vlad. And tell them the truth about the appraisal, they deserve to know. About the letter…," Heracles scrutinized the sheet of paper and tore it into tiny pieces. "I trust you will be discreet."

"Are you sure?"

"Please, just do what I asked you to."

Two days later Mark Podolski arrived at Kovalskis' estate with the violin in hand, strongly standing by his decision to remain discreet – per Heracles's wishes. However, facing Magdalena's strong, unchanging and unwavering decision to donate the violin for the auction, he deemed it most appropriate to reveal the truth regarding John's written will that he had found in the violin case. It felt like he owned it to a man, who despite his slightly authoritarian and dictatorial attitude, had a big heart underneath. One that he learned about long ago, when he clung to the very said heart and rose after his fall. He was still wondering, however, who this erudite philosopher was, and for what reason it was him, not his only son or beloved granddaughter, that John wanted to hand the violin to.

Clutching the violin case, Vlad quietly slipped into the room and found a place in the back. He gazed over the whole lecture hall and took a trip down the memory lane, looking back at his university days. Sometimes it would happen that tired after an all-nighter, he could be found half-asleep in the last rows or just rocking back and forth, barely registering the passing of time and the lecturer's weak words. Whatever he was witnessing now stood in stark opposition to this sudden, nostalgic retrospection. Everyone was focused, their gazes fixed at the lecturer who would sometimes spontaneously call his students out to defend their beliefs.

Man's got style and panache, he thought to himself.

"If you were all to visit Greece now...," Heracles looked over the lecture hall. "And I was your guide through the antic world, first I would bring you to a charming brasserie for a glass of ouzo...," he stopped, waiting for the amused audience to calm down. "And then to Delphi, to the ruins of the Temple of Apollo. The place where the Seven Sages of Greece created the oldest didactic text of Greek wisdom: "Know your time. Be...," he motioned his hand, waiting for the students to finish the thought.

"...yourself!" Someone in the crowd responded, brining an appreciative smile to Heracles' face. Satisfied with the results, he continued the wordplay with his students.

"Make accusations..."

"...face to face."

"Speak..."

"...from knowledge."

"Exercise..."

"...your mind."

"Shun..."

"...what belongs to others."

"Nothing..."

"...in excess."

"Pray..."

"...for what is possible."

"Struggle..."

"…for glory."

"Respect yourself." Heracles waited for a while. "These maxims are short, I'd even say concise. Yet so wise. Am I right?" He looked at the audience.

They all nodded, agreeing.

"I'd like you to pay attention to one more inscription," the man put his hands in the pockets of his pants and waited a second. "It is inscribed in the pronaos of the temple and requests the visitors to know themselves. To be exact... know thyself. Learn who you are. Those believing in the Delphic god adamantly looked for an answer to one question: who are we? Precisely…," he looked directly into the eyes of the audience, and then spread his hands and asked loudly: "who are we?"

For the next half an hour, Heracles listened to their arguments, conclusions, theories, as always forcing them to defend their opinions.

"Before we wrap up, I'd like you to undergo a procedure… not a bloody one. It won't hurt, I guess," a hesitant chuckle grew in the audience. "Memory erasure. How do I plan to do that?" Heracles raised his brows, as if waiting for a hint. "Alright. I'll give you a certain pill. Choose any route of administration that suits your preference, you might swallow it. And what happens next? You go to sleep and wake up the next morning without the burden of your memories. While you don't have any problem with your personal identity, for you know what your name is, what you do for a living, but…," Heracles raised his index finger, "you don't know your past. To your family and friends you are still the same person that you were before taking the pill that erased your memory. To yourself, you are also still the very same *you*, because your continuity was neither interrupted nor damaged. So we are still *us*, except that there's a void in the place of our memories. Ladies and gentlemen," he addressed the audience loudly, "here's a question to think over: can you still be *you* without any history of yourself?"

Heracles stepped down from the lectern, unbuttoned the middle button of his jacket and sat down in the empty chair in the first row. No one except him took that place during his lectures. Merely a symbolic gesture. By doing so, he let his students know that pondering over existential matters knows no division concerning age, experience, social status. Everyone is equal, everyone has the right to air their concerns and opinions.

"Memories last, even without our consciousness," Heracles stated after a few minutes, buttoning up and returning to the lectern to face the audience. "They last in our preferences, talents, fears... Memories shaped us. Made us who we are right now, whether we want it or not. Oh, and one more thing," he added in the end. "The pill that I mentioned today has not been invented yet. Don't mistake it for Alka-Seltzer, you are supposed to take these the day after." His statement was followed by laughter and ovation.

The students had left the hall a good few minutes ago. Heracles did not move an inch, leaning on his hands against the lectern covered with his notes. When it seemed he's found his place in the society, just like now, he would suffer from sudden bouts of nostalgia that forced him to obsessively reflect on his own life. His past, as if it were a massive wave, was dragging him into the ocean of reminiscence. Each time, it was harder and harder to keep afloat. He was returning to these ephemeral images, still visible on the fading film of his life, that would appear frame by frame on the back of his eyelids.

"Impressive. Maestro, brava!"

Heracles raised his gaze from the notes. Vlad was walking

towards the lectern, one hand hidden nonchalantly in the pocket of bright-colored pants, with a violin case black as his jacket held in the other.

"Well, well!" He was genuinely happy to see him. "I had no idea my lectures draw such personalities."

"These kids are so enchanted by you," Vlad said and put out his hand to greet his friend. "Careful or it might go to their heads."

"No worries, I don't think this will happen. They are far too intelligent and too conscious. Anyway, today's youth needs no authority figures."

"Well, many authority figures would agree."

"Alright, stop talking nonsense. You better tell me what brings you here."

"This!" Vlad raised his hand with the violin case. "I came to hand it over to you."

"Hand it over? Man, let it go. It's not for sale, and even if it were, I have no intention of buying it. What would I do with it anyway? Purchase a glass cabinet for it? None will replace the one it was displayed in. In your father's study."

"Stop fucking around with me. I didn't cross the country so that you can make a fool of me. You know it was his will! And you should respect it!"

"No, Vlad. You should respect the memory of your father, a philanthropist, and donate the violin to an auction or just gift it to some talented child with your Polish roots. Just take a look around, I'm sure there's plenty of them."

"Are you even listening to me?" Vlad's voice was bursting with determination. "This violin belongs to you."

"Listen. I really won't accept it. So stop pushing. Understand?"

"No. You stubborn idiot, it was my father's will for you to get it. So stop bickering with me or else I won't invite you for Christmas."

"Jokes aside, man. Look at me," Heracles brought his face towards Vlad. "I have no idea why John decided to give this instrument to me. But I-won't-accept-it. Do you understand?!"

"Do you really have no idea why he was so intent on specifically giving it to you?"

"I told you before." Heracles looked at the case with firm indifference. "No!"

"You bastard! Stop pretending it's all Greek to you!"

Hearing that, Heracles burst into an uncontrolled, almost pathological fit of laughter which was very inadequate to the situation.

"Sorry," he finally muttered, wiping away the tears with the back of his hand. "Listen, I've got a meeting with a student in a few minutes. Give Magda, Betty and Kate a kiss from me, will you?"

"Kiss yourself, you weirdo," Vlad said, clutching the handle of the violin case, and headed towards the exit.

He was walking slowly, as if hoping that Heracles would try to stop him. The man followed his friend with his gaze, still standing in the same place, so Vlad had no other choice but to turn back again.

"I would just like to know why the hell you won't accept it? Why?" he shouted towards Heracles.

"Good afternoon...," a seemingly lost student peeked inside the hall. "Excuse me, is professor Papadopoulos still here?"

"No," Vlad snapped, noticeably annoyed. "He's not here. He's already left."

"Wait, but, what do you mean? After all…," he stretched his neck to make sure he was right, "I can see him."

"That's not him. It's his brother. Twin brother."

"Wait, but…"

"Oh just piss off!"

The young man adjusted his glasses with his middle finger, turned around and left the hall.

"You've taken this a little too far, don't you think?" Heracles hissed.

"You don't want this violin? Fine. You don't care about my father's will? Fine as well. But I refuse to leave and I won't let anyone interrupt us before you answer one simple question: why?!"

Heracles looked at him in silence.

"What?" Steadfast in his resolve, Vlad continued. "Come on, tell me, why?"

"It's none of your business."

"What did you say?"

"It's none of your business," Heracles repeated. "Come on, just leave. I've got nothing to say to you! And I won't let you insult my students!"

"None of my business?! For years, you've been spending almost every Christmas at my home. You were a witness at my wedding and you were at the birth of my daughter, the very same girl you taught how to ice skate, make faces and drive me nuts. You mourned with me and my mother after my father's death… And you're telling me it's none of my business?! Huh?… Who the hell are you?! Who? Because I don't know you. And you know what? I have a feeling this violin thing is somehow related to your past that you're so cleverly evading. I think that my father saw that in you. Please recall your own words that you instilled in the minds of these kids with such virtuosity: *Can you be yourself without your own history?* And answer that question. Admit that before yourself, freaking Mr. Professor! And do you know why do I care so much about it? Do you know why?! Because I'm your friend. And you won't have another one like me, ever. You son of a...! And this...," he propped the violin case on a chair nearby. "If you don't want to have it, you can just throw it away. I don't give a shit what you do with it. Oh, and one more thing: our friendship is hereby suspended!"

"Vlad, you can't suspend friendship."

"Our Plainfield home has always been your home, but until you are ready to open up to me, tell me what you've been hiding for so many years from me and my mother... people who swung the door open wide to their home and made you part of their family, it's better... it's better for both of us if you don't show up."

Vlad walked away, leaving behind Heracles and the violin for many years to come.

Heracles still missed this tempestuous, bold Polish friend with a face of a pureblood Catalonian, a master of the challenging art of tactful and graceful swearing.

The possibility to read through books and find in them everything about life was merely a substitute for the life he had lived before, when he used to be friends with Vlad. But it seemed to be enough for him.

He was a jovial sixty-year-old in good health and perfect physical condition, jogging, swimming and practicing martial arts. Loneliness never really got to him, as he was always busy; his house was always open and friends, neighbors, the owner of a small store where he shopped and his hairdresser – they would all drop by to talk. Green velvet covers of the two sofas in his living room were worn down by students who would suddenly hop up and sit down again during heated discussions, and then bustle around the kitchen to cool down and have a refreshing cup of tea.

Heracles reveled in discovering new books that completed his home library (not that it hasn't been overflowing with volumes to start with). In the living room, right underneath the ceiling, there were bookshelves that saved a bit of floor space, sparing the necessity to install bookcases. Rare volumes were stacked underneath a sizable glass coffee table, creating an original installation with the furniture.

The largest collection of books, however, could be found in the study – a place that was off limits to everyone. In the middle of the room, there was a massive desk with an armchair. A top-to-bottom bookshelf with architectural fronts housed stacks of books, albums, and niche journals on ancient thoughts and modern art. There was also a custom-made glass cabinet, styled after the case in John's study; inside was Heracles' nemesis, an embodiment of the scars on his soul, a message from the past: a gold-coated, fake Stradivarius.

This violin tormented his memory, heart, soul, reminded him of another violin, leading him straight to the haven of blissful memories only to wake the dormant pangs of conscience and throw him into despair.

That Saturday evening, he was sitting – all annoyed – in front of the computer, meticulously authorizing the interview that he gave to some charming young lady, a contributor to one of the scientific quarterly journals. There was plenty to correct, as the woman, no matter how lovely she seemed, took it too far in the interview, imposing absurd questions on his private life that had nothing to do with the main topic of their conversation, namely *Philosophical Reflections on Economy.* "*Professor, how important to you is Aristotle's idea that lack of stable relations between a man and woman causes the weakening of social bonds?*". He was about to cross out this question, murmuring *what a load of…* under his breath, when his phone rang.

"It's Kate."

"I'm very glad, but Kate who?"

"Oh, uncle Heracles! Don't you recognize me? Kate Kovalski."

"My, oh my! Your voice changed. By any chance, are you all grown up now?"

"You bet! I grew so much I can even kiss my fiancé, what's more, I can even…"

"Stop, stop! That's got to be you. Always talking too much."

"And you would always patiently listen to me. I hope it will be the same this time."

"We will see. Where are you?"

"In front of your house."

Sweet little Kate! The moment she was born, he loved her as if she were his own daughter. The upbringing part, however, was handled by Betty, Vlad, Magdalena and John. He would only provide entertainment. Whenever he arrived in Plainfield for Christmas, Kate would run to welcome him and then followed him like a shadow just waiting for an appropriate moment to invite her uncle to her room for a tea served in tiny teacups at a tiny table, in the company of two adorable dolls. When she was five, he told her almost all of Greek mythology, and when she was seven, he taught her how to play hockey. She always sought his presence and he was constantly looking for her. He would have never even suspected that this little girl could soften his character so much.

A young woman standing at the threshold of his home, her hair slicked back and her lips crimson red, bore little resemblance to that tiny Kate with a wild mane of curls and mouth constantly open in astonishment.

"Hi, uncle Heracles."

"Is that really you?"

"Without a doubt."

"You grew up."

"And you grew old."

"Brutally honest as usual. Hello, darling," Heracles embraced her shoulders with his arm and pulled her closer.

"I missed you," Kate admitted.

When she snuggled in his embrace, he had an impression she breathed a sigh of relief.

"Tell me," she broke away from him. "Why did it end up like that between you and my dad? How could that have happened? And it's all because of this dumb violin!"

"Here, come…," Heracles pulled her hand. "We're not going to stand here like that. What would you like to drink?"

"No, thanks, I just dropped by for a moment."

"Oh, I thought…"

"Sorry, I know it's not very nice to appear after all these years and run away so soon, but I'm not alone in Boston. We came here with Lukas to pick up his younger brother, he's studying at Tufts, and…" Kate took a glimpse at a gold watch on her wrist. "Well, time flies, our plane to Chicago leaves in two hours."

"Hm…," Heracles crossed his arms. "I know what Lukas' little brother is doing but I still don't know who Lukas is."

"Lukas is my fiancé, you've got to meet him. I'm sure you

will like him. He's a swimmer, just like you back in the day. When you come to Plainfield, I'll introduce you."

"Plainfield? Kate, I'm not coming to Plainfield."

"You know...," Kate took a step forward. "Regarding my father... he misses you. We all miss you. And honestly, the only reason I joined Lukas was because I wanted to tell you that. I've been planning it for years, but..."

"Did he forbid you to do so?"

"He told me..."

"Sshh... don't tell me what your father told you in anger. Just tell him that... that... or don't say anything."

"I won't tell him anything, that's for sure. He doesn't even know I'm here and I'd rather it stayed that way. You know, I envy you two. I've never met anyone that I could be friends with the way you two used to be. Please, come. I've got to go... oh, and there's one more thing: I lied. You haven't aged a day, you look great. Are you still on your own?" Kate asked and looked around. "I understand it's a matter of choice, not necessity. Am I right?"

"You would like to know a lot given how short this visit is."

"Alright, then we'll pick it up next time, with a bottle of decent wine in hand, wrapped in blankets on our porch in Plainfield. Till the next time, uncle Heracles."

"Kate!"

"Yes?"

"What are you doing in life? Who did you become?"

"What am I doing? I'm sharing my knowledge of Greek mythology with my students. I teach history in college. Who did I become? I'm still the same girl that's waiting for her beloved uncle to play hockey with."

"Wait a second," Heracles disappeared in the office, returned with his phone and handed it to her. "Would you be so kind and type here your dad's number? Maybe it will come in handy one day."

"Provided he will still have the same number," said Kate, giving him a meaningful look.

A few months later, the violin in his hand, Heracles arrived at the estate in Plainfield. But before he decided to come there, he had to put himself to a test – an attempt to fully consciously recall the past.

He didn't even shave in the mornings, by noon he just gave his lectures to be done with them, which was entirely not his style (rumors have started to spread across the university that he was either sick or, finally, in love), then he would quickly return home and sit down at the desk littered with his students' essays, where he would channel his thoughts in the same direction he's used to for the past few weeks: absent-mindedly tracing book spines with his fingers and then, ultimately, staring at the violin: an heirloom of a person he respected, loved, considered a great friend and maybe, subconsciously, sought a father figure in. The sentimental bond with this instrument was damaged by something like a persistent droplet of water that hollowed his fossilized memory, as if wanting to invigorate it at any cost. Its presence directed his thoughts backwards, towards the past – and returned like the first love that you carry within till the end of your days.

All of this made him reach for a glass of scotch in the evening, as if it could bring him answers to all his questions. Nights, however, were reduced to insomnia.

And one day he succumbed to the temptation: he touched

the violin and humbly dropped his head, unable to stop thinking about this young guy who would stand underneath the wide crown of the chestnut tree – madly in love and so hopeless – and wait for porcelain sounds of the piano that came bursting through the raging storm.

᷍

He was getting used to the violin. Its touch, sound, closeness. Daily, patiently, slowly. Passages... arpeggios... month by month. His playing was skillful and he was determined, but it all lacked soul; that divine spark that once ignited him was gone.

And so an October night came, bursting with the scents of fall – a night heavy and deep as the one years ago. Heracles approached the bar and poured himself a glass of cognac that he kept for special occasions, concluding that it was high time he started celebrating his sixtieth birthday. Relishing the exquisite taste, he made an important decision.

He shaved off the beard he'd been growing and set off for a journey – not on a bus, not on a train, where he could marvel and take in the views and scenery, as he would always do. Heracles boarded a plane and started counting down the hours to meet his friend, looking through a tiny window at barely a sliver of the vast expanse of the sky.

Halfway through the staircase, Vlad felt his cell phone vibrate in his pocket. For a few seconds, he wondered whether he should answer the call – he didn't know the number and was in such hurry, as the meeting of the supervisory board was about to start in half an hour. He stopped at the landing of the third floor and swiped his finger towards *accept*.

"Hallo."

"Hi, it's Heracles. What's up?"

Vlad stepped aside to make way for passersby. He remained silent for a long time before ultimately deciding to speak.

"I'm wondering if someone if playing a stupid prank on me right now."

"If you've got nothing better to do, come to Rock'n'Roll at Clark and see for yourself."

"Rock'n'roll on Clark Street here, in Chicago? Isn't it a McDonald's? Listen, I'm at the office right now. There are quite a few decent restaurants around, I'll book a table for us. Six o'clock sounds good?"

"No. I'd rather we talked here, at Rock'n'Roll."

"Why specifically there?"

"Because we've got to talk sober."

A bald, well-groomed man, probably around the age of fifty plus – though he could have been sixty as well – appeared in the glass door of a modern, ecologic interior furnished with plant screens. When he took off his elegant coat, the scent of a luxurious fragrance wafted through the area. The man was clad in a navy-blue suit adorned with a red pocket square speckled with a tiny print, and an impeccably white Italian-collared shirt. The sleeves showed just the right amount of rigid cuffs secured with square, yellow gold cuff links. He draped the folded jacket over his arm, his gaze ran across the room and he finally headed towards a nonchalantly seated man clad in a black shirt. Not even trying, he was drawing everyone's attention: a nasty scar on his right cheek and the raven brows clearly cutting from his short gray hair, now raising in surprise upon noticing the bald man.

They both just wanted to put out their hands in a welcoming gesture but fell into each other arms instead.

"This place has changed much more than we did. I think I was here with Kate once, she could have been ten at the time."

"Well, your little Kate has changed too."

"Did she give you my number?"

"I asked for it."

"Right. But it was she who visited you, not the other way around."

"She was supposed to be silent as the grave. Did you resort to torture to get the information?"

"Well, she was the one who came to me with it."

"Always had a big mouth, this one. Her fiancé, Lukas, is basically screwed."

"Was. He's not the fiancé anymore."

"Oh. I thought it was something serious."

"Times change, Heracles. People are not like swans. More and more people refuse to stay with the same partner for their entire life, becoming one entity, one thought, maturing together for the longest time, sometimes up until death. Now it's an endangered species."

"What about you and Betty?"

"I'm the lucky one. We're both the representatives of this endangered species. We'd love to have grandkids, Betty seems to be particularly ready for that. We're definitely not going to get it going with an aggressive campaign to find a potential father of our grandchildren, though. Kate will make the choice herself, and even if she chooses not to do anything, it will be her decision too. And you? Did you pass on your talents, inclinations and diseases to someone?"

"I...," Heracles took the last sip of cola and put the empty cup on the table. "I, a childless man, won't pass anything to anyone. Nothing will be left after me. Just void." He leaned forward to place his hands on the table. "I could use some coffee, want some too?"

"Sit down," Vlad heavily got up from his chair. "I'll pick it up and I'll take a leak on my way there."

Heracles leaned back in his chair and looked around the space. A pretty couple intrigued him. A pale girl with a pixie cut exposing a delicate long neck was talking to an Asian man sitting opposite her. Whatever she was saying, she was doing it in such a way to make her companion interested in not only the topic, but mostly herself – her gestures, mimics – as if she put both her body and soul into it. It could be clearly seen that she cared about him, while he was lazily and nonchalantly sipping his drink from a straw. *Touch her hand, you emotionless son of a gun!* Heracles thought.

When Vlad returned to the table, their discussion revolved around serious matters (Trump still had no idea how come he became the president and what should he do now because his mishaps just kept on happening – but hey, maybe next year's presidential election will change something), close to their hearts (the elderly lady Leokadia, who was the Kovalski's housekeeper, passed away, Magda remained in good health, Betty was still beautiful and Kate was independent. Work, business, travels). They did not utter a word about their last encounter. Both of them were aware that at that moment, their relationship suffered a fracture that they both perceived as a betrayal.

A long silence followed and they both looked each other in the eyes. Carefully, hesitantly. And they both found in their respective gaze everything they've missed: a friendship that underwent a harrowing, lengthy ordeal of time. They still, however, had the ability to read each other's minds, predicting moods and gestures.

"You're looking good," Heracles finally broke the silence.

"Well, but as you can see," Vlad touched his head, "I lost my hair somewhere and I'm not even trying to find it."

"Meanwhile, I'm still gray."

"Well, your appearance works in your favor. Are you seeing someone?"

"I live on my own."

"I know, that's what I heard from Kate. I'm asking if you're seeing someone."

"No. Probably not."

"Probably?" Vlad leaned forward. "But you do remember that sex is as important for health as a balanced diet, right?"

"My memory is still good. I even remember that you wanted to write a book once, obsessively searching for a good theme."

"It's ancient history. As years go by, you drown in banality and literality, forgetting about the daydreams of youth."

"Music, poetry, literature, these are not daydreams. At any age. They help us escape the banality and literality of mundane, daily life. What do we need old age for if we're ashamed of youth... or we're running away from it," he added and leaned back.

"And what about your youth, Heracles? Your meticulously hidden past? Are you no longer running away from it?" Vlad confidently sat back in his chair, waiting for an answer. "This is what you wanted to talk to me about today, right?"

"See for yourself."

"But why so late, Heracles? Why? We were friends, weren't we?"

"People who are friends with each other can be silent on certain things. Just so that the friend won't feel an obligation to rush with help."

"An obligation?" Vlad laughed, without a hint of joy in his chuckle. "Dear professor," Vlad laced his fingers together on the table and looked into Heracles' eyes, "friendship is not an obligation."

"I agree, it's not an obligation. But…" he looked down and shifted in his seat. "I'm not sure if you happen to feel the same way, but there are moments in your life that you just wish you could have lived them differently. If, you know… you could foresee the consequences of your actions, your bad, dumb decisions."

"I'm not sure what you're getting at, but I can tell you one thing: if we could predict it, life would unravel in an entirely different direction. There's one question, though: would it be better? You can never know that."

"For me, though, being aware of this resembles a burden that I will carry till the end of my days," Heracles explained. "And everything else that has happened, happens and will happen in my life will be of secondary importance."

"Tell me, then," Vlad enquired, "what made our friendship of secondary importance for you. And explain the other things that happened in your life, for example, women that fell victim to loving you. Huh?" And then, leaning back, he added: "Was she pretty?"

Absent-minded, Heracles was not answering.

"So, was she pretty?"

"What?"

"I'm asking what did she look like?"

"What?" Heracles was staring at a white cup with coffee, rubbing his finger along the rim. "She looked like someone you're going to miss your whole life," the man said, his eyes still fixed at the drink. "Fragile, but not vulnerable. Natural. And so wonderfully unpredictable. Her laughter alone was enough of a reason to stay by her side until death parts us. But all of this was just a secondary thing. There was something more... she slipped out of my hands and I keep on asking myself: why? Why did I let her do that, was there anything I could do?"

"Tell me about it," Vlad asked, his tone surprisingly gentle. "Tell me."

"You know how it is," Heracles sighed. "You just keep on living and then bam: your future is determined by fleeting moments and occasions; longer, shorter, sometimes these are just split seconds... that shape you, set out the direction, decalogues, or quite the opposite, stir up wild chaos. And then you spend your whole life looking back over your shoulder trying to see whether all of it really happened. That's how it was with me, and I was barely seventeen. Not old enough to understand the world, yet mature enough to fall in love. Until that moment I couldn't boast any scar left by a former affection. I was just a seventeen-year-old smartass who thought he would become a world-class violinist..."

Heracles Papadopoulos had an official take on his past that he used to share to satisfy the curiosity of the people he met. And while it does contain a grain of truth, it was not entirely true. The time has come to tell it all:

He had just turned seventeen when he packed his Storioni, a luthier's old violin, and set off with his mother for a journey across the ocean and through the Iron Curtain, so that he could finally meet his father, Michaj. Michaj, who – had it not been for the circumstances in which he happened to live – could have learned from best maestros and then fill the world's largest concert halls with his music. But he was merely a poor self-taught busker, a child of "a nation with no homeland", a nation that passed the knowledge of its memory by the word of mouth, a nation proud to belong to its own group and live according to its own rules; rules outlined in the unwritten code of Romanipen.

After the war, Michaj and his Romani family settled in Lower Silesia. First in Legnica, then Wrocław. As a child he used to be a rascal, constantly rebelling against his brothers from the settlement. The violin turned out to be an outlet for his emotions with which he never parted. He would wander the city streets with it, his virtuosity enchanting passersby who generously filled his hat.

Legend has it that one summer, when the country was ravaged by a devastating drought, he grabbed his violin and played a devilish czardas. Heavy clouds rolled over the town and the sky opened up, pouring buckets of rain on the streets. Ever since that moment, people started talking that his playing brings life-giving rain, that it heals and soothes.

One autumn, Bronisław Fabisiński, a gadjo, heard him play at the Wrocław market square. Fabisiński, a figure on his own, was an important persona within the artistic circles, a true aficionado of classical music.

"This fragile body hides a genuine talent. It's a raw diamond that requires polishing and care to make your brethren proud," Fabisiński declared to Michaj's parents and took care of him.

Michaj started touring all over the country, becoming one of the export products of the Warsaw Pact countries. The borders of communist Poland were particularly tight at the time, but some artists, writers and scientists made their way out of the Pact, making use of awarded scholarships, not even having to adjust their ideological views, their morals largely unharmed. That's how a Romani violinist from Poland ended up touring the city of lights and love – Paris. It so happened that a student of an American university, Nikoleta Papadopoulos, was there at the same time.

Nobody knows how, but everyone knows that for sure two young people, speaking entirely different languages, eventually met. Making nothing of all the cultural, social, and many other differences between them, high on wine and a balmy, summery Parisian night, they gave in to overwhelming affection.

After returning to the States, Nikoleta realized she was pregnant. One month before her due date, she boarded the plane to visit her homeland of Greece and got off the plane clutching her tiny son to her chest, whom she named Heracles to honor the flight's captain.

Contrary to the Greek saying *tu pedhin mu to pedhi dhio fores pedhi mu* (my child's child is twice my child), Nikoleta's parents did not accept their grandson, the son of the Romani busker.

The woman returned to the States, quit Harvard and started overcoming adversities on her own. Those adversities also included Heracles' rebellious character, as the boy turned out to be one of those who start fires that parents are forced to put out. Not only did he like to fight, but contrary to his opponents from the street, he also had no problem clearly articulating his arguments and upsetting his adversaries.

When he was just a little tot, Heracles showed exceptional musical skills. Nikoleta turned a blind eye to her child's talents, as deep inside she dreamed he would one day study law at the university she was forced to quit so early – at Harvard.

Also, it has to be said that Nikoleta was not one of those mothers, who when discovering a spark of genius in their child, do their best to ensure that it realizes all their unfulfilled dreams and ambitions. All she wanted was to ensure that her son gets a good education, assuming that a decent university equals a decent profession, and thus a stable life.

When Heracles was busy chasing his own identity, causing more and more trouble every day, Nikoleta finally resorted to purchasing a violin for him – and Heracles finally understood where he was headed.

At first, he tried to learn how to play on his own, so headstrong in his striving, but then agreed with his mother that he needed a master who would properly position his arm and then help him glide the bow over the strings. And Nikoleta found such a teacher for him.

Carried by music, Heracles started to neglect his friends from the streets and they slowly began to turn their backs on him; classical music seemed so fake and pompous to them.

He was thirteen when he learned about his father. But he did not learn the whole truth… from that moment on, he grabbed the violin even more passionately, as if hoping the fate would write the remaining chapters to the story of one meeting, that of his parents – a charming Greek woman and a Polish violinist.

They finally met a few years later, mostly thanks to Nikoleta's determination and help from a certain Romani organization. As it turned out, apart from the fruit of love which bloomed during that Parisian night, aside from all the memories, not much was left of the affection, as both Nikoleta and Michaj picked up the pieces and found happiness with new partners.

Four weeks in Poland consisted mainly of making up for lost time. Time when a raw, genuine transmission between generations should take place: Michaj and Heracles had barely one month for everything that fathers and their sons should have countless moments between the birth of the latter and death of the first: to set out the map of life.

It would be an exaggeration to say that the first meeting brought tears to their eyes and immense joy. Sure, the father was overwhelmed by these emotions, but the son remained indifferent – Heracles expected a genuine heir of the uhlan fantasy, whose body was still echoing the flutter of hussar wings that raised fear and admiration at battlefields near Vienna, that saved Europe and maybe even the whole world from the wave of armed Islam, and it happened barely one hundred and eighty years after a Genoese sailor mistook North America for India – such was the history lesson that Heracles received from Franek Sopuch, a bricklayer from Poland who worked at the construction company that belonged to Tom, Heracles' step-father.

"Do you play our Stradivarius?" Vlad asked.

"It's not a Stradivarius," Heracles reacted, gazing at the sun setting down outside. "You know that."

"Of course I know. But it's always nice to think it could be one, right?" His animated brow shot up. "You finally acknowledged it, like a father and his illegitimate son. I'm glad to hear that."

"Was that a neat swipe at my father?"

"Forgive me," Vlad seemed genuinely concerned. "It wasn't supposed to sound like that, that's not what I meant."

"Come on! I know."

"So, how's it going? Is playing the violin like riding a bike, once you learn it, you never forget it?"

"I wish. It's a bit more complicated, though. But this violin takes it easy on me. It's going... well, let's just say my playing is bearable," Heracles admitted humbly.

"So," Vlad started and leaned back in his chair. "You're no son of Zeus? Or Aphrodite?"

"Sadly, I've got to disappoint you. I'm not even a demigod. Just an ordinary man, the son of a Romani man and a Greek woman. Who, by the way, parted their ways."

"Well, then…," Vlad crossed his feet underneath the table. "Your family home is not located in the heart of an olive grove with views overlooking the Schiza and Sapientza bays?" He leaned forward and looked at him reproachfully. "Do your roots make you uncomfortable?"

"Nonsense!" Heracles scolded him. "What are you talking about? Uncomfortable?! Well… when I saw my father, I stopped in my tracks. A man in a black silk shirt adorned with flowers embroidered in silver thread. Add to that picture a thick chain on his neck, cowboy boots and a black hat with a quirky brim. He looked like he just came off some sort of stage. I was puzzled, my mother should have warned me. I would have reacted the same way to an Eskimo… Indian… whoever…

"Wait, wait," Vlad moved with his chair. "So you're saying you were bewildered because he looked nothing like your idea of a true Polish person? And how, according to you, should a genuine Pole look like, huh?"

"What's that got to do with it? What are you suggesting?"

"This," Vlad slapped his chest with his hands. "Look at me."

"Namely…"

"Do you remember what they used to call me at Harvard? Italian, Catalan. Most often Guido."

"Jesus Christ," Heracles pinched the bridge of his nose between his fingers. "Man, what are you suggesting?! Prejudice? You've known me for so many years. All these insinuations… what for?"

"I don't know…," Vlad began, shaking his head. "So many years have passed. I don't know what should I think. I don't know… maybe if I drank something, I would understand, but with a clear head…?! We haven't talked in years. Just because of… actually, because of what?"

"Listen, let me explain something…"

"Why…," Vlad leaned with all his body onto the table. "Why the heck did you make such a mystery out of it? It was nonsense, something completely unreasonable and stupid. Because here, in the States," the man started tapping the table-top with his finger, as if trying to accentuate the importance of his statement. "Here everyone comes from someplace far away. Apart from the Native Americans, obviously, they actually come from here and always have. Elvis Presley was also Romani! Did you know about that? Just like Charlie Chaplin!"

"Let it go, Vlad! You're taking it too far. If there's any good in me, it originates from this genetic, cultural blend… I'm perfectly aware of that. The problem is, I have never told them that… and I never will. Neither my father… or mother."

"So that's what it's about!" As if sighing with relief, Vlad leaned back in his chair. "The great remorse of every generation: I didn't say I loved them, I didn't apologize… forgot… disregarded…"

"Listen to the rest of the story," Heracles reproved, although patiently. "Because that's not what it's about."

Young Heracles was not particularly impressed by the way Poland was in the second half of the 1970s. Gray people with stone-cold expressions on their faces, landscapes muffled by communist ideology. The Romani family of his father, on the other hand, was bursting with colors. Somehow he felt uneasy in this new, unknown world. Despite his status as a renown violinist, Michaj and his wife, brothers and other members of his extended family, lived in an old tenement house with a shabby façade, water spots here and there. Dark, cramped apartments overflowing with more or less needed bric-à-brac were filled to the brim, resounded with chatter and conversations that Heracles couldn't understand. To add insult to injury, one of his cousins kept on following him around. Was she a close or distant relative? He didn't even remember, but she would constantly grab his hand and mutter something under her breath, invading his priceless personal space.

"What in tarnation is that?"

"Palm reading," his mother explained.

"What does it mean?"

"She wants to predict your future."

"I don't believe these old wives' tales. Just tell her to get lost."

"Tell her yourself. We're both equally hopeless when it comes to her language," Nikoleta smiled mischievously, and then turned serious and spoke again. "What about you try being a bit nicer? I know you can do it. We're their guests. And by the way, I think you should let her do it. Don't be afraid, she's not going to hurt you."

He kindly agreed to the fortune-telling but didn't understand a word. When the girl had delved into his twisted fate inscribed on his palm in a constellation of short and long lines, she seemed petrified, murmured something and ran away.

Meanwhile, Heracles was busy avoiding a certain guy, who happened to be a nephew of Michaj's closest neighbor. He didn't have anything against the neighbor himself – the man looked like he could be a hundred years old and seemed quite likeable. A black hat, gray moustache, cane and a pocket watch on a chain big as a compass. He would spend hours sitting on the bench in front of the house, his hands clasped on the cane, watching the world like a sage engrossed in his own thoughts.

One day Heracles sat down next to the neighbor and started talking to him in English, just for laughs. The old man smiled and responded in Romani. They conversed for good ten minutes, both having a blast. Old man's nephew, a man of average height, with a gaunt face and devilish gaze, overheard their chat and started giving Heracles dirty looks, as if he were calculating something. Ever since that moment they would often engage in staring contests, estimating their capabilities.

The boy, apparently a distant cousin of Heracles, was named Borys and was younger than him – but he seemed bolder. Whenever he was angry or annoyed, he would go around and say *czuri*.

"A knife."

"Sorry, what is it?"

"I think it means *knife* in Romani," Vlad explained.

"Czuri… a knife… makes sense," Heracles admitted. "The dude was particularly skilled when it came to knives. He could throw it whenever he wanted with clockwork precision. He would often do it in the face of that girl that predicted my future. It was driving me mad, but you know… my bare hands and his sharp *czuri*… I had no chance, I felt some kind of respect towards him. Respect with an undertone of fear for your own life. How could I compare to him?!" Heracles stared blankly at the tabletop. "You know… he was the king of his own land. I was just a weirdo from another world hanging around his kingdom. He had a sharp czuri, I had a bow made of horsehair," Heracles crossed his feet and rubbed his face. "One time he threw the knife right next to my mother. The father was away, he had some stuff to do regarding his concert, so I had to take the matters into my own hands. I don't really remember how did it happen that his knife ended up in my palm. I don't know… did I steal it, snatch it…? I don't remember, not that it matters at all. Anyway… he was walking around, looking for it around the backyard as if searching for the remnants of his reason. I had a feeling he was about to cry. He took out a cigarette, lit it up, mused and started walking towards his home. And I followed him, up to his apartment…"

Heracles pushed Borys inside and kicked the door shut. The cigarette fell out of the boy's mouth in a way a petrified child loses their lollipop. He wanted to say something, but towering over him, Heracles pressed him against the wall, showed the knife in his hand and brought his mouth closer to Borys' ear.

"If you start shouting, I will kill you," he spoke with clenched teeth. "Understand?"

Borys nodded, his eyes wide.

"Now listen, you jerk. If I see you one more time bothering women, particularly my mother, I'll kill you like a dog with my bare hands! And then I will shove this freaking dirk up your ass!" Heracles said and threw the knife at the floor; to his surprise, it plunged and landed right between Borys' feet, proudly boasting its richly decorated handle.

Heracles communicated with his Romani family through gestures and smiles. Nobody there knew English, he could make nothing out of the Romani language, and when it came to Polish, he knew just a few words: *Cześć. Dzień dobry. Dobry wieczór. Jak się czujesz? Kurwa.*

Sometimes, in his own country, he couldn't comprehend those weird phrases spoken by his colleagues, the children of immigrants; these utterances resembled a blend between curse words in the language of their homeland and slang English. During his stay in Poland, Heracles became convinced that with its rustling sounds, it's got to be the world's toughest language, just behind Chinese. And closely followed by Romani.

He would get along with Michaj the best, communicating in a language that knew no grammar and syntax; a language that did not succumb to manipulations, a language that was perhaps the most humane of all, as it would leave a lot unsaid, creating space for one's own reflections. That language was music. The bodies of their violins were a place where they hid similar feelings: the intonation, rhythm and tempo of the pieces they played made them realize that their reflections – those of a father and son – are nearly identical.

Heracles' violin, given to him by Tom, was unique. It was an old, destroyed Storioni that was revived by a skilled luthier. Michaj played a ten-year-old custom-made violin crafted by Józef Dorduła, a reputable luthier from Zakopane.

"We enjoyed playing together so much..." he continued. "We would improvise and have great fun while doing so. Sometimes my uncles would join us. My father was a genuine virtuoso, I was enchanted by his rendition of Monti's *Csárdás*. I've never met anyone perfect the violin to such an extent despite receiving no formal musical education. He could play pizzicato with his left hand, just like Paganini, can you imagine? Such virtuosity, such skill... you don't owe it just to good genes, great talent, it's down to constant perfecting of your abilities, for years and years. You know...," he said, rubbing his eye. "When we weren't playing, he would take me and my mother for a spin around the neighborhood."

"I bet he drove a Skarpeta."

"What?"

"It could be a Skarpeta, meaning a Syrena or a Warszawa," Vlad explained, an undertone of nostalgia in his voice. "As far as I know, these were the cars on the streets of Poland back in the day."

"Could be," Heracles dismissed it. "But I remember that he was a horrible, unpredictable driver, always gesturing, nervously releasing the clutch… he would be looking at my mother in the corner of his eye and merging onto the main road at the same time. *Please*, I was thinking to myself at the time, trying to keep a straight face and squeezing my knees together, *just freaking focus on the road ahead.* Can you imagine it? He never used blinkers. One day…," Heracles leaned forward, "we drove to a neighborhood with post-German villas lined along the street. We parked near a home with a chestnut tree in the garden. My dad pointed at the home, said something to himself and mused for a while. A man came out of the house next door. My father must have known him because they waved at each other.

Vlad looked at Heracles face' – stern, experienced, distanced, yet radiating youth – and wondered how come they both turned out to be such idiots to put their friendship on hold for such a long time. And how can they summarize it all now: everything that they missed together? But he had time. He called off all meetings he had planned for that day. Even the important one which was bound to finish with a glass of champagne sipped with music lingering discreetly in the background. When he called Betty to let her know, she broke into tears. Tears of joy.

"To this day, I've got the image of that book engraved in my mind," Heracles continued. "Bound in black leather, with gold inscription. When I touched it, I felt as if it put a spell on me...," he brought his hand to his temple. "I think there's something... like, nature equipped us with the ability to predict that our life is changing in a given moment. And I felt that. The book was written in Braille, so I figured out this knife-wielding motherfucker must have stolen it from someone blind. And I immediately wanted to return it. I don't know why it moved me so much... I don't know," he leaned forward, his clasped hands resting on the table. "I bargained over it with Borys. I gave him a quartz watch, it was nice...," Heracles cracked a smile. "Tom gave it to me. I threw in a pair of worn-out jeans, and then he showed me the house and the tree that he scaled to enter the room through a window. I've seen this house before. A post-German villa with the copper roof."

Heracles sneaked in at night when everyone was fast asleep. The book was in a haversack slung over his shoulder; he adjusted the backpack and looked up: the wide branches of the tree spread into every direction. The first branch was far beyond his reach. Heracles mused: how did this runt cutthroat climb it? He ran his palm over tree bark splitting into tiny pieces and felt a peg of some sort underneath his fingers. He pulled himself up and then grabbed one branch, then another. He was climbing higher and higher, carefully checking whether another branch was strong enough to support his weight. Suddenly, lightning tore the midnight sky, flooding the darkness around him with light; a mighty thunder followed. Finally, it started hailing and a strong wind picked up, tearing the branches. *What do they say about lightning?* Heracles thought erratically. *It always strikes the tallest tree! What the hell am I doing here?!"*. After two minutes he raised his head and looked around the branches: dense raindrops were dripping from leaves that resembled a spread palm. Adrenaline bursting through his veins helped him reach the destination much quicker than he initially estimated. The window was cracked open. Heracles jumped from the window sill onto a wooden floor and strained his eyes; the room was filled with darkness. Soaked through and cold, afraid to move and make any noise, he spent a few minutes behind the sheer curtain, giving his vision time to adjust to the shadows. Shapes started to slowly emerge: a grand piano, a bed with messy sheets, a wardrobe in the corner. And there was something else. Two fireflies twinkled right next to him; he sighed with relief when he realized it was a cat: it was sitting on a chair underneath the window and focused on licking its paw, completely unfazed by the intruder's presence. He, on the other hand, attempted to focus with all his senses on his task. Heracles reached into the haversack for the book and started wondering where he should put it back. The bed? The piano? The chair…? Or maybe the window sill? He walked the creaky floor towards the bed and placed it underneath the pillow. Just as he wanted to turn back and go to the window to quickly slip out, he changed his mind at the last moment. He returned to the bed, wanting to place the book on the pillow so that the owner could immediately see it. Then he scolded himself: *I'm such an idiot, the owner is blind.* So he was back at turning towards the window. With one leg outside, fumbling in the dark and trying to find a secure spot on the tree to support his body, he heard a sound coming from behind the door. His blood ran cold, sensing the impending disaster. The door leading to the room creaked and a petite figure entered the room. Judging by the pajamas she wore – baggy pants and sleeves that were too long – it could have been a boy. Though seeing the ability to move so gracefully, with the ease of a grasshopper, in complete darkness, it could have been a girl as well. His stomach sucked in, breath held, Heracles was standing behind the curtain and closely following her movements. As he was hiding there and thanking God that this person has not turned on the lights, it dawned on him that it must not only be a girl – it must be the owner of the book that Borys stole.

How stunned he was, when ignoring the storm outside and being completely unaware of the tempest raging in the heart of a person standing behind the curtain, the woman sat at the piano and let out music that soothed Heracles like a tranquilizer injection. In his subdued imagination, just moments ago marked by a vivid memory of a mighty thunder witnessed from the tallest tree in the vicinity, he saw the reflection of moonlight in a smooth surface of a quiet lake.

Beethoven's Moonlight Sonata, he thought with satisfaction, as he could play it too, equally good, but on a violin. Making nothing of the profound moment, the torrential rain was bashing against the window sill.

"I stood there for good two hours," Heracles continued. "The woman was just tireless. She played lyrically, classy, with precision, intuition, so movingly lost in thought. Some absurd jealousy overcame me, because how could you play this good being blind? Or maybe that was her advantage, her disability, that's what I was thinking. And just as I was considering the sense of practicing the violin blindfolded, Beethoven's *Hammerklavier* exploded. She was banging on the ivories as if she were wandering through different realms. When she finally reached the triumphant end, I wanted to jump up and applaud her. And to finish it all up…," he smiled, shaking his head. "God, I still remember the shiver that traveled down my spine… she ultimately and ruthlessly knocked me off my feet, playing Dvořák's *Humoresque Number 7*. It was my signature piece, I could pull off a world-class interpretation of it, obviously right after Michaj, as he and his violin were a complete, Romani Paganini. Before I heard it, I believed no instrument other than violin could reflect the light-hearted tone of this piece, the lightness, the frivolity… but everything that this tiny person did to the humoresque, her fingers dancing on the keyboard of an enormous piano, sounded like a mockery of all my imaginations. I've never experienced anything like that. Music was bursting into my veins, devastating my youthful vulnerability. I was tormented by conflicting emotions… at one moment, I wanted to cry, seconds later, I wanted to laugh… I wanted to come up to her and pick her up the way an older, caring brother would hold his little sister. And then, as if contrary to these light feelings, I felt humiliated, because I knew very well that even if I stopped wasting time on eating and sleeping, devoting myself completely to the violin, I would never produce anything as good as she did," his voice resounded with amusement. "And then, as if it were nothing, she just laid down in bed. I stood there for a moment, curious how she would react to the returned book. I think I expected her to break into tears; meanwhile, she hugged it tight and fell asleep, as if it were a teddy bear. When I finally left and felt the ground under my feet, I realized it had stopped raining. Deep inside my soul, music was still playing… and I broke down. I'm telling you, I didn't know why, but I just bawled my eyes out. Was it because of sadness or joy? To calm down, all shaky, I started breathing deeply, filling my lungs with all the moist air that was there underneath that tree. You know, it's funny, but I still remember that smell, the peculiar scent of wet soil.

Vlad remained silent, not sure what to say. Over all the years of their friendship, he's never seen Heracles this emotional: moved, his eyes glistening with tears... he simply traveled in time to that room and listened to the music.

At last, Vlad crossed his arms, raised his brows and sighed.

"Incredible...," as soon as he opened his mouth he knew he was about to make a complete fool of himself, but he still preferred this to the melancholy on Heracles' face, "how talented children can be. Musically. Once I was so impressed by a ten-year-old Chinese girl, she played the clarinet so beautifully... yes, I guess it was a clarinet?"

"It wasn't a child," Heracles explained. "I realized that when I went there the second time."

"You went there again? So it's not the end of the story?"

"No."

"So what, did you appear in the doorway and in English kindly introduced yourself?"

Heracles raised his brows high, his aspect mischievous.

"No way, did you come in through the window again?"

"Is it really that surprising? You'd come in too. I was young, a bit reckless..."

"...and definitely dumb! Someone could have taken you for a thief and shot you down."

"Well, maybe. But I was not the one who got a beating, unlike you, Casanova. Remember when you stole a violin from your aunt to impress a girl and then you were beaten up by her communist fiancé at the cemetery, huh?" Heracles clasped his hands on his stomach. "By the way, unlike in the States, firearms are not that easily obtainable in the country of your ancestors."

"Thanks for the information," Vlad piercingly gazed at him. "Alright, what was next. The woman enchanted you and…"

"It didn't happen during our first meeting, though," Heracles elaborated, looking sideways at the pale girl and the Asian man. This time he was far more into her than half an hour earlier. He wasn't taking his eyes off her. *Take her hand, you idiot, don't lose time.* "Back then I pitied her more…," he continued "or maybe I was a tad jealous. You know… poor girl, wronged by the unfair fate as it gave her immense talent, yet took her vision away. Something else drew me to her. Night concerts. I, a musician's son in my genes, possessed the sensitivity to discover that… that the whole beauty of music does not stem from a genius, finely composed piece. It is rooted in the way it affects us. Thousands of times that I listened to the pieces composed by great classics performed by world-class maestros, yet I never ready to go crazy about it… Vlad," he shook his head, "I went crazy about her."

"You mean music or the girl?"

"It was one and the same for me. When I was walking the wet streets home, it started dawning on me that I have changed."

Doubt flashed in Vlad's eyes.

"Listen," he rubbed his nose. "Aren't you canonizing this pianist a bit too much?"

"Vlad, I'm saying how it felt at the moment. Just try to see all of this through the eyes of a vulnerable seventeen-year-old."

Overwhelmed, trembling, Heracles returned to the old tenement house. As he entered a tiny vestibule, he lit up a candle on a shelf – left there waiting for someone returning in the dead of night, to avoid using the electricity and waking up the others who were sleeping. In its warm glow, he looked at the mirror and carefully studied his face. Heracles no longer resembled an irritated, bored guy who was counting down the days until the departure. There was something unique in his reflection. He glowed with light, the energy that he needed to find an outlet for. Dvořák's *Humoresque* kept on echoing in his mind; he wanted to pick up the violin and play it even better than his father. But he also knew that no matter how much he desired it, it was impossible for he would have to devote his whole life to this dream.

With the candle in his hand, Heracles entered the guest room they occupied with his mother. He laid in a makeshift bed on the floor made of colorful throws, blankets and small cushions, buried his face in someone else's pillow and pondered over everything he experienced on that day.

And then night bled into morning and dawn found him there, still fully clothed.

The window in the woman's bedroom was always open ajar. Heracles even befriended her cat that he initially envied, seeing the delight on his face whenever the animal would weave through her legs. He didn't remember the moment she became aware of his presence, but he could recall the blissful warmth that flooded his young body at the very thought that she likes it, has nothing against it, that she's not afraid, that she trusts and awaits him. That dark room was Heracles' enchanted garden, a wide-open gateway to a haven of new, bright experiences. Slowly, so as not to spoil the wonderful moment, he started to shorten the distance between them. He wanted to feel her, touch her... but the most he dared to do was to bring his searing lips to her long neck, his warm breath letting her know he was there, and he was so close. But she still played the same game: let's pretend you're not here.

"Once it seemed I took it too far," Heracles continued. "I thought she would turn around and slap me across the face. I was kind of prepared for it – how long can one pretend to be a ghost? She was driving me mad. The cat could rub against her legs as it pleased, and what about me? I wanted to be the cat."

"And? How did she react? Did she hit you?"

"She stopped playing. She seemed surprised, but not nervous. She grabbed her neck and said something softly."

"What was it?"

"How could I have known? It wasn't in English. And me... what was I supposed to tell her? Hi, hello, how are you? That's all I knew in Polish. So there I was, silent as a mouse. But she...," Heracles smiled, "talked a lot. Once she got completely undressed in front of me."

"Jesus Christ."

"She did it the way... a patient undresses in front of a doctor. A daughter before her mother," he added, noting the way Vlad was looking at him.

"Mother?"

"The stars and the moon were shining so bright, as if on purpose... like they wanted to highlight the magnetism of her beauty."

"Today neither the moon nor the stars shine like that. The progress of civilization messed up our sky. Or maybe there are no appropriate objects that deserve out-of-this-world lightning."

"She had a stunning body... my body reacted appropriately, but... I was tormented by both desire and utter lack of knowledge about all that stuff. And she... she was unaware of the way she attracted my attention."

"What do you mean she was *unaware*?" Vlad responded, his voice slightly raised. "Every woman is aware of that. If I didn't know you, I'd think you were talking nonsense."

"You know me, so you can rest assured that I'm not talking nonsense," Heracles responded wryly, not even bothering to explain further. "Soon I realized she took off these funny boyish pajamas only to get dressed again, this time wearing something different."

"More sexy?"

"She put on a flannel shirt and a ridiculous pair of dungarees that covered her silhouette. Then we went downstairs and out of the house. It was dark, she didn't mind it, but I... she walked confidently, chuckling at my clumsiness whenever she heard me trip. All of this made me forget I had a flashlight in my pocket. Christ, I'm telling you! I nearly lost my teeth, I thought I'd crash into some tree. No lights, no cars, just typical countryside silence and deep darkness in the dead of night."

"Where did you go?"

"She took me to a cemetery."

"Oh snap! A cemetery?! After midnight?"

"Well after midnight. We sat by her mother's grave. We were sitting on a bench, surrounded by dead people, and she talked so much... that blend of amusement with tenderness... I listened to her, though I couldn't understand a word she said. I felt like I could tell her all the things I have never told anyone else. She radiated this peculiar warmth that spread into all, even the darkest corners of my soul. And then there was rain, and we ran holding hands... Her laugh resounded with otherworldly joy and it was just so profoundly moving. I ruthlessly took advantage of her being blind, as I could get away staring at her for as long as I wished. Even if only in the gleam of the flashlight, I would simply beam her eyes with it, I'm telling you… she was taking my breath away, she was so stunning."

"Beautiful, mad artist," Vlad concluded. "As they say, craziness is a result of great vulnerability."

"She was different. She wasn't crazy. Vulnerable, yes, but not crazy. She was profoundly honest, so genuine, natural, she wasn't pretending to be someone else…I knew I meant a lot to her, maybe she even loved me… God, even now, after all these years, I cannot really describe everything I felt back then, but…," Heracles rubbed his cheek with an open palm. "Damn, it's so hard for me to talk about it," he admitted miserably.

"So don't tell me everything now," Vlad proposed and looked at him, as if waiting for Heracles to take his turn, but he just sighed in response. "Okay, you will finish the story, but some other time. Anyway, I'm always here for you."

"No!" Heracles finally broke the silence. "Let me finish this now. Now or never. Understand?" He was visibly moved. "My mom and I were to return home soon and I've just started to like it there in Poland. Admittedly, in the beginning, everything about that place rubbed me the wrong way. That tenement house with its cracked, soaked-through walls, my makeshift bed on the floor that resembled a bed of a stray dog, these loud Romani people, sad Poles… and then I indulged in these views, sounds of the daily life, I grew to like these people. I felt I could live among them. Me, them, my violin and the girl with the grand piano… but I knew it was impossible because I would have to give up the life I had before. And I knew it was impossible, I wasn't ready for that sacrifice. I was about to start a music conservatory. I worked my fingers to the bone to get there. A few days before the departure, I told my father everything. That I just wanted to return the book, but that girl was playing so wonderfully... I mean... I told him... the language barrier was quite a challenge, but what do you've got your hands for? He knew the man living in the home next to her. The one I mentioned already, that my father greeted when he took me and my mother for a ride around Wrocław. I wanted to know why she was blind," he continued. "How did she learn to play this good, what's her name... anyway it turned out this colleague of my father worked as a janitor at some college or university. He introduced us to a man who spoke English, he was very kind and keenly agreed to be our interpreter. And so I learned my girl's name was Joana."

"Joanna," Heracles corrected him. "Double n."

"Joan-na... Joanna," Heracles repeated, "lost her vision when she was still a child. Probably as a result of dire experiences following her mother's death. Apparently, it was possible to restore it, she was waiting for surgery at a decent eye clinic, I think it was even renowned abroad. Her father and grandmother were taking care of her, but they seem to have been somewhat peculiar. They didn't let her go anywhere, only to the cemetery where her mother and grandfather were laid to rest. They locked her inside that home as if it were a fortress. Everyone in the neighborhood knew that family and used to respect them very much, probably due to her grandfather. He was a professor in Lviv but ended up in Wrocław as a result of post-war resettlement efforts. That's where he was supposed to continue his scientific work at a university. Music was his great passion, Joanna probably inherited it from him, she received no formal education. Nobody taught her, nobody, she was a prodigy. Like my father," Heracles added. "People just got used to her nighttime concerts, the way they get used to urban legends. Can you imagine it: with the window wide open, the sounds of music were resounding on the sleepy streets and nobody was bothered by it, not even by the pounding like *Hammerklavier*. A hellishly tough, challenging piece. The riddle of the sphinx for nearly all pianists, as Berlioz once said."

Deep inside his soul, Heracles felt that if he left, he would never see Joanna again. Still, he imposed on himself a kind of a remembrance discipline, so to say. Namely, music was the only thing he wanted to keep in his memory. Nothing more than that. A day before the departure, as he was packing his things up and trying to organize his thoughts at the same time, he attempted to conjure up some common sense and decided he should not visit her on that last night. He feared that this meeting might evoke emotions that he would have to fight or simply succumb to; he didn't want to suffer, didn't want to ponder over it again and again. He couldn't afford the luxury of any fleeting moments of weakness. Maybe what awaited him was a life of basking in the limelight at the world's finest concert halls.

And yet, he was suffering.

"Son, take a seat, please." Nikoleta gestured towards the place next to her, on the bed.

"Can't you see I'm busy? Clothes, notes...," he said to himself, looking around. His gaze fixed at the violin case, he came to it and took out the bow and a small box.

"Will you play with Michaj today?"

"I won't," Heracles responded a few moments later, rubbing the amber rosin on the tight hair of the bow.

"That's new," Nikoleta frowned. "Are you going somewhere?"

He turned around to look at her suggestively before he returned to applying the rosin on the bow.

"What was that look supposed to tell me?" she asked, blinking.

"No, today I'm not going to visit her today," Heracles closed his eyes tightly and opened them again. "It's the end."

"Noow that's some good news! It was so irresponsible of you to go there. It wasn't only yourself that you put in danger."

"Yes, I know, I put her at risk as well. How many times should we go over this, mom? We've been through this before."

"Ehh... you know... climbing that tree, slipping through the window... like a thief! Michaj could have gotten in trouble because of you..."

"...mom..."

"You were incredibly lucky you weren't busted. People could have thought you took advantage of that girl and her disability. In small communities like this, people are incredibly supportive. They would tear you into pieces."

"Thanks, mom. At least now I know what fun I missed. But you know what? They would be right. In a way, I did steal from her. Every single time I visited her."

"Oh, stop talking nonsense, don't drag philosophy into it."

"I stole talent from her, giving nothing in return. Anyway, I don't want to talk about it anymore. We're leaving tomorrow, so everything is over now." He rapidly closed the violin case, fixing his gaze on it as he did so. To his annoyance, he felt his eyes well up.

"Heracles, I know it hurts, but... soon it won't be painful, I promise. It will be just a nice holiday memory. A memory that is... you know, brought back by music... when me and Michaj, back in Paris...," she bit her tongue.

"I need to talk to father."

"He's not home."

"Where did he go?"

"I think he's at Wasyl's."

"Thanks, mom," Heracles kissed the top of her head. "Change of the plans."

"What do you want to do, you little hothead?!" Nikoleta shouted, as he already opened the door and walked into the tiny vestibule.

"Pay her."

"But, but… how? In dollars?!"

No other instrument lies as close to the heart as the violin does. Joanna saw the source of its extraordinary sound in it; the sound that resembled a human voice, sparkling with laughter and wailing in distress. She wanted to hear a violin concert. Live. Not on a recording, not on the radio, live. Without even realizing it, Heracles made her dream come true. Michaj and his uncles, Wasyl, Dziani and Iwan, helped him with that. Under the stars, in a forest clearing, they played for her a concerto for five violins. When the warm glow from the campfire danced on her face, all captivated by the music, Heracles' heart fluttered in his chest like a butterfly captured in the hands.

Even though for years to come Heracles would isolate the memory of Joanna from the remaining parts of his life, during these first months after his return to the States nobody and nothing could fill the void that she left.

He's never been the one to share his emotions, embarrassed to the core by sentimentalism. Somehow, more and more often, he would fall into a downward spiral of reflection and melancholy, especially upon hearing the pieces that Joanna played. The music of these nighttime concerts followed him everywhere: it was on the radio, in the streets, in the subway... and in school, at Boston's New England Conservatory of Music where he was working on his talent.

A cellist happened to be his roommate in the dorm room; he was a big guy from the Deep South who divided people into those created by God (and God, according to him, was white American – though there was no proof for that) and the others that descended from nowhere. One day Heracles snapped. The procedure to transfer him to a different dormitory took one month during which he developed an injury to the fifth metacarpal bone, widely known as a boxer's fracture. His chauvinist roommate, on the other hand, ended up with a split brow and a bruised face. Everything due to different views.

As time passed by, Heracles grew tired of hours-long practice. Without the support of hard work, his talent seemingly started to fade away. He himself was one huge emotionally unstable mess, living in something that resembled drug-induced fog, his shattered heart the source of all suffering. The visits to his New York home were kept to a minimum to avoid tender conversations about Michaj that could accidentally trigger his memories of Joanna. Heracles convinced himself that everything that ever mattered to him was out of his reach. All of this caused him to go astray and start experimenting with drugs and sex.

It was two in the morning; Heracles has just returned to the dorm after one of these extravagant parties that brought a hangover, not only a moral one, on the next day and inevitably ended in him swearing to never touch that crap again. Suddenly, he was asked to pick up a phone call.

"Hello?" He asked, doing his best to stand upright.

"Heracles!" His mother's wailing voice filled the line. "Michaj... your dad, he passed away."

Phone in his hand, he was standing there until only a long continuous signal could be heard on the other end. He put the receiver down, returned to his room and threw himself face-down onto the bed as if diving into an abyss. When he woke up in the morning he took three Aspirins, chased them with coffee and got into the car to drive home to his mother.

It wasn't until a few weeks later that they finally managed to travel to Poland, this time with Tom.

While Nikoleta and Tom were carrying their baggage inside, Wasyl, Dziani and Iwan embraced Heracles and mourned Michaj together.

"He succumbed to a second heart attack," Heracles leaned back and rubbed his face. "We didn't make it to the funeral on time. You know... all the red tape... As far as I remember, it took a few weeks before we went there. At least we visited his grave," he added.

"Right...," Vlad concluded reflectively, took a sip of cold coffee, put the cup back on the table and wiped his mouth. "Regrettable. And what about the girl?" He asked carefully. "Did you visit her?"

"We were supposed to stay in Poland for seven days," Heracles crossed his arms. "We were given the same room that we had the year before. Mom and Tom would fall asleep in no time, I would be fighting my mind. You know how it is, every single day you're trying to make up your mind and try to push unnecessary, sentimental thoughts aside; you learn there is someone that you cannot have anyway because you two are worlds apart, and then the fate puts them at your fingertips, so close. But, on the other hand...," he leaned forward, his clasped hands on the table. "There's this realization... that being doused with a bucket of cold water ... that you cannot do anything because in a few days you will be back on your own planet. I was lying there, staring in the darkness...," he picked up the cup, "fantasizing how would it be if I climbed up that tree, then went through the window... I was imagining her face, so sweetly surprised...," he brought the cup to his mouth and glanced at the pale girl and the Asian guy. They were getting up. Just before leaving, the man did not even hesitate and greedily embraced her; she appeared startled. *You screwed up, dude. And I told you: the hand first. Grab her hand. Delicateness, heck. You've got to build the tension up.* Cursing in his thoughts, Heracles put the cup down on the table. "Some two, three days before the departure I became extremely restless," he continued. "I would lock myself in the room, pace it and wonder what should I do. On the one hand, I wanted to see Joanna one more time, even if it were to be the last time in my life. Just because I could and, as I chose to believe, she wanted it too. But on the other, I tried to think clearly. This hopeless obsession could ruin the rest of my life. And I could not let that happen."

And yet, he did.

The untamed feeling of the youth prevailed. Because when you are young, you cannot wait. You want to have it here and now. Heracles wasn't thinking about consequences and future; he was thinking about whatever was happening to him at the moment. So he was there again, in the pitch-dark garden, seeking the shape of the familiar tree.

When he turned his flashlight on and saw Joanna sitting at the piano, he realized she was the one he has chosen to be happy with. The outline of her shoulders and neck… she was playing *Humoresque*, as if time stood still as if nothing has changed, neither him nor her, and everything else has been pushed aside. Before the painful realization that she was a Capulet and he was a Montecchi, Heracles wanted to take her out of that room and take her somewhere far away. And then another wave of infatuation overcame him, this time awakening not only his soul but also his body – and desire.

He surprised her with the first, passionate kiss, depriving her of air. The following kisses stopped the questions, all of them incomprehensible to him. At one point he felt that he stepped on something soft; the cat's tail. *It's nothing*, he thought to himself, as if stepping on a cat's tail was something entirely normal between two people that desired each other. They both ignored elderly, kind Sphinx who sacrificed his own tail, sensing that the frail common sense of these two youngsters will soon succumb to the mighty power of primal instincts.

They made love intoxicated by the scent of the storm raging outside the open window. With his tender hands, Heracles unleashed in Joanna the energy beyond her control, the woman astonished by her body's reactions in moments of elation. The flashes of lightning brought her face and shapes out of the dark.

Later on, they cuddled on the floor. Trying to catch their breath, they made wordless plans, ignoring their waking voices of reason that wanted to warn them against the consequences. Joanna, completely exhausted, drifted off to sleep. Heracles got up, looked at the dawn framed by the window and gazed at Joanna. Never in his entire life had he seen anything this beautiful. He settled next to her on the floor, wanting to fall asleep and never be able to wake up from that dream.

Quietly, Sphinx trod towards them, curiously looked at the couple, sniffed them and stretched out among their tangled legs.

Heracles went silent, and that's when the phone rang. Slightly irritated, Vlad fished his cell out of his pocket and glanced at the screen. It was Kate. Without saying a word, he put the telephone back on the table.

"You won't answer it?"

"It's nothing important."

"I was in a hopeless situation," Heracles continued. "Torn between the sudden elation of the heart and the voice of reason. I chose the first one."

"So what did you choose?"

"I chose to stay."

"In Poland?"

"I was ready to give up everything. My country, university, mother… just to stay with Joanna. Because if I hadn't done that, I would hit the rock bottom. I was thinking: that's not what life is about; it's not about giving up something that makes us happy. In the name of what? Suffering? Because of what? I didn't want to suffer. I wanted to be content. I just wanted to be happy. Heaven was seemingly at my fingertips, but I was yet to learn I have already been to hell."

He stopped for a while.

"The next day, Wasyl took us for the last ride around Wrocław. He wanted to show Tom some huge entertainment hall, a true jewel in the crown of Wrocław modernism, erected back in the German era. Sure, Tom owned a construction company, but he was an architect by education. Intriguing buildings and their history always were of interest to him… The sky opened up, the rain was battering the windshield so badly you could barely see outside. We kept on driving the rainy streets, passing gloomy tenement houses stripped down to the bare brick. I waited for the right moment and said that I was staying and I was not coming back to the States because I fell in love. At first, they thought it was nothing but a dumb joke, then blamed the hormones for wrecking my common sense, then came fury and my mother went into grave despair. As usual, I felt hopeless facing her tears, but, at the same time, I wanted to be with Joanna. No matter the price. But they just wouldn't let it go. Tom would constantly bring up my common sense, blaming it on feverish youth; my mother coined the worst scenarios: a wasted life, wasted chances as if I already were a famed artist that shunned the world's greatest concert halls at the peak of my career... giving up my freedom, choosing life under communist rule. They acted exactly the way I would behave if I were in their shoes, just some twenty years later. Everyone except Wasyl reacted impulsively. His hands firm on the steering wheel, he just kept his eyes glued to the road. And then the tension grew, I grabbed the door handle threatening to jump out of the car. Wasyl, puzzled by this whole situation, kept on shooting nervous gazes on me, into the rearview mirror to see my mother and Tom. He didn't need to understand English, it was enough to look at us to realize it was bad. Still, he tried to focus on driving and keep his cool. I remember him wanting to break the tension when he started to sing, at first in Polish, then in Romani, he was even impersonating Elvis. And then...," Heracles looked to the side and sighed. "And then, after a dozen or so days, I woke up at the hospital, my head wrapped in a bandage, my leg in a cast, the doctors pumping me with painkillers. A woman was sitting next to me. She didn't have to say a word, I already knew,

I felt it, yet I still could hear Wasyl singing in my head... they all died. Except for me."

Silence ensued.

"I don't know...," Vlad looked down and shook his head. "I don't know what to say. Man. I'm so sorry."

When the wounds started to heal, he was sent with his cast back to the States. Apart from scars on his soul, the accident left him with gray hair – sudden stress, Marie Antoinette syndrome – and two scars: an awful one on his cheek and a smaller, shallow one on his chin.

Everything came to him in the empty home. Heracles refused to think about the future, for according to him, there was none. Tom's untimely passing put an end to his construction company, but a few former workers, shook to the core by Heracles' fate, proposed to help him out. One of them attempted persuading him to move in with him and his family; Heracles, deafened by pain and pangs of conscience, wanted one thing only: for everyone to leave him alone.

"I didn't want to live. I hated myself. There was evil in me. Wars aren't the only thing that awake animal instincts in decent humans. Love does that too. So I wanted to erase Joanna from my memory; I convinced myself she was equally responsible for this tragedy and that I hate her," Heracles closed his eyes for a while and slowly opened them. "This love scarred me here," Heracles touched his heart, and then his forehead, "and here. I was left alone. I had to make it work somehow because I wasn't brave enough to take my own life. I gave up the violin and then... and then it so happened I transferred to Harvard."

It seemed that none of them knew how to behave, what

to say and what next step should they take in the silence that ensued.

"And then you met me," Vlad finally shuffled in his chair and crossed his legs. "I'm so sorry. I didn't know. We all have our demons and we deal with them in different ways. Some drown them in alcohol, others shoot up with drugs, some hand them over to therapists. But really, these demons never leave us alone. You finally brought them to light. Shit, man, I have no idea what should I do right now. But I guess the most appropriate thing would be to ask… why so late, why now? Why didn't you tell me earlier? Alright, excuse my formidable behavior. I'm no freaking therapist and I'm pretty sure I'm just talking out of my ass. Thanks for opening up to me and telling it all. Thank you."

Upon seeing Vlad's concerned face, a thought storm started raging in Heracles' mind. While telling the story of his life, he omitted a particularly important period of his life. He started weighing whether he should share it or not. But after a while, he figured that if he said A, then he should say…

He was all alone and life hurt. The inheritance money started running dry, mostly on his "oblivions", as he called all abusive substances. He would take anything he could get and that could make him forget everything. And he succeeded, up to the point when the lack of his ordinary dose would trigger symptoms of withdrawal; muscle spasms, vomiting, throbbing aches. Upon satisfying that craving, he would wander the streets looking for god knows what and befriending shady people. Had he not been a strong and skilled fighter, he would surely succumb during one of his many brawls. Soon Heracles became recognizable in the community and realized that sooner or later he will end up the way those similar to him did; but for some weird, incomprehensible reason he was still alive.

Everything was put up for sale: furniture, bric-à-brac, memorabilia, Nikoleta's jewelry and Tom's architectural photography books. The only thing left was his violin that Tom used to win the way to his heart that one winter, asking if Heracles would mind it should he become his stepfather.

Heracles followed a known path in the empty apartment, wandering between the bed, fridge and bathroom. And a day came when he eyed the violin, his glance hungry and devoid of any sentimentalism, deciding to head to Boston and sell it to a luthier that he had met during his time at the conservatory. The man owned a small antique shop frequented by youngsters wanting to sell more or less valuable family heirlooms and get some money to fund their lavish youth.

In the early morning hours, Heracles hitched a ride in an old van, with an older man and young woman in the front seats. They were quiet, discreet and did not ask any questions, which suited him. After a few hours, cold, with pain piercing through his bones and his head buzzing, Heracles found himself on a slightly deserted stretch of a familiar street. At such an early hour most stores, except for produce markets, were still closed. Given that owners didn't raise the iron roller shutters until noon, the neighborhood was almost desolate. Heracles was circling, looking for a place to wait until the antique shop opens; at a certain point, he even started pondering whether he shouldn't turn back and go away. Eventually, he sat on the pavement with his back against a wall, held the violin tight against his chest and dozed off. When he woke up, feeling hungry, he popped into a corner store, brought a candy bar and headed towards the antique shop.

For over an hour, he stood in front of the display where

gold-plated china, figurines, dusty crystals, matte silver jewelry and old books with damaged, decorative covers basked in the sunshine. These ancient items radiated some soothing energy; a dormant history of homes from which they found their way behind the dirty window, now put up for sale. Heracles was looking at all of them, his hesitation nearly inflicting pain on him: should he come in or not? His stomach in knots, the man held the violin against his chest. He didn't have the case anymore; he gave it to Little Jack, a homeless street player. It happened on that Saturday when he dropped by with the promised dose of morphine and noticed Michaj's violin, immediately marveling at it despite the fact it was carelessly strewn on the floor as if it were nothing but trash.

Heracles liked Jack. Just like him, Jack went astray and lost everything. The only difference was that Jack's parents were still out there, just not for him anymore.

On that Saturday Jack left Heracles' apartment with the violin case and bow. But without the violin itself…

"It's a beautiful violin you have here," Heracles heard behind him and turned back.

He had to squint and cover his eyes, as the sun shone directly into his face. He was facing an elderly man, bringing to mind an image of a noble poet-thinker who had long ago buried the dreams of his rebellious youth. Not that anything in his appearance brought to mind the springtime of his life: a hunched back, veiny hands. His eyes, however, were still young. The man was wearing a flannel shirt, a corduroy jacket with elbow patches and a checkered bowtie. Heracles gazed at him, his glance – opposed to his young age and the stranger's graze – that of an elderly man.

"It's a beautiful violin", the man repeated. "Worth much more than the money they will give you in this run-down antique store. You don't have to sell it," he said, smiling.

"Will you just leave, old geezer? I'm not interested."

"No, no!" The man raised his hand in a comforting gesture. "I didn't mean it like that, you misunderstood me. I just assumed that deep inside you don't really want to sell this violin. It's very dear to you."

"Really? And you know it because…?"

"Because I've been observing you. You've been staring at this window for," the man turned his wrist and glanced at his watch, "let's say for more than an hour. And you hold this violin against your chest as if you were cuddling a child. It is dear to you."

"Do they pay you for observing people on the streets and harassing them?"

"In a way, yes. Though not necessarily on the streets. I've been trying to comprehend human existence for years now. What, how and why?"

"Isn't this nonsense a waste of time? Humans are worse than animals. Deep down its impulses that rule them. So here are the answers to those questions of yours: what, how and why."

"Meh," the man shook his hand as if he were waving away a fly, "nothing new under the sun. A truth as old as the hills, I'm afraid. But… here's a certain *but*. Namely, man still remains a creature that is not entirely known or comprehended. And it will probably stay this way until the end of the world. So there's still plenty to work on, don't you think?"

"Are you a philosopher?"

"Correct. Johnson," the man extended his hand. "And you, the man with the violin, who are you?"

"I'm nobody."

"Nobody! A very charming name, indeed. So all the masks have fallen off and now you can be whoever you wish. May I know what is more important to you than this violin, since you want to sell it?"

"Morphine," Heracles whispered, his throat dry.

"For what?"

"Not for therapeutic use," he admitted honestly.

"Oh, a tough one. Still, I guess," Johnson smiled widely, "it's not a hopeless case. I've got for you something much better than this shit. And you could keep your violin."

Out of all available treatment options for morphine abuse, professor Johnson had chosen the aggressive method for his favorite future Harvard student. He locked him in the basement of his house, where emotionally labile and infuriated Heracles came raging at Tom's violin and smashed it against the wall. Then, professor Johnson got him Methadone. In the meantime, Johnson's wife, Eleonora, ensured that their protégé did not succumb to hunger and thirst.

The professor and his wife turned out to be the best therapists. Hard physical labor did the rest. Heracles helped out a construction crew that was building a house for Johnsons' daughter; he dug the foundations, installed the sewers and isolated the underground part of the building. He kept his nose to the grindstone, all grateful for that hard work. At the end of the day, he was too exhausted to dwell on the past.

After all that he's been through, Heracles refused to pick up the violin again. Professor Johnson realized that a spark would be enough for the devastating addiction to take over his protégé's life again. Life hasn't been particularly kind to this young man; feeling sorry for him, the professor convinced Heracles to apply to Harvard, where he was a philosophy lecturer. Heracles was accepted and soon he met Vlad Kovalski.

Now, sitting opposite his best friend's face, he felt an inner cathartic wave overpower him as he dug into the deepest corners of his mind, unearthing – word by word – his memories from the rubble of pain and pangs of conscience. Memories of Michaj, Nikoleta, Tom, Wasyl and Joanna.

Vlad's phone lit up and a text tone followed.

"Sorry, man, I need to return this. It's Kate," the man got up from his chair and left.

Heracles gazed at the nearby tables, all taken, and looked at the windows. It's been dark outside for a while; he glanced at his watch and realized he should be leaving for the airport soon if he doesn't want to miss his flight. He's started to analyze everything that he'd just said, opening his soul up before Vlad, when a sudden thought emerged in his mind. It wasn't that it was something new, as it's been bugging him for some time now, but in the light of today's encounter, it started to take a new, brighter shape. And what if...

"Okay, I'm back. Sorry it took so long, Kate wanted to make sure everything's fine between the two of us. She insists you should stay the night in Plainfield."

"Today, I'd rather not. I promise I will come back soon. But not on my own. I'll bring the violin."

"And? Will you finally play for us, maestro?"

"On one condition." Heracles smiled and looked into an empty glass.

"What?"

"I'd like to ask you for a favor."

"Sure. Just tell me what it is," waiting for Heracles' response, Vlad raised his brow.

"You'll help me find Joanna."

His mouth wide open, Vlad leaned back in his chair and blinked in astonishment.

"Excuse me? You've got to be messing with me!"

"I'm not."

"Wait... wait. How long have you been sick? You look so healthy..."

"Well, if you can't...," Heracles took a jab at his ambition.

"Oh!" Vlad rolled his eyes at the ceiling. "Of course I can! But think about what you want to do! What if you're oneirically distorting the memories of that pianist? It's been a while. She has probably married, has children, grandchildren... Do you want to win her back? Or maybe she already passed away?"

"I will be fine with everything, except for the last one." Heracles leaned back in his chair and looked around the restaurant. "I don't want to win her back. I just want to make sure she had a happy life... and learn if she recovered her sight. I don't want to win her back," he repeated.

"Well, I'm not sure how Freud would interpret that. Do you believe in God?"

"I'm not sure I follow. What do you mean? You know the answer anyway. Nothing has changed regarding this subject."

"So, as an agnostic, you don't question His existence?"

"I don't confirm it either."

"You're screwed, then. You don't even know where your soul will go after death: to heaven, to hell, to purgatory... or nowhere. But I know where you will go: you will rot in hell, divine Heracles! I'm telling it to you as a Catholic. You will turn this woman's life upside down! Sorry, man, I really would do a lot for you, but this one thing… forget about it. And don't even try to blackmail me! You have to visit Plainfield next Saturday, and you better remember to bring the violin! Otherwise…," Vlad pinched his mouth and shook his head, "Kate and her mother will bite my head off! Not to mention my own mother!"

Ever since Heracles asked Vlad to help him find Joanna, he's been meticulously organizing his time. Jogging, shower, violin, university, violin, coffee. And violin again in the evening, the late night practice keeping him awake better than coffee. Like never before, he finally felt that it was not the violin that belonged to him; it was the other way around. Overnight, it started to resound with tones reflecting the state of his soul; pure and clear. He wouldn't practice scales and runs anymore. He played specific pieces – by Tchaikovsky, Dvořák, Shostakovich, Prokofiev, Vivaldi… as only this way he could develop a unique, natural relation between emotions, pitch, and vibrations.

From the moment of his admission; the confession that did not happen within the harsh walls of a temple but at a homely McDonald's, not before a righteous priest but to his closest friend, Heracles had enough time to thoroughly analyze his life, both before and after the accident. Ultimately, he came to a certain conclusion: taking him out of the depth of his addiction, professor Johnson helped him with his second rebirth. After the conversation with Vlad, he was born for the third time, and he was not in for another resurrection. Heracles was ready to give in and accept life with everything it comes with, that is everything it had in store for him and anything it had mercilessly thrown into his way so far. Life is about the ups and downs, because what would it be without them? This life?

The prospect of losing love; the awareness that he would not be able to live a normal life without it once brought Heracles to the edge; this led to tragedy, and that resulted in frantic attempts to carefully select the material to craft his memories. He wanted to forget Joanna so badly. Knowing she was not the one responsible for his parents' death, he spent years blaming her for that in some irrational way. Having finally reached the moment in life where we ultimately understand the old-age truth that the memories of the past – which we will never relive again – are all we've got, he started to think about Joanna more and more frequently. Stunning, young, chatty, with her subtle smile and then in deep thought, distant when sitting at the piano. He would stand in front of his students, lecturing them about Plato… and kept on thinking: *what about Joanna?* At night he would toss and turn: *did she manage in life?* He would sit over a pint of beer with his laid-back friends… and his mind would drift away again: *who is her husband? Assuming she has a daughter, does she look like her?*

He could have denied her existence but he never forgot her. Never. It's ironic that out of the whole pandemonium of faces he's got to know so good in his life, hers was the one that shone the brightest and strongest, even though he never saw it in the light of the day, marveling at it at night. The truth is, over forty years ago a feeling beyond any control overpowered him; infatuation.

One time he had trouble falling asleep. He got out of bed, went to the study, pulled out a chair at the desk and sat down. For a long moment, Heracles stared at the violin and took out a clean notebook from the drawer. He grabbed the violin and stroked the bow over the strings. Carried by creative elation, he improvised, immediately noting everything he came up with.

For days to come, he would perfect it and try to give it a perfect shape.

Within one week, struggling with sheets of paper, a fountain pen and the violin, carried by the wave of memories, Heracles composed a sonata, pouring into it all his talent, enthusiasm and memories of Joanna. Its first sounds and phrases – subtle, gentle, yet so promising – grasped one's heart like an invisible hand that would lead through a dark garden, then through the branches among rustling leaves, and finally through an open window into the piano room, where wrapped in other sounds, in complete darkness, without words and on tiptoes, the great affection bloomed.

He played whenever he could, for hours and with a passion so great he barely noticed that Thanksgiving arrived. Once again, just like for years before, he spent it with Plato and a piece of roasted turkey with cranberry sauce brought by some kind soul. He chased the meal with a glass of Scotch, never missing a chance to take a glance at the violin.

And then Black Friday came, bringing the shopping mayhem and intrusive bank commercials serving enticing advertising slogans: *Give a unique gift to your beloved grandparents who deserve the best!*. Thick brochures and Christmas classics lingering here and there reminded him that there was only one month left until Christmas. And that he had no intention to spent it over books, with Plato, munching cookies baked for him by some kind soul.

As usual, he fumbled through a few pre-Christmas parties, listened to three concertos and five carol choirs, and then set off on a long bus ride (nearly thirty-hour-long) to spend Christmas with Vlad's family.

Having traveled over 930 miles from Boston to Chicago,

and then some sixty more from Chicago to Plainfield, he finally arrived at a familiar home adorned with thousands of twinkling lights, red bells and green garlands. Breathing slowly, the air turning into puffs of white clouds in the cold weather, his soul felt so light that he wanted to wrap the whole neighborhood in a tight embrace.

The Kovalskis were not informed about his visit, as Heracles wanted to surprise them. However, the moving welcome and affection they showered him with, resembling a reunion with a prodigal son that is given not only the blessing of forgiveness but also a welcome home feast, clearly indicated that his arrival was very much anticipated.

Despite her advanced age, Magdalena – her hair gray, her frame seemingly smaller and slightly stooped – was still the same joyful, graceful woman with wise blue eyes and an aristocrat ring to her. Betty, who welcomed him with her open, untamed honesty, gained a few pounds and started resembling her mother, Merlin. In the diffused chandelier light, Heracles noticed familiar emerald earrings on two sides of her firm, smooth face. Kate, her hands on her mouth, stood on the sidelines, blinking quickly. Heracles embraced her neck with his arm and pulled her closer to him.

Christmas Eve was celebrated the Polish way. It wasn't a blend of cultures and traditions, it was simply Polish to the core: there was a white tablecloth, Polish beet soup and sharing a wafer. The atmosphere at the table adorned with silver candlesticks and tasteful ornaments was somewhat tense. The feasters' gestures and words were seemingly too careful, as if in fear of doing or saying something that could hurt Heracles. He, on the other hand, was making every effort to breathe a little freedom into the festive evening.

"Heracles," Magdalena finally spoke, "I noticed you brought the violin with you. I wouldn't want to offend or, God forbid, bring back painful emotions, but…," she hesitated for a while. "Would it be impolite of me to say a few words about it?"

"Oh, mom," Vlad interrupted her unexpectedly. "Before that, may we let him," the man stopped upon Heracles' meaningful gaze above the glass of water that he brought to his lips.

"No, dear Magdalena, of course not…," Heracles put his glass down on the table. "I assume that all of you gathered here know everything about me," he smiled at Vlad while saying this. As if confirming his words, his friend raised his glass. "So, go on, what is it that you would like to say?"

"Well. I'd like to start by saying that sometimes elderly people think of murdering someone," she remarked with studied dignity, glancing at her son. "Most often someone from their closest family."

Betty and Kate took a quick peek at each other, covering their mouths and chuckling.

"You know…," Magda continued, addressing Heracles again. "I still cannot believe that it was my John, a grounded, straightforward, at times maybe even a bit crude, who saw through you first and sensed your vulnerable, artistic soul. Now I understand why he insisted on handing this violin to you. He would constantly repeat that there is something mysterious to you. Do you know how did he called it? Oh…," she sighed deeply. "My John, my dear husband boasting the genteelness of a boxer, called it beautiful. Can you imagine…," Magda looked around at their faces. "John saying it, a beautiful mystery. Over the years we spent together, he's not called me that. Not even once."

Everyone broke into laughter. The housekeeper came in, carrying a platter of fish.

"Well, well," Vlad rubbed his hands. "Carp. Dad would be glad."

"I don't really like it," Kate admitted. "It's all because of these awful bones."

"It's a mandatory dish, though, so stop fussing. Tradition is tradition."

"Heracles, he called your mystery beautiful," Magdalena continued, "as he suspected you can play the violin. He couldn't have taken into consideration your traumatic experiences, as he just wasn't aware of them. I feel so, so sorry that you…," her blue gaze was so warm, honest and disarming, "had to go through all of this. The mystery was not beautiful. It was tragic, and yet still, young man, you managed to build a beautiful life for yourself. You are a renown and respected professor at Harvard. And, I don't want to brag, but you have a wonderful family," she expressively waved her hand, pointing at everyone sitting at the table. "Most of all, Heracles, you are a good man. I'm just not sure of one thing, but I believe you will dispel my doubts in a moment. Will you do it for me and play the violin? You know, all these weird modern songs that resemble creations of a haunted mind took their toll on me and I'd gladly listen to something marvelous."

Heracles wiped his mouth with a handkerchief, slowly got up, approached Magda and planted a kiss on her hand.

"Thank you for everything."

"Pfft," Vlad snorted. "I bet he's most thankful you called him young. This old fart is over sixty!"

"Son, when you reach the eighth age of man, like me, everyone under the age of seventy is young. Oh, and one more thing…," Magda grabbed Heracles' hand before he returned to his seat. "The girl who played the piano so wonderfully… Joanna… you cannot blame her for what happened to your parents and uncle. I'm certain that you made her fall in love with you and let her believe the feeling was mutual. And then you suddenly disappeared. Can you imagine? Can you imagine what did she have to go through later on, poor thing? Just because of doubt! Maybe you broke her heart. But…," her eyes lit up. "The world is so tiny right now. Nothing more than the global village. You're travelling to Europe to and fro…. Admit it, weren't you ever tempted to visit Poland?"

"It's just that…," said Vlad, prodding the fish with a fork. "What for?"

"Oh come on, what for?! To face the past. And by the way son, since you already spoke up uninvited… you could take advantage of your contacts and track this girl down."

Heracles' brows raised in anticipation of Vlad's reaction, who straightened up and put his cutlery down on the plate with a loud clink.

"Well, no! It's ridiculous and immoral and we have already agreed with Heracles on that!"

"Vladyslav, don't you dare talk to me like that! I know what's moral and what's not. I myself taught you that! Do you want to tell me that Heracles had asked you for help and you refused?" Magda squinted her eyes, still blue and still wise.

"No, no…," Heracles broke into their conversation. "It's me. I'm not sure whether it would make sense," he lied smoothly.

"Of course it would!" Betty, who sat silent until that moment, spoke confidently.

"I think so too," Kate gave Vlad a meaningful glare.

To avoid a further word scuffle, Heracles finally grabbed the violin.

He stood up relaxed, his feet slightly apart, took a deep breath and broke into devilish czardas. The whole space of the dining room filled with sounds. Tones that danced from high and sharp into those deeply vibrating. Emanating from the ceiling, walls, floor, ricocheting around the glassware on the festive table with a crystal clear echo.

"Dear Lord…" Betty sighed quietly. She grabbed a napkin and took her glasses off to wipe away the tears.

Vlad, sitting sideways on the chair, his arm propped on its back, kept a wary eye on his mother, as if he worried she could break into dance.

Twenty six hours. That's how long it took the New Year 2020 to crawl across the whole globe. From the Republic of Kiribati to Baker Island, the world lit up with marvelous firework displays. First Day Boston 2020 was no different from the previous ones – ice sculptures, a parade, concerts and fireworks. Like every year, Heracles' students persuaded him to join them and revel in the midnight countdown together; they welcomed the New Year under the stars, surrounded by popping champagne bottles at Copley Square. Somehow, he enjoyed these expeditions – mainly thanks to his joyful companions whose youth seemed almost contagious. They were his children, though brought to this world by other people. Like a good father, he nurtured them, built relationships, shaped, educated, and then released into the world.

Heracles quickly recovered after New Year's eve, packed his things and visited Plainfield again, where he spent six days among the people that replaced his family. He would go horse-riding by day and play the violin after dinner.

On the last day of his stay, they went to visit the new Chicago headquarters of Vlad's company. It stretched along an entire floor in a luxury skyscraper in the heart of the downtown. The sophisticated ambience of the interiors muffled the sounds of the bustling streets outside; lavish marble, soft leather, a palette of blacks, whites and metallic shades.

"So, how do you like it?" Vlad asked, pushing his hands into his pockets. A spectacular view over the maze of city streets and Lake Michigan – its level highest in years – stretched before them behind the glass wall.

"Well… it's stunning! All it takes is listening closely to the whispers of the city and writing about it. You've always wanted to do that."

"Piss off," Vlad gave him a scorned look and moved aside to pour scotch into two glasses.

"Never."

"Why do you keep doing it to me?"

"Because I love you."

"Get lost!"

"In a few minutes."

"Already?" Vlad blinked rapidly. "Your plane doesn't depart for three hours. Alex will drive you to the airport."

"That won't be necessary," Heracles responded and crossed his arms, gazing at the cityscape.

"Listen, about that woman from Poland…"

"About Joanna."

"Okay… about Joanna," Vlad corrected himself bluntly. "If it's so important to you, I could ask here and there."

"It is."

"Why?"

"It's hard to explain," Heracles sighed, his eyes glued to the panorama of the city. "Just like that… it is important to me."

"And eternal world peace is important to me," Vlad clapped back, waving his hands animatedly while holding on tight to their drinks. "Still, is there anything I could do about it? Abso-freaking-lutely nothing! Just deal with it. There are certain things beyond our control. Digging up basic information about her… I mean… her address, occupation, social security number, favorite dish… you know it's not much of a challenge for me. But there's no way I could learn whether she's still thinking about you, if she remembers you, if she has dreamed about you, even if only once. Heracles, listen to my good advice, let it go, ok? You've already been to hell and back. What do you need this for?"

"Vlad," Heracles turned around to look him in the eye. "I want to go there to learn who I am."

"Oh sure, you and your philosophical musings! Learn who I am! Maybe start from the other end? Think about who you are not and you will find the answers to your fucked up existentialist question."

"Spilling it, aren't you."

"Because I'm freaking fuming!"

"I meant the Scotch, you stained your cuffs," Heracles smiled mischievously, taking his glass out of Vlad's hand. "I'm no Jew, Catholic, Muslim, Greek, Polish or Romani. But I'm a little bit of all."

"You're human. So why do you want to go there if you already know that?"

෴

More and more often, Heracles would evoke the memories of his mother, exploring the whole range of her contradictions, both these in her appearance – noble Grecian features, straight nose with a smooth line running from her forehead, tawny complexion and her hair, resembling wheat fields on a summer day, sparkling in the sun with subtle shades of gold – and her mentality – her open mind, kindness, benevolence, liberalism, longing for freedom, individualism, and, the surprising tendency for malcontentedness.

There was much regret to the fact he didn't even have a single picture of her. A month or so after the funeral, Heracles piled up all family photographs, letters, and diaries, set them on fire and watched the sorrowful cry of his soul turn into ash.

It's been a while until he realized that his mother is an absence that was always present in his life. He carried in his genes the shape of his Grecian nose and a soul that yearned for freedom. Years later, he would seek her image in his dreams – to no avail, as she would always fade away.

That night he could finally see her so clearly in his dream. So clearly and so beautifully, that he wished this image stayed with him when his time comes to leave the earth; a blonde Grecian goddess, light dancing on her face, who would take his hand and lead him wherever his soul was destined. Even if it was a void.

The dream disappeared. When he opened his eyes, it was a Saturday morning in January. Heracles got up, almost wobbling on his feet as a migraine struck him, turned on the radio and pulled the blinds up. A flock of black birds interrupted the stillness of the desolate street as they suddenly took flight from the roof of the neighboring house. Heracles went to the bathroom, took a shower and shaved. Putting on a watch on his wrist, he listened to the quiet mumbling of the radio; it broadcasted an information service. The journalists discussed a mysterious disease from Wuhan: coughing, dyspnea, fever, muscle pain, finally really nasty pneumonia. With a network of contacts within the local academic community, Heracles was familiar with the city. Few of his acquaintances were there as part of the "Talents" project. Appropriate forces deemed the program to be more of economic espionage; nonetheless, many academics were against restricting cooperation with China, bringing up one of the priorities in the world of science, namely openness.

Once he dealt with the watch, Heracles approached the radio and turned the volume up.

"Since mid-January, the virus has spread to the whole territory of China…," informed a female voice with impeccable diction. Alright, so it will spread outside China in no time, Heracles thought to himself. The world is just a global village, everything's close, as Magda charmingly noted during Christmas Eve in Plainfield.

He was pouring himself coffee when his new iPhone rang. It was Vlad.

"Hello, Hera, what are you up to?"

"Drowning a migraine in my coffee."

"Uh oh, sorry to hear that. Hope it wears off before February 15."

"Should I consider it an invitation for Polish vodka?"

"Well, why yes?! It could be Polish vodka too, in its natural habitat."

"What do you mean…," Heracles froze, his cup of coffee mid-way to his mouth.

"Exactly what you're thinking about."

"So…," he put the cup on the table, took out the chair and sat down. "Does that mean she's alive?"

"She is, except that…,"

"She has a husband?" Silence. "It's not that surprising, right?" Heracles added after a while.

"No, it's not about that… she didn't regain her vision. She's still blind."

"Oh… it's so bad." Heracles leaned over the tabletop and rubbed his forehead with his hand. "Did you learn anything else?"

"She took the surname, Adamczuk, after her husband. She lives in Warsaw and I have her address."

"In Warsaw…? What about her family house, the one near Wrocław?"

"It belongs to her, she's inherited it from the previous owner, her father or grandmother, it's quite a complicated story."

"If you say she lives with her family in Warsaw, is the house vacant or is there someone renting it?"

"I know she didn't sell it and that's it. But if it's so important to you, I can ask."

Heracles got up from the table and started pacing the kitchen in circles, pushing the phone against his ear. He opened a cupboard and immediately closed it.

"Hera?" The voice on the phone broke the silence.

"Yes?"

"I said I could ask about this house."

"No, that won't be necessary. Or… okay! Ask! I mean, I would like to know the address. I'm not sure I would recognize the place now."

"Do you want to see Joanna or the house?"

"First, the house."

"What for?"

"I don't know. I just want to."

"So you want to visit both Warsaw and Wrocław?" Silence followed the question. "Okay, as you please. I also made them ask about your Romani family. Your father was destined for a stellar worldwide career, but it was cut short by his untimely passing. Did you know he was supposed to play at the Olympia in Paris?"

"At the Olympia in Paris? He should have played in Carnegie Hall. He was a genius."

"The tenement house that you lived in during your stay in Poland is not there anymore. Ten years ago they tore it down and built a school and a football field there. Your uncles emigrated to Germany after 1989. And that would be it. Oh, and one more thing. She, I mean Joanna, she's a widow. She's been one for years."

Heracles sat down at the table again, wiping nonexistent sweat from his forehead.

"Hera?" he heard again.

"Yes?"

"She has a son."

"A son?" Heracles got up again, paced the kitchen, peeked into the fridge and closed it after a second. "How old...?"

"Come on, you know."

Heracles lost his temper. "I'm asking, how old?"

"She's your age."

"Christ, Vlad! Get your shit together! I'm asking about the son!"

"He's a big boy."

"I adore your sense of humor, but you're taking it too far this time."

"No worries, man. Stop picking on me." Silence ensued

between the two of them. "She was already married when her son was born."

∽

They checked into the Hotel Bristol in Warsaw, a magnificent place with a neo-renaissance façade located near the Presidential Palace. Both of them fought the jet lag and set off to wander the streets where the "wounds of remembrance" could be seen on the walls of tenement houses and promenades paved with yellow, red and gray granite – as in Canaletto's paintings.

Vlad confidently walked these streets; after all, he's been there at least twice a year, so nothing seemed strange, shocking or astonishing to him. He changed along with this cityscape, the world of his ancestors, treating it all like an integral part of his own history – which just unravels as time passes by, without drawing much attention. On the other hand, what Heracles sought in the city were metaphysical experiences, traces of war and communism; he was stunned by the transformation. Fascinated by the places that witnessed history, he would touch bullet holes, barbed wire and bricks in the wall.

The next day, they flew to Wrocław where they caught a cab to Pawłowice. A suburb on the outskirts of the city which, as the taxi driver said, boasted a beautiful palace complex from the 19th century and a charming lake – much to Heracles' surprise, who remembered only the house with the chestnut tree in the garden and the cemetery, both wrapped in deep darkness.

Arm in arm, they walked the pavement, their silhouettes illuminated by the sun, exceptionally warm in the surrounding winter. They discussed everything and nothing: the neighborhood was clean and neat, people were kind, there was a friendly dog... and oh, a strange church building – what a hybrid of architectural styles! Heracles' heart tingled with disappointment. Everything seemed so distant. Distant. And he fed his hearth with the naive hope that the past years did not entirely wash away the mirage of the days gone by. He wanted something to linger; something that did not lose this elusive aura that could envelop him in a subtle veil of memories and whisper into his ear: *hello, dear, I recognize you. Glad you're back!*

"Listen…," Vlad spoke up after a moment of silence. "Why is my writing suddenly so important to you, huh?!"

"You'll see, sooner or later you will do it."

"I will humbly acknowledge your comment. It makes me feel appreciated too… It's a shame my father can't hear that. According to him, counting and calculating profits and losses were the only things I could do."

"That's a harsh judgement."

"Not at all. On a five-star scale, I would give my father three stars for being a father. And five for being human."

"Why do you judge him against different measures?"

"Maybe because I'm hanging out with you? And look at everything through the eyes of a philosopher? And, by the way, how would you judge my philosophy? Am I wrong when it comes to my father?"

"What are you getting at?"

"Nothing. I just want you to agree with me. But if you don't, I won't be offended. Shoot! I'm like…," he clenched his fist, "like this iron! Like the late John Kovalski! And by the way…," Vlad pushed his hand inside the pocket. "Soon, I'll be sixty. At this age, you cannot be offended so easily."

"Alright…," Heracles started, running his hand through his short hair. "As a philosopher, you suck. Because you spend too much time thinking about it. But you're okay as a friend.

You talk and you talk like a chatterbox, and I know what you're getting at, but there's really no need to worry."

"Well…"

"Listen to me! You don't have to distract my thoughts, I know why I'm here. Thanks!" He slapped him between the shoulder blades. "I'm going to be fine!"

"Are you sure…? And by the way, you know… you're cruel. *As a philosopher, you suck.* How could you tell me something like that?"

Heracles chuckled.

"And you claimed to be tough as iron, that you won't be offended because when you're sixty…"

"I didn't celebrate my birthday yet!" Vlad snapped back, pretending to be outraged. "I'm going to be sixty this September!"

"So what? You've already reached the stage of old age."

They were still far away when the broad crown of a mighty tree emerged on the left. The branches reached over the copper roof, now painted with a tint of green patina, covering the house with a white façade. There was something to this old house. Something that made it seem that among the sea of all the homes in the area, both these new, pleasant to the eye, neatly trimmed, and these old, with refreshed facades and boasting new terraces made of glass and steel, it was the only building that seemed to be so necessary and right where it should be.

"Well, well," Vlad marveled. "Seems nice, but it's utterly ruined. I can see from here that the plaster is coming off the walls, the gutters are broken… human memory is like pigeons. As long as you're alive, they will eat crumbs out of your hand and respect you. But when you die, they shit on your grave."

Heracles went silent. He wasn't listening to him anymore.

After a few minutes, they approached the front oak door.

Vlad raised his hand but just when he was about to knock, he looked at Heracles and noticed him tense up.

"Are you sure?" He frowned.

"Yes. Or... wait!" Heracles grabbed his arm. "Let's go to the garden first!"

"Are you sure you want to do that? Trespassing someone's property? I don't really think it's a great idea. Think logically!"

"Listen...," Heracles took one step closer. "Had I thought about it all logically, I wouldn't even be here. But since I am...," he looked into Vlad's eyes, his gaze that of a person ready for every sacrifice. "Wait for me here, I'll be back in a minute," he added.

"I'm not going to stand here like an idiot. I'm going with you. Jesus Christ!"

They walked around the house. Just when they turned the corner, a miserable view fell upon their eyes: a lonely chestnut tree, bushes, a rotting veranda next to the house overgrown with bare vines.

"Christ! Told you...," Vlad blabbered on, "you should contact her first in Warsaw and tell her you want to see this ruin. Maybe she wouldn't want it, huh? This looks so pathetic!" A string of Polish curse words followed. "You're a stranger to her...," he kept on talking, "and anyway, so much time has passed. Man, she must have forgotten you! And even if... even if she remembers, she can resent you for disappearing into thin air. Just like that. She doesn't even know who should she reminisce about, and even if she heard about the car crash, there would be no grounds to link it to you, right?"

"She remembers me."

"Oh," Vlad chuckled ironically. "How, the hell, can you be so sure about it, huh?! From what you've said, you never spoke a word to her. She doesn't even know your voice. What are you muttering there? What for heaven's sake?! It's you who threw all the logic out of the window."

"Get a grip on yourself and stop panicking. As for Joanna… I was her first."

"And…?"

"What do you mean, and? Every woman remembers her first partner. Out of all people in the world, do I really have to explain that to you?"

"Thank you, professor, for this professional lecture. You visited her once, twice, seduced her and took off! That's how she remembers you! And now let me give you reliable advice: let's get the fuck out of here before someone busts us! I feel as if I threw a rock through their window!"

"Give me a second."

"Hera…," he took a step forward. "It's someone's property, do you understand…? Okay. You don't." Vlad said, as Heracles was busy examining the tree: closely inspecting the branches as if he was attempting to do something while caught in a time warp, waiting for the rustle of twigs sprinkled with reddish buds of leaves to give him something more than just memories. The man was touching the bark splitting into splotching flakes, finally finding a peg he used to pull himself up to reach to the branches and climb higher. "Okay!" Vlad raised his arms. "I'm going, then."

Only then Heracles gazed at him.

"Going where?!"

"Gracefully and culturally, I'll knock on the door and politely ask if my friend could visit the room upstairs and have a look around because he crossed the pond to do so and he's a tad too old to be climbing trees."

"Have you lost your mind?" Heracles looked him directly into the eyes. "What are you up to?"

"No worries. I'll tell them we're here because of the advert. Did you even notice it? There's a sign on the fence that she put the house up for sale. Maybe they will let us in and you could have a look around. So you stay here and talk to the tree while I talk to the people inside... Hey, Hera," he shouted, peeking from behind the corner. "Remember that...," he glanced at his watch, "our taxi will be here in an hour and our plane to Warsaw leaves in two hours. Keep it short and concise with that tree and for the love of God, don't attempt climbing it because it's gonna take you hours. We should also let your lady know that we want to visit her in Warsaw, don't you think? Heck, right, that's what we should do because that's what fucking phones are for!" Vlad added, but immediately disappeared upon seeing the look on Heracles' face.

Vlad rang the doorbell – but no sound followed. He pushed down on the door handle; the door creaked and cracked open. Vlad found himself in a small corridor in the faint light of a dust-covered lightbulb hanging on a piece of black cable.

"Hello? Anybody here?" the man shouted.

A man came running downstairs; he could be around forty, with fair hair and a dark complexion.

"Oh, the village administrator must have sent you," the stranger concluded and put out his hand.

"Not really. I was just passing by and saw the ad that the home was up for sale. Oh," he extended his hand. "Władysław Kowalski."

"Excuse me, I thought it was someone... anyway, it's not that important," he kept on talking shaking Vlad's hand. "I'm

Adam Adamczuk, son of the property owner. So," he clapped and rubbed his hands, "you say you're interested in buying?"

"Precisely."

"Great. So I guess you would like to have a look around?"

"Precisely."

"So…," he kindly gestured towards the entrance door. "What about we start from the garden?"

"Perfect, my associate is already there. Oh, no worries," he immediately reacted as a surprised expression appeared on the man's face. "He's no looter, he's actually fond on old trees. Honestly, it's the chestnut tree growing behind the house that drew his attention… you know, my friend is a foreigner, a citizen of the United States. He buys promising properties in the European Union, renovates them, obviously according to the guidelines of heritage protection authorities, and then…"

"…and then he sells them at horrendous prices as jewels. I understand," the man concluded and led Vlad towards the exit. "The house went fell into ruins because my mother's father had neither the means nor will to protect it. You know, my mother moved out many years ago but still holds an exceptional emotional bond with this place. When it comes to the next homeowner, it matters to her who it is. It matters to me too. Just look…," once they were outside, the man pointed his finger at wild bushes by the fence. "Back in the day, rhododendrons and azaleas grew there…"

During their meeting in the garden, Heracles and Adam went on without all these emotions, feelings, intuitions, that would tug on their hearts like a blabbermouth wanting to share a great secret. They kindly greeted, introduced themselves, and that was it. Fear flickered in Vlad's eyes; he kept to the sidelines but suddenly started wondering what would be better: facing all the improbable and astonishing life scenarios or not being even aware of them?

Straight from the veranda, they went into a room furnished with a bed, two armchairs, a table with two chairs and a wardrobe. Adam explained in perfect English that it used to be a dining room, but his great-grandfather had it transformed into a bedroom for him and his wife. Then they entered the kitchen and all the remaining rooms on the ground floor. Heracles showed little interest in the presentation, following them like a shadow with his hands clasped behind his back. At some point, he vanished into thin air.

"It's unusual," Vlad noticed and looked around, "that there are sliding doors everywhere. It's not common in old Polish houses."

"Correct," Adam admitted. "Except that this house was built by Germans," he noted. "And regarding the door, you're right, it's very convenient. Thanks to it you can turn all the rooms into one large space."

"Very clever. It's a remarkable property," Vlad said, wanting to give Adam a reason to be genuinely content. "You sure must have plenty of purchase offers."

"Honestly: not really. We put up the advert today in the morning. Apart from you, there's one more candidate, but he's been coming forward with the offer for a long time. It's the local village administrator who would like to set up a hotel for seasonal workers here. He's been trying to convince mom to sell it to him for years. Mom lives in Warsaw and scarcely visits this place. Or should I say never. Ever since my grandfather's death the administrator has been taking care of the property, hence his hopes that mom will finally give up. He wants to pay whenever we are ready, even if that means today."

"And that does not seem right to you," Vlad clasped his hands behind his back. "You would like to keep it, right?"

"Well... maybe I have different plans."

"What plans? And how does your mother feel about it?"

"Too many questions!" The kind and approachable version of Adam turned into a combative one. His feet slightly apart, the man crossed his arms. "What are you looking for here? And where's your friend?" He raised his brow.

Vlad rocked on his heels and, confused, glanced to the side. Heavy silence ensued; one that makes it possible to hear the ticking of a wristwatch – subtle, yet so intrusive tick-tock, tick-tock trying to break into one's veins. Suddenly piano music flowed from the upstairs, bringing bemusement and splitting the atoms of uncomfortable tension between them. Adam jumped out of his place and Vlad followed him upstairs. When they entered the piano room, Heracles was already there.

Usually, the color black deepens the aura of sadness and mourning. But for Joanna it seemed to be a perfect color, highlighting her dignity. She retained her youthful freshness and noble features became more graceful. Serene, tranquil, she felt the eyes of silent spectators on her, yet she just kept on playing. With this last act; a regular, soothing musical gesture, she said her goodbyes to the house and the piano, a hundred-year-old Bechstein. Joanna wanted this moment to last forever; to delve deep into her heart and find a reason confirming she did not lose a dozen or so years of her life surrounded by these walls soaked with... she couldn't even describe what. And what if it was love that was here? Even if it were barely a substitute for it? Not the sugar-coated, annoyingly sentimental, but genuine one? She forced herself to think about her father. Suddenly she realized that being away from her family home for so many years, it was not the room, her grandma, not even her mother that she missed. With indifferent astonishment, she discovered it was her father that she yearned for the most. Dad, I gave you a grandson. I fed him meals that your mother, and then your grandmother cooked for you. Dad, I managed to raise him to be a good man. And you helped me in doing so by being a good grandfather to him. Even if you never believed in me, it helped me reach beyond the borders of my disability again and again. Dad, I made mistakes. But these were my mistakes and I lived my life my way. You have to know, you have to know, dad... that I forgive you and that... oh, daddy, I miss you so much..."

Upon concluding the piece, she heard the rustle of uncertain movements and quickly wiped away a stray tear from her cheek.

"Mom," Adam spoke after lengthy silence bursting with respect. "The village administrator did not come, but I'm here with two gentlemen. One of them claims to be interested in purchasing the house."

"Oh, so Roman didn't send you?" Her voice still sounded unbelievably kind.

"No, dear madam. No," Vlad responded. "Please let me speak on behalf of my friend who is standing here next to me...," he turned towards Heracles to look at him; he was standing with his head low, his expression vigilant and stern as if he has just realized something incredibly important about him and Joanna. Astonished, Vlad stared at him dumbfounded for a brief moment – he even wanted to say something but gave it up and addressed Joanna, continuing his statement. "My friend is an American and unfortunately, he doesn't know any Polish. As I have already told Mr. Adamczuk, Heracles purchases old properties, restores them and either sells them or keeps them as investment capital," he lied smoothly.

"Oh. I understand," a slight tone of disappointment could be heard in her voice. "So it's business. Something I know nothing about, just like my son. We're just musicians, the kind of people that are detached from such a grand scheme of things. So you say," she slightly raised her head and Vlad felt like she looked at him, immediately making him uncomfortable, "that purchasing a property like this is an investment?"

"Of course," he responded firmly, wondering whether maybe she wasn't completely blind.

"And, as I understand, it's one of these transactions that it's hard to lose on?"

"Precisely!"

"And what if this house does not live up to that principle?"

"Well...," he said, running his fingers through his hair and staring intensely at the floor. "My friend is ready to take the risk."

"Unfortunately, I'm afraid he won't have a chance to find out if taking the risk was worth it. You see, I've just decided to take the offer off the market. But I'm sure you will find another, equally interesting properties to expand your estate, which I wish you with all my heart," Joanna got up from the chair and grabbed the white cane. "Adam," the woman addressed her son, who was straightforwardly staring at Heracles, as if wondering where could he have seen this man before, "please see the gentlemen out. I would like to apologize to you for the trouble but please, put yourself in my shoes. It's a family home, after all, it's hard to part ways with all of this."

"Oh, it's understandable. In case you changed your mind," Vlad reached into the inner pocket of his jacket and fished out a leather case," please let me know. By the way, you are a marvelous piano player. My friend is a great aficionado of this instrument," he handed his card to Adam.

"And a fan of old trees," Adam joked. It seemed that his cheerful disposition came back with his mother's decision to keep the house.

"A fan of old trees…? What kind exactly?"

"Chestnut trees, ma'am."

"Oh!" Joanna's mouth opened in astonishment. "Really? An aficionado of music, trees… your friend must be a very interesting person."

"He sure is," Vlad reassured and took a glance at his watch. "Time flies in good company. Unfortunately, our time's up, we're in for a long journey. The taxi's waiting," he suddenly addressed Heracles, meaningfully raising his animated brow.

"So…," Joanna put out her hand to say goodbye. "Safe travels. It was nice meeting you both."

Surrounded by silence, Heracles took her smooth, petite hand for a lengthy moment. A sensation she struggled to verbalize started flowing through her veins.

Once upon a time, my love touched your lips, Heracles mused, the thought being the only thing that was left to him.

Heracles was born in truly extraordinary circumstances. On a plane. And 61 years later, in circumstances no less extraordinary, he nearly perished.

The landing gear of a fully booked plane from Warsaw to New York had just been extended for a safe touchdown at the John F. Kennedy airport in New York City, when one of the passengers, a respected Harvard lecturer, felt an acute, sharp pain in his chest, radiating to his jaw, throat and shoulders. It was a massive heart attack, an event subsequently widely reported in press and news services.

Doctors at New York's Presbyterian Hospital spared no efforts to save the patient's life; the efforts, however, were futile, as Heracles seemingly could not decide between life and death. Following an angioplasty procedure, he was transferred to ICU, where his heart rhythm was closely monitored. After a week, the day came when he finally opened his eyes. Whenever he closed his eyelids, though, as he spent most of his days sleeping, he always visited one place. Again and again.

(His heart pounding in his chest, he was hiding behind the curtain, the velvety sounds of the sonata dissolving in the air. The sonata. His sonata. Familiar shapes started to emerge from the dispersing darkness: the piano with lid resembling a bird's wing in flight, the wrought iron bed, the chair and the cat's eyes. Suddenly, an unexplained twinge of unrest pierced his soul: the landscape was incomplete, there was something missing. His eyes used to the dark, he moved his gaze, looking around intensely. Suddenly, the door opened, Adam entered the room and turned the light on. Only then did Heracles realize what it was that he was frantically seeking: she was seated on the chair, petting the cat in her lap, her face shrouded with subtle mantilla as if she were a distraught wife mourning her husband.)

And then he woke up.

One afternoon his eyelids lifted, seemingly with no effort on his side, and he saw a character from his dream. Adam? How many thoughts, experiences and thrills could be triggered by one quick glance, even if it lasts for just a split second?

As a kid, Adam was one of these sharp and clever boys. Upon learning how long a pregnancy lasts, he meticulously counted on his fingers, knowing his parents' wedding date, how long did mom and dad have to wait for him to join them earthside. And it turned out it's been two months.

Both an old wooden abacus and a modern calculator showed the same result. He figured his birth must have been a miracle of nature. Later on, when he was a young man well aware of human nature, he became certain that his parents conceived him seven months before their marriage. On the day of his eighteenth birthday, he learned the truth.

Devastated by the news that the person who brought him to life resembled the ghost who would silently haunt his mother after midnight, he persistently tried to picture his father. Which was not easy, as the only figure appearing before his eyes was Wiktor – the only father he knew and loved. Years later, he gave up these attempts.

The breakthrough came on the day when two American weirdos appeared at their old family home in Pawłowice. Standing to the side in Joanna's room, Adam glanced towards Heracles; the man was silent, his head down as if he were examining his conscience. Somehow, his face felt familiar to Adam: the nose of a Greek sculpture, narrow, straight, with a smooth line running from the forehead, and then there was his olive skin and that voice (when they spoke a bit in English in the garden) – low, vibrating, resembling that of Eddie Vedder, the lead vocalist of Pearl Jam. The band Adam admired in his youth and still appreciated; his wife, Zuzanna, joked that his fascination with the band was so strong, it was reflected by a charming, quirky element in the Adamczuk family – the voice of their son, Konrad, resembling that of Vedder.

So when Adam was bluntly staring at Heracles for as long as he wished, musing about all these issues, he came to the conclusion the man reminded him of Konrad. *That's what my son will look like in some thirty, forty years.* The significance of this thought grew until a certain suspicion started drifting in Adam's head, pushing him to travel half the world, across the ocean. But before that, he reached for Vlad's business card and sent him an e-mail, asking for Heracles' contact details. Guided by his instincts, he even provided the reason for such a dire need.

The message did not knock Vlad off his feet. Actually, he already knew that back in Pawłowice. Clutching his cell phone as if it were his lifeline, the e-mail displayed on the screen, he wanted to run to the Presbyterian Hospital and cry out the happy news to his unconscious friend: *Hera, do you know, man, do you know that your family just grew!? You have a son, a grandson and a daughter-in-law!*

The thing was, he could not do it. The only things Heracles needed were silence, peace and the presence of a loved one, for his heart was on the verge of giving up. It could not bear beating and pumping anymore.

Vlad booked a hotel room near the hospital, where he would spend the nights. During the day, he could be found by the bed of his vanishing friend, resorting to various methods of motivating him to fight for every, even the most shallow breath.

Much to the horror of a nurse fumbling around the ventilator, he would whisper into his ear: "Get up, you fucker, get up and give me a beating!".

His mind was haunted with horrible pangs of conscience that he had even attempted to discourage Heracles to search for

Joanna, to get it out of his head; but he was so afraid, so afraid Heracles was in for disappointment as it could be nothing more than his memory bringing up some distorted memories. And then he would lose him again. His only friend.

"Hera, you're strong, you always were. Enjoy life as long as you can, you've got a son! Go back to your students!" Vlad would repeat that like a mantra, refusing to accept the inevitable, bargaining with both fate and God over him.

Then doubt and bad feelings overcame him; precisely on the day when Adam appeared next to him at Heracles' bed. He heavily got up from the chair and left the father and his son alone.

The air outside was crisp, the wind forcing Vlad to turn up the collar of his jacket. Then a sudden realization came upon him; a realization that it's been years since he has looked at the night sky. He lifted his head, looked to the stars. And started crying.

The night dragged endlessly as Vlad awaited the phone call. He just knew they would call from the hospital. There was not a thing in the world he wouldn't do to delay that moment.

In human life, there are moments when Time and Earth stand still. Borrowed time given to us to catch our breath, reflect on the things that are the most important in our life. When Heracles recovered after the massive heart attack, perplexed by an avalanche of memories uncovered from the depths of his mind, he was ready to leave the only thing that kept him anchored. Harvard.

Still, there was no way Heracles would leave without bidding farewell to his students.

Heracles moved his gaze across the lecture hall, unable to leave behind one thought; when he entered the very same hall many years ago to give his first lecture, awaiting him were anxiety and stony silence. Today the mood was different, there were smiling faces and anticipation in the crowd.

"Ladies and gentlemen," he finally broke the silence "this is my last lecture." A gasp of disbelief swept through the audience. "Your reaction is certainly flattering, although I do have a feeling that after you listen to the lecture, all of you – and I know you well – will chip in for a ticket and send me to the airport, begging me, for heaven's sake, not to come back. Or, at most, to return as a tourist," Heracles managed to cheer the students up a bit with the last sentence. "My name is Heracles Papadopoulos," he continued, "and you obviously know that. Today I will tell you something you were not aware of. Because I want to explain something to you. And find understanding," his hand pushed deep into his pocket, he paced the lectern and stopped in his tracks. *We have two lives, and the second begins when we realize we only have one.* May this quote by Confucius guide us through today's lecture..."

Heracles put his suitcase down on the floor, took out the chair and sat at the desk to turn on the computer. When the study filled with the dim, grayish light of the screen, he glanced at the violin and then at the picture on the desktop. A boy, his dark fiery eyes and his narrow nose, resembling Grecian gods, holding a guitar. Hello, grandson! He smiled at him and opened his e-mail.

Ewa Pruchnik

Hello,

My name is Konrad and it appears that I'm your grandson:)

Just so that we're clear, I know what was in grandma's message – she was dictating it to me and I was writing, translating it directly into English. A cross-generational teamwork of sorts. But before I did that, I did some Internet research. I wanted to learn something more about you, though Vlad already shared a fair share with me – though I'm not sure if I should believe everything he says:). By the way, your friend is incredible! I don't think there are friendships like this anymore, right? Alright, I think I got carried away and I'm talking like an old fart. Sorry! I just wanted to tell you one thing: from what I learned about you, and I'm not talking about the dry info published on the websites of these important American universities where you gave lectures or even from the short notes on the book covers next to your pictures (look at that rhyme! Well, I'm not gonna change it now, I've never been particularly fluent in the art of epistemology) – I wanted to know the opinion of young people. People like me (yes, I contacted your students – the world is tiny and the Internet is huge like outer space). The one conclusion I came to was that you are an intriguing person. I've got to admit I'd like to meet you in person. If you feel the same way, I guess the old home of my grandma, Joanna, would be the most suitable place to do so. I'll be waiting there for you, just let me know. Whenever you are ready:)

Konrad

Dear Heracles,

Thanks to your friend, Vlad, I finally got to know who you are. Deep down I want you to know that none of my words can express the sorrow I feel for the tragedy you experienced years ago in my country. It's reasonable for me to think that I have contributed to it, albeit unconsciously. Please, forgive me. I can only hope that time brought you comfort and healed at least some of the wounds.

We both love music so much, and it taught me to reminisce about the traces you left and gather all the memories they triggered. Sometimes I would wonder whether you also still remember me. I hoped you did and that life did not let you leave too far behind these nights when our love bloomed in darkness, without a word, at our fingertips. It seems I wasn't wrong.

As you probably already know, Adam is your son. The violin stole his heart, just like it happened with you and your father Michaj, a Romani virtuoso.

Recently, Adam told me that there is a huge mural of Michaj in the heart of Wrocław. How many times did he pass by it, completely unaware that the man donning an oversized hat and clutching a violin is none other than his grandfather? Isn't life full of surprises?

Heracles, please find enclosed with the letter a photo of Konrad, our grandson - a bright, open-minded young man who knows no insecurities and prejudice. He's not too fond of Chopin, though – his words, not mine – he respects him. It's just that Konrad prefers music different to that admired by his parents or grandparents. Though I cannot see it, I

*sense how much alike you two are; bold, courageous and
vulnerable at the same time. You share the same facial
features, hairline, noses, brows, wide jaws. That I know for
sure, Heracles. I've got it all at my fingertips, that's how I
remember you.*

"Hi, what are you up to?"

"Reading. You interrupted me at the most engaging portion."

"What book is it?"

"Best I've ever read."

"Right, sure! Are you reading Joanna's letter again?"

Silence.

"I've got no clue why I'm doing this for you but… I made
it. Your flight departs on March 17 from Chicago, it's some kind
of an operation called *Lot do domu*. Polish aircrafts are carrying
back home Polish people from all around the world who want to
escape the pandemic. Listen… are you sure you want that? What
about… what about we turn this whole situation around, huh?"

"What do you mean?"

"Well, not you going there but them coming here?"

"No way."

"How can you be so sure of that? You didn't come forward
with that proposition!"

"They wouldn't agree."

"Okay, let me ask again – how do you know that?"

"I just know."

"Christ! Man, you've just been through a severe heart attack,
you're giving up on your recovery efforts… you won't survive
that flight! And what if you catch this virus?!"

"Stop screaming, Vlad. Thank you so much for everything

you've done. As soon as the world goes back to normal, visit us. In Poland."

"What the heck are you talking about? Should I bring grave candles?"

...it's beginning to smell like spring here, though it's still winter. Soon the birds will return and build nests in my chestnut tree. And I will sit underneath, in its shade.

The perspective of spending the rest of my life at this house makes me feel equally scared and hopeful. I need to listen to its old walls to find answers to the questions that have been bothering me for so many years. There's this sense of certainty that my old friend, the chestnut tree, will help me out. I carry the good shade of this tree within myself. Every single day, it takes my hand, forcing me to get up, walk and pace the bright places through the darkness.

Joanna

EPILOGUE

TWICE. HERACLES MANAGED to outsmart his death twice. Once, so many years ago in Poland, when his parents passed away and he miraculously survived.

The second time was that heart attack aboard a plane. I saw, I witnessed myself as he faded away. Banging my head against a brick wall, thinking it was the end, but somehow my divine friend again evaded death. It wasn't the *third time's a charm* kind of situation for him.

They spent twenty days together. What a coincidence! Joanna told me that according to her calculations, they met exactly twenty times when they were young.

The second heart attack was it for him. Just like it was for his father, Michaj.

The coffin carrying his body arrived from Poland in the tender company of Adam and Konrad. And Joanna? Joanna is waiting. I promised her I would give him back to her.

Now I'm no longer upset with them; I understood that things had to unfold this way. For their whole life, humans seek experiences that move their hearts, this everlasting pursuit triggering joyful ecstasy and satisfaction, as it equally often turns out to be the easiest road to despair, frustration and self-destruction. So often we want what kills us; slowly, methodically or suddenly. It all depends on us. Things we chase, things we seek. Everything is in a rush, constantly moving. And that, as one philosopher used to say, is the only thing that is constant – change. Among this rush, it is a virtue to stop and listen to the voice of the past, as it always calls us by our name. Such is the truth that my friend unveiled to me. His past had been calling him for his whole life and he could not ignore it anymore. One time he told me that there are two things that define us: heredity, so the past hidden in our genes, and our mysteries. I find it hard to argue with the statement.

As I'm writing these words, he's here before me, in an urn. But he does not belong here. The place where he belongs is underneath that chestnut tree. As soon as the world is vaccinated, I'll fly with him and spread his ashes. He will listen to Joanna's piano. As a philosopher, he could not have come up with anything more beautiful than that.